A LEAGUE
OF HAWKS

AN IAN QUAYLE SPY NOVEL

CALIBER
BOOKS

Also from ALAN CAILLOU

CABOT CAIN Series
    Assault on Kolchak
    Assault on Loveless
    Assault on Ming
    Assault on Agathon
    Assault on Fellawi
    Assault on Almata

TOBIN'S WAR Series
    Dead Sea Submarine
    Terror in Rio
    Congo War Cry
    Afghan Assault
    Swamp War
    Death Charge
    The Garonsky Missile

MIKE BENASQUE Series
    The Plotters
    Marseilles
    Who'll Buy My Evil
    Diamonds Wild

IAN QUAYLE Series
    A League of Hawks
    The Sword of God

DEKKER'S DEMONS Series
    Suicide Run
    Blood Run

The Charge of the Light Brigade
A Journey to Orassia

Rogue's Gambit
Cairo Cabal
Bichu the Jaguar
The Walls of Jolo
The Hot Sun of Africa
The Cheetahs
Joshua's People
Mindanao Pearl
Khartoum
South from Khartoum
Rampage
The World is 6 Feet Square
The Prophetess
House on Curzon Street

CHAPTER 1

Ian Quayle was in a very happy state of mind, and why shouldn't he be?

He was at the wheel of a car he delighted in, his little soapbox Mini-Cooper 'S', a tiny toy of a machine that would hold an easy 125 MPH on its ridiculous four-cylinder twin Stromberg carb engine.

He was holding it down to eighty or so as he drove through the twisting lanes of the Surrey byways, clip-bordered on both sides with immaculate hedges, the trees above him arching over to meet each other and casting dappled shadows in the evening sun.

The sun was new; most of the day it had been raining.

He was a little under six feet tall, Ian Quayle, broad-shouldered and narrow-hipped, but wiry rather than muscular, all the wrong muscles getting the exercise through his mania for digging the garden all the time rather than working out in a gym...

A high, intelligent forehead, and piercing dark eyes under rather bushy eyebrows, almost angry eyes that burned when they were staring at you and wondering what the hell you were talking about; they were eyes that stated emphatically that he had no time at all for idiots, and if you thought that was a kind of arrogance—then the hell with it and with you too.

He was what the girls he knew liked to think of as 'desperately handsome' though this was a term he could never possibly accept, and he had the most awful scowl when he got uptight—which was often. His hair was thick and dark and sort of curly, almost always a mess because he just couldn't be bothered with stuff like blow-drying.

And he smiled easily, the way a nice guy should; but the smile often didn't reach his eyes.

In short—if you *studied* that good-looking face, with its excellent features, and if you had any understanding at all, then you could see a facade of *so-who-cares?* under which lay a strong foundation of stubborn determination.

He'd recently passed the thirty-four age barrier, and hated every minute of it. But he took great comfort in the knowledge that some of his girls, at least, were convinced that he wasn't a day over thirty-three...

The Mini was behaving splendidly, the countryside was lush and satisfying, and the antiseptic functionalism of his London flat was far behind him and forgotten. Most of all, he was desperately in love, (for the moment at least, hoping it would last the weekend,) with the lovely girl beside him.

She was exciting, long-legged and very blonde, with straw-colored hair that was long and straight and all over the place, and the kind of facial bone structure that could drive a susceptible man to distraction. Her flesh tones were English peaches-and-cream, her eyes were huge and pale blue with perpetual surprise in them, and she had the happiest laugh ever, which she used all the time, often for no reason at all. And she wasn't unnecessarily intelligent.

She'd said, "As long as it's understood I won't stay the night, *ha-ha-ha*...And if I should have to, then I want my own room and no battering down of doors in the horny early hours of the morning, okay?" dissolving into laughter again just at the thought of it.

But she was really very lovely, with promise even in the way she walked, with the loose and easy articulation of a camel. He'd met her at one of Eddie Forbes' parties, and her name was Paula.

Paula what?

For the life of him, Ian Quayle couldn't remember her surname, and did it matter? He thought not.

He said now, making conversation, "You'll just *love* the cottage. It's Fifteenth Century, with the most gorgeous thatched roof you ever saw in your life, absolutely fantastic."

Paula was silent. He couldn't know it, but she was thinking about her long-time boyfriend, whose name was Harold, a rather overweight young man who made his living at the greyhound track. He'd just told her he'd never marry her, ever, let's keep things as they are, great for both of us...She was very upset about it.

Ian Quayle said, musing, "The countryside. I keep trying to persuade myself that I love Mother Nature. But you know what Mother Nature is, don't you? Don't you?"

She came back to reality. "I know what what is?"

"Mother Nature. And you're not listening to me, are you?"

"Sweetheart, of course I'm listening to you! I'm hanging on to every word you say!"

There was a Jag up front, hogging the winding road, and Ian put his foot to the floor and overtook it on the wrong side like a bullet shot from a rifle. He saw the needle sweep round to a hundred and ten momentarily, and eased off again.

"Mother Nature," he said, "means the squirrels eating all my cob-nuts, it means the birds taking all my plums and peaches, the maggots boring into my tomatoes." He grunted "Mother Nature is the bloody foxes taking my chicken and the weasels getting the eggs. It's what's got to be called ecology, and you can take Mother bloody Nature and stuff it."

"Are we nearly there?"

Paula was tired of the confinement; Harold had an American car a mile long, and a lady didn't have to stick her elbows out of the window to make room for the rest of her body.

"Two more minutes."

"And there really are more people coming tonight? I mean, it's not just the two of us? These days, a girl has to be awfully careful."

"Awfully careful' can ruin a great evening, but don't worry, there'll be hordes of people coming. Your Eddie too."

"Eddie Forbes is *not* 'my Eddie,' he's hardly ever laid a hand on me," Paula said petulantly. And there was the laugh again. "Just his work, he measured me a couple of times, and said I had the perfect model's figure. I thought that was very nice of him. And for a party like this...You don't think my dress is too revealing?"

He took his eyes from the road for longer than was safe.

"No. Your birthday suit would not be too revealing. And here we are..."

He hit the brakes and swung the wheel around, skidding the Mini over the mud into just the right position. He said, "Why don't you get the gate for me? And leave it open for the others."

He drove through to the little whitewashed cottage with its heavy thatched roof and ancient timbers, a pure delight. And by the time she rejoined him he had taken the wooden case of champagne from the back and was struggling with it to the front door.

"The key," he said, his hands occupied, "it's in my left-hand pants pocket."

He felt her fumbling for it, saw her fitting it into the lock.

"It's already open," Paula what's-her-name said, and he answered her abruptly, "Oh balls!"

"It *is*..."

Ian Quayle said patiently, "I come here every weekend. I go back to town every Monday morning, and I lock up before I leave, it's a matter of habit."

"Ian, I swear, it's unlocked."

And it was.

He followed her into the living room, set the case of champagne down on the table, and stared at the Deruta ashtray there; a cigarette in it had not been properly extinguished and was still smoldering...

He had always known that the work he was doing now just might have its attendant dangers, but it still came as a shock to him, and he said quietly, "Paula, go back to the car. Start it up, be ready to drive off at the first sign of trouble. There's someone here who shouldn't be here."

Paula stared at him uselessly. "Oh my God...I always knew that you were up to some kind of nonsense. Eddie told me. He told me in no uncertain terms: 'Ian Quayle's involved with MI5, or something equally ghastly.' And now, I'm sure of it."

Quayle looked at her. "MI5? Isn't that one of those comic Intelligence agencies? I swear to God, I never even heard of them, ever. Now, get into the car. It may be nothing at all, but if there's a problem, I want to know that you're safe."

"Sir bloody Galahad..."

"Will you shut up, for Christ's sake, and get moving?"

Paula saw the look on his face and did as she was told, worrying about it.

Quayle took a poker from the beautiful old stone fireplace, explored the kitchen and the serving-porch, creeping around in silence and wondering how he would make out if he actually had to hit someone over the head. He found nothing untoward, and returned to the living room, paneled in dark oak, and stared for a moment at the still smoldering cigarette.

And then, for no reason at all, he suddenly *knew*...

He said aloud, "Oh shit."

He put down the poker and went up the stairs. When he came to the bathroom he found the door open, and Wendy Hayworth was stretched out in the tub, soaking herself luxuriantly. She looked at him as he stood in the doorway with one hand on the jamb, staring down at her and trying to contain his hostility.

He said coldly: "Good evening, Wendy, it's nice to see you looking so well. Would you mind telling me how the hell you got in here?"

Smothered in soap suds, she smiled, an extraordinarily attractive young woman lying there naked, bubbles caressing her breasts.

"Darling," she said, "I picked the lock of your front door. It's really not very efficient. All it needs is a bobby-pin."

"A *bobby-pin*? Wendy my love, they haven't even manufactured bobby-pins in a hundred years."

"Well, isn't that the truth?"

She was stroking herself, Yardley's Lavender moving back and forth sensuously. "It so happens that I carry a little something with me, made of high-carbon steel just like me. It picks any lock ever made. And you're supposed to know about these things."

"If I were a Field Officer, I would. But that's not what I am, thank God. I'm giving a party tonight. It's honestly not a good time for you to drop by. And I didn't see your car, or I'd have let the air out of the tires."

"I hid it behind the barn, darling, wasn't that discreet of me? And I know about the party, of course I know about it! That's part of my job. I just assumed that your invitation got lost in the mail, you know how the Post Office is...Would you like to scrub my back for me?"

"No."

He sighed. "There's a dizzy blonde downstairs, waiting

10

for me to go down and tell her that we haven't been invaded by undesirables."

"*Undesirables*? Ian, you choose your words marvelously well. You really are a sonofabitch, aren't you?"

Ian Quayle scratched at his head. "Yes, that may well be. I haven't thought about it too much."

"Scrub my front, then. You see how I humble myself before you?"

"Not even that, just now. Her name's Paula. She's waiting for me, convinced that my life is in the greatest danger, but braving it all out very nobly indeed."

He hesitated. "She seems to think that I'm with MI5."

"With those assholes?" Her stare was very solemn. "It means that your security is not as good as it should be, Ian. Have you been talking in your sleep, maybe?"

"You know me better than that."

Wendy stood up in the bath. "The back and the front," she said, holding out the luffa. And when he did not move, she turned her head a little to one side and said, "And are you going to sleep with this unfortunate creature tonight?"

He shrugged. "That was the general idea, I suppose. She thinks I'm marvelous."

"Strange, isn't it, how some people can be so grossly misinformed." She stepped back out of the tub. "A towel, at least."

He found one and wrapped it around her, patting her dry. He took her in his arms and touched her breasts very lightly with his fingertips, and said gently, "Put something on. Come down and help out, we have to make canapes for a hundred thousand people. They'll all be descending on us in an hour or so."

"That ought to leave us time enough. It doesn't always take that long, you know."

"I bought shrimps, and feta cheese, and cucumbers, prunes and bacon for Angels on Horseback, olives, a little bit of black and a lot of red caviar, enough cold cuts to feed an army...Brie and Chevres and Double Gloucester, and Stilton too. We'll see what the chickens have done, and stuff some hard-boiled eggs..."

"And I'm supposed to share all this domesticity with your dizzy blonde, is that it? What's her damn name again?"

"Paula something-or-other, you'll love her. She's cute."

"Cuteness is not a quality either of us likes."

"Just promise me you won't pick a fight."

"Like hell I will."

He sighed. "Come on down soon." He kissed her breasts, left her standing there, and went downstairs to find Paula sitting in the Mini with the engine turning over quietly. He said, grinning broadly, "False alarm, so come on back in the house. It's just a friend, I found her in the bloody bathroom."

"*Her*?" There was a very sour look on Paula's lovely, petulant face. "But how did she get in? Does she have a key?" She looked away. "I suppose that's none of my business, right?"

"Right. Her name's Wendy Hayworth, she's a...well, a sort of business associate, and she's nice. You'll get along fabulously well together."

"I'll bet."

"So let's start turning groceries into food."

They gathered up the shopping bags, and as they went into the house, Paula said, "It would be foolish, wouldn't it, to ask what this Wendy-bird would be doing in your bathroom?"

"She was taking a bath," Quayle said, astonished.

"What else would she be doing there? And we have to get the eggs."

He led her to the chicken run at the bottom of the garden and counted the hens there, seven of the Rhode Island Reds and four of the little black Barnevelders that laid the biggest brown eggs in history. He swore softly. "There are supposed to be fifteen all told..."

They found a dead fox, its throat torn out, and Ian Quayle said, "Charlie."

"Charlie?"

"George's dog."

"George?"

"Albert's son."

Paula just stared at him, and Quayle said patiently, "Albert is the farmer who lives just down the road, he looks after the place while I'm up in town, feeds the hens and so forth. His son is George, who has a dog named Charlie..."

"You forgot to tell me the name of George's mother."

"Oh shut up."

"Just wondering."

"Charlie is the ugliest damn dog you ever saw. He hates foxes, squirrels, weasels, stoats, rabbits, ferrets, badgers, hates everything in Mother Nature's arsenal of bloody nuisances. Let us now give thanks for Charlie, without whom we'd have no eggs at all."

They found a total of thirty-seven eggs in the nesting boxes and took them back to the house to hard-boil. And then Wendy was stalking down the narrow staircase...

And Wendy Hayworth was something else again...

At the age of 29, she was the most beautiful creature ever designed in God's carnival of animals.

She was tallish, and slender, and very *willowy*, positively swaying with every movement she made. And as though a stunning figure wasn't enough, the good Lord had given her a face to be stared at and remembered too, even to be drooled over.

It was a Renaissance-type face that could have been a model for Botticelli, with calm blue-green eyes that burst into flame unexpectedly when she got angry; with a wide, intelligent forehead, an aristocratic nose, and lips perhaps a little too full but very promising.

Her hair was long and silky, almost straw-colored, just a

little darker, and it was kept under disciplined control most of the time, piled up on top of her head by one of London's most expensive hairdressers; she always thought the result was worth the big hole it made in the housekeeping.

Just once in a while, she liked to let it down (in more ways than one), and on those occasions it just about reached her waist.

Her complexion, with or without a touch of make-up, was flawless. But above all, there was that solid air of competence on a face that just made you stop and stare in admiration; and maybe *wonder* too...

She was a very, *very* striking young woman.

Ian Quayle said, "Ah, may I present Wendy Hayworth, Paula, er, Paula, er..."

"Paula Hammond," Paula said swiftly. "How very nice to meet you." She was smiling broadly. "And I simply adore that outfit, it's really most becoming, absolutely gorgeous."

Wendy had put on a very simple cocktail dress of off-white silk, most skillfully cut, a Kamali original, and she thought: *Well, perhaps she's not so bad after all, at least she knows good clothes when she sees them...*

"I have exactly the same model at home," Paula said.

"I really should wear it more often, but...well, I always feel it's a little old for me."

There was only the briefest pause, and then Wendy said smoothly, "Of course. The knack of wearing good clothes does demand a certain maturity, doesn't it? I mean, big boobs and a see-through blouse don't necessarily add up to elegance, wouldn't you agree? But don't despair, darling, I'm sure there's still hope for you. It's quite amazing what the plastic surgeons can do with an oversized bust these days."

They were on their way to the kitchen, and Ian said loudly, "Will someone please start slicing up the cucumbers? Not peeled, a quarter of an inch thick, a piece of feta cheese and a smidgen of caviar on top? Toothpicks stuck into them..."

"I'll take care of the cucumbers," Wendy said happily.

"I just hate to think what Paula might want to do with them."

Quayle sighed. "Oh Jesus."

He threw up his arms. "Plates in the cupboard there, and there's parsley growing right outside the kitchen door. And why don't we all have some champagne while we're working? Wendy? You know where the glasses are."

He took a bottle from the case and held it up to show them. "Bollinger 60," he said, beaming, "the best of all of them. And I got a hell of a good deal, a hundred quid for a case of a dozen. How can they sell it at that price? A street market in Soho, the only place to go shopping."

"Stolen," Wendy said flatly. "Shame on you, Ian Quayle."

He nodded, glumly. "I'll admit, I didn't ask any questions, and maybe I should have. But...a hundred pounds a case, you can't lose, can you?"

The cork didn't pop when he opened it, and he said cheerfully, "Ah, it's colder than I thought it would be..."

He filled their glasses, and Paula was the first to sip it.

"Delicious," she said. "But isn't it supposed to be, well, a little more bubbly? I'm not complaining, of course."

Ian Quayle raised his glass and said, "Here's to the health of us all, and down with the peasants everywhere."

He took a drink and set his glass down. "Oh Christ. Jesus bloody Christ." He looked at Wendy, and said: "I got screwed, luv, didn't I?"

Wendy nodded. "Slightly carbonated water, Ian, colored with the faintest touch of tea. Yes, you got ripped off."

Quayle swore, and examined the bottles carefully. They had all been skillfully recorked and sealed, empty bottles (with their all-important corks), bought from the City's clubs and restaurants and put to profitable use.

"A hundred quid's not easy to come by," he said glumly. "And where did it go? Down the bloody drain, that's where it went. Oh well..."

But there was plenty of red wine and white in the cellar, and they carted up thirty-odd bottles between them, some vintage, some fair, and some that would be acceptable as the night wore on. The canapes piled up, and by eight o'clock when the first of the guests started arriving, everything was ready.

The first was Eddie Forbes, youngish, personable, and a health nut who liked to pump iron when he wasn't making more money than he could spend. He owned a fashionable modelling studio in Shepherd Market where he trained a horde of pretty young things in the art of being desirable, or at least desired.

He was tall and slender and quite feline in his movements, dressed in a blue jumpsuit with a twist of red cloth at his throat, and he shouted boisterously, "Never enough birds at your parties, Ian! So I brought two of them, two for the price of one! May I present our genial host, Ian Quayle, Felicity and Phoebe, two of my star pupils destined for a marvelous future. Do me a personal favor, Ian, use them in your next picture."

Ian Quayle was about to protest that he had nothing at all to do with the film industry, when Eddie said quickly, "I told them what a fantastic Producer you are, told them how much money your last picture made. What was it called? Ah yes, '*The Bridge of Thighs*,' critical acclaim everywhere. So help them along, will you? And in case you hadn't noticed, they're twins. But *identical* twins, and you know what that means?" His voice dropped to a worried whisper, and he said, "I slept with Felicity last night, and you know, this morning, at breakfast, *Phoebe* told me how much she'd enjoyed it. It's weird, truly it is."

Twins they were indeed, identical to the border of bewilderment, the popular model figure with no flesh anywhere, but satisfying bone structure. They were both red-headed and dressed in Britannia jeans with green silk shirts open down to the waistline, and they looked very fetching indeed, their splendid torsos deeply tanned. Tanning salons, Quayle ruminated, were springing up all over London now, a month of Mediterranean sun compressed into three half-hour sessions.

"Oh, you're going to have such a good time tonight, aren't you?" Wendy Hayworth said, and he realized that he'd been staring. He made the introductions, and Paula said, gushing: "Yes, I've heard of you, of course, that wonderful studio in the Market."

He gave her his card, looking her up and down. "Most of my models have chests like young boys, but once in a while we get a call for the, ah, the fuller figure. My own personal choice. So why don't you give me a ring?"

There was the honking of a Colonel Bogey horn outside to announce the arrival of Monty Brewster in his ancient red Maserati. He had a semi-conscious young woman with him, holding her up, and he said her name was Linda. "Can you believe it? On the way down she polished off a whole fifth of Johnny Walker, right out of the damned bottle. Can we find her a sofa for a couple of hours?"

Almost on their heels, Valerie Dupuys arrived in her ivory Corniche, dressed in white shorts because of her fabulous legs, and a black cashmere sweater from Sulka because her upper parts weren't that good. She had her current boyfriends with her, Malcolm and Boris. Malcolm was a nobody, but Boris was a defector from the Bolshoi, tall and straight and with long blond hair down to his shoulders; he was trying to worm his way into Covent Garden even though, frankly, his dancing was quite pedestrian.

And then a Vanden Plas limo pulled in, with no less than five ladies aboard and a single man with them. It was Ian Quayle's good friend Martin Fox, and he said, laughing, "Don't expect me to introduce them, Ian, they're merely here in the interest of pulchritude. I just told my secretary: "Find me some good-looking heifers," and that's what she did. They're nice, aren't they? Their names, I think, are Millie, Wilma, Astrid, Letitia, and Elise, but God alone knows which is which. And could I have a quick whisky-splash? They're a bit exhausting."

In no time at all, the party was getting to be a great success. The canapes were quickly devoured and as quickly replenished, the wines were well received, even the cheap ones, and soon after half-past eleven the rain came thundering down on the Fifteenth-Century roof, leaking in everywhere.

"Buckets, everyone," Ian Quayle shouted, draining his Pouilly-Fuissé, "buckets and saucepans, everybody!"

There was a general exodus to the crowded kitchen in the search for receptacles (Martin Fox gleefully found two chamber-pots from upstairs), and they were placed just so by a score of guests to catch the heavy dripping through the thatch; very few of them were particularly sober now.

And in the middle of it all, the old grandfather clock struck twelve, and Ian Quayle began singing, a little off key:

'*My grandfather's clock was too tall for the shelf,*
So it stood ninety years on the floor.
It was taller by half than the old man himself,
Though it weighed not a penny-weight more...'

Wendy Hayworth said quietly, taking him aside, "Midnight, Ian, the witching hour. Harris and Mrs. French will have just arrived, on time as always. They want a word with you."

He stared at her. "What?"

"You heard me. They'll be in the greenhouse, waiting. I thought it might be a suitable meeting place, discreetly away from the mob."

"Suitable my ass! The greenhouse is full of my herbs.

They'll take one look at Mrs. French and wither away, just wither away and die! I won't have it!"

"They're waiting for us, Ian."

He could hardly restrain his anger. "Well," he said, "you bloody well tell them to piss off back to town, I don't want to talk to Mrs. bloody French tonight, or even with Robin Harris. So tell her."

Wendy said tartly, "I can hardly tell your boss and mine that you don't quite feel like talking to her right now! You damn well tell her yourself, if you've got the nerve."

He sighed. "You have a point there, all right. But I'll be damned if I'm going to skulk around the garden when I've got a houseful of guests to worry about. Especially when the rain's just pissing down. If Mrs. French wants to talk to me, then she can talk in the house or not at all."

"God damn your eyes," Wendy said, "you really are a troublemaker, aren't you?"

"Yes, I am, you should know that by now."

"Very well then, I'll go get them. So where do I find a brolly?"

"In the umbrella-stand in the hall, where else would it be? In the frig?"

"Bastard..."

Wendy found an umbrella where it was supposed to be, and went out in the rain to rescue from the greenhouse the two uninvited guests whom Ian Quayle, at this moment, simply wanted to have nothing to do with at all.

He was absolutely convinced that Robin Harris and Mrs. French meant nothing but trouble.

And just when he was feeling on top of the world...

CHAPTER 2

Even though the walk from Mrs. French's Jag to the front door had been a short one, the rain had been heavy enough to ruin her immaculate hairdo. Robin Harris hadn't brought an umbrella, and he knew he'd never be forgiven.

Introducing them, Ian Quayle said, "Boys and girls, may I present, ah, Arnold and Lucy Watts? Dear friends from way back."

Mrs. French said, smiling out of the freezer, "And how very nice to be here." Her eyes spelled murder.

Always the gentleman, Robin Harris murmured, "Good to see you, Quayle. Sorry about the intrusion, but it really is necessary."

No one paid them the slightest attention.

Mrs. French's cold blue eyes were roving, looking over the guests with overt disapproval, and she said tightly,

"We have to talk, Mr. Quayle. And at once, there's a certain urgency."

She was in her forties, an extraordinarily beautiful woman of carefully constructed elegance, wearing a well-chosen cocktail dress of some distinction, jet-black and shimmering, not an original but from Harrods, where all the best people shopped; it was not too rich, nor yet too casual either. Her glorious auburn hair was piled up on top of her head, only the upper layer damaged by the rain.

Quayle looked at the hair, and said mildly, "I've always admired your coiffure, did you know that? I just have this awful feeling that if I were ever to make love with you, perish the thought, you'd say, 'Don't touch my hair,' even when I was on top of you, probing..."

"The most dreadful thing about my chosen profession," Mrs. French said coldly, "is that it brings me into too close contact, sometimes, with the most vulgar people in the world. Could we find somewhere to talk?"

"Wendy suggested the greenhouse, but my herbs are growing there."

He took great delight in the knowledge that she didn't know what he was talking about. "One of the bedrooms, then. If the idea of a bedroom won't discombobulate you too much. But I won't leave my guests for too long, it has to be brief."

"I doubt very much," Mrs. French said, "that your guests will even miss you, Mr. Quayle."

"Could be..."

He said to Wendy, "Do me a favor, luv, look after things for a while, will you do that?"

But Wendy Hayworth shook her head slowly. "No. I'm in on this meeting too."

"Oh." He grunted. "I should have known. Well, the hell with it, they all know where the drinks are."

He led them up the staircase, a little bit off true where the foundations had sunk in the last four hundred years; it made for a certain instability. He opened the door to his own blue and white bedroom, and Martin Fox was there, humping away with Monty Brewster's barely conscious Linda. One of his own five girls—was it Wilma, or Elise?—was crouched on her knees, beside them, fondling Linda's opulent breasts and murmuring, "If you ever recover your senses, my sweet, look me in the eyes and tell me how much you adore the touch of my fingers..." They were all naked, all having a wonderful time together.

"So sorry," Ian Quayle said, and they paid him no attention at all.

"Disgusting!" Mrs. French said as Quayle led them hopefully to the second bedroom. He murmured, "We just might be stuck with the greenhouse after all."

But mercifully the second bedroom was empty, and he closed the door behind them and said, "Okay, I'm all ears."

Mrs. French sat primly in the only armchair there, Wendy Hayworth stretched herself out on the bed and stared at the ceiling; and Robin Harris just prowled.

Ian Quayle leaned against the door and waited, watching Harris, just waiting for him to speak.

Harris was very much the gentleman, and he was greatly concerned because he knew that his Number Two, Mrs. bloody French, was slowly easing him out of his high position and taking it over for herself, a brash and arrogant woman without his experience, without his sense of diplomacy, without his understanding of the old values.

There'd been a time when all that mattered was the right school, the right clubs, the right *acceptance*. But today, very different criteria were taking over, criteria, he thought, that weren't always desirable in the make-up of MI6. A highly-secret organization such as this could only be staffed with *gentlemen*; else, where would it all finish?

Sometimes, Robin Harris thought, uncertainly, of Burgess, of Philby and McLean, and of Blount; they were gentlemen too, but they had betrayed their country.

And now, Mrs. French...

Who was she? Where had she sprung from?

"Ah...Grammar School," Sir Gerald Trendwilly had said over a pint of half-and-half in one of his rare public appearances.

He was head of MI6, and liked to wear a god-awful phony beard when he appeared for the whole world of foreign spies to see and photograph.

"Grammar School," he had said again with the greatest contempt. "She has limited Latin, no Greek, no classical education at all. She thinks that Epictetus is the name of a restaurant in Soho. She's a one hundred percent virgin, y'know, I suspect her tastes are for those of her own sex. Disgustin', isn't it? But that's something we'll never really be sure about, I suppose."

He had downed his beer, and had said miserably, "But she'll have your job, Harris, within two years. In five—she'll probably have mine. It's not a prospect a gentleman can face with equanimity. What about another half-and-half?"

Robin Harris looked at Mrs. French now in the heavily timbered second bedroom with its rose velour drapes over the windows (which Wendy had chosen), and her imperious nod was his signal to speak.

"News from Rome, Quayle," Robin Harris said. "A very senior Police Officer there has been murdered."

"It happens all the time," Ian Quayle said, mocking him. "There's an outfit there called the Red Brigades, you may have heard tell of them."

He could not disguise the sarcasm in his voice. "They and the cops take it in turn, knocking each other off. What fun. It makes it their business, not ours."

"And how did you know," Mrs. French asked, "that it was indeed the Red Brigades who killed him?"

"Possibly not..." Robin Harris began, but Quayle said angrily, "In the last four months, by my most recent count, twenty-seven Police Officers or judges have been murdered by the Red Brigades, it's a natural assumption."

"Twenty-four," Mrs. French said, and he turned on her furiously.

"Twenty-seven! Don't argue with me about figures, that's part of my business! I'm sure it will astonish you, but I happen to know what I'm talking about! If you want, I'll rattle off all their names, one by one. And I've a feeling that you don't like to lose arguments, so do yourself a favor and don't start one."

She was cool as could be. "You really are a very arrogant man, Mr. Quayle, aren't you?"

"Yes, I know that. But what the hell does the murder of a police officer have to do with me? I bleed for him, of course..."

And Mrs. French said swiftly, sweetly, "I'm so glad, because you have reason to. His name..." She paused, and then: "His name was Mancini. *General* Mancini."

Quayle was stopped dead in his offensive tracks, and he felt the blood draining from his face. He whispered, his voice hollow, "General Mancini?"

Wendy said gently, "That's right, Ian. Carlotta's father. I'm sorry. The General stepped into his car, the driver turned on the ignition, and the car exploded. What can I say? I'm sorry."

"He was working for us," Robin Harris said, "our top agent in Italy. You never knew that, of course. But it makes it our business now."

Quayle sat on the bed and held his head in his hands. He whispered, "He was such a good man...And Carlotta? She adored her father."

Mrs. French was even smiling. "You mean you knew them? The General and his daughter? Ah yes, I remember now."

She was driving home the pain for the sheer joy of it, and Ian Quayle rounded on her furiously. "You bitch! You bloody, one-hundred percent gold plated bitch! Are you trying to tell me you didn't know? At this moment, I hate you more than, more than..."

He could not continue, and Robin Harris said quietly,

"The Red Brigades claimed responsibility for the murder. But we heard on the grapevine of a rather elusive thing called 'The League of Hawks.' You're the best research man we ever had on our staff, Ian, and we hoped that you might perhaps have heard of them."

In the long silence that followed, Mrs. French said tartly, "Pull yourself together, Mr. Quayle, if you can. Tears for a dead man you once knew really don't amount to very much."

Ian rose to his feet, and his voice was rising as he said, "I never even met General Mancini, you bitch, as I'm sure you know. I'm concerned about his daughter Carlotta, whom I knew...and loved."

He was shouting now. "And God help me, if you push me any further I'll break a golden rule and do violence to a woman. A woman, *sort of.*"

Mrs. French too was livid, and for a moment it seemed that she was going to strike him. But Wendy was suddenly between them, and she said urgently, "We need your help now, Ian. For Carlotta's sake? Please?"

"Then keep that damned woman out of my hair!"

"Your boss, Ian, and mine too."

"No," Robin Harris said quietly and quite unexpectedly. "*I* am the boss, let's not forget that. So calm down, Quayle, and tell what, if anything, you know about the League of Hawks."

Ian Quayle took hold of himself; he rather liked the gentlemanly Robin Harris. He took a deep breath and said: "I never heard of them. There's something like a hundred and fifty documented terrorist organizations worldwide, and thirty-eight percent of them are operating in Europe, I make that fifty-seven or so. But a League of Hawks?"

He stared at the floor for a moment, and then said slowly, "There was a *League of Owls* once, but even that's only a distant bell ringing, a *Napoleonic* sort of bell. Napoleon the Third, I think, back in the nineteenth century. But owls, not hawks. Can't be the same thing."

He was still confused over the news of General Mancini's murder, and couldn't quite bring his formidable powers to bear on the problem. He said, worrying, "Research is my business. Sometimes, you pick up little fragments of information and file them away at the back of your mind, that's what research is about. Sometimes, it takes a little while to focus them, to put them into their proper perspective. Hawks? Owls? I just don't know for the moment."

"But you'll find out, Ian," Wendy said. "Won't you?"

"Maybe." He turned to her. "And they're about to suggest that I go to Rome, right?"

"Yes, that's what we have in mind."

"But this is field work, and I'm not trained as a field officer, thank God. I like to sit in my London flat, or here in the cottage, and do the research I'm paid for."

"Well," the abominable Mrs. French said, "if it's a question of what you're *paid for*, we could probably offer you a pound of two more for finding out just who killed your girlfriend's father."

"Drop dead, bitch," Ian Quayle said without rancor.

"Just don't bloody *talk*."

He said to Wendy, a bright young woman in whom he had the utmost confidence, "All right, I'll go to Rome, if only to see Carlotta again after all this time. Jesus Christ, it's damn near twenty years!"

"Twenty-one, actually," Mrs. French said. "I know how precise you like to be with your figures..."

Twenty-one years! A third of a life time!

He'd had a furious affair with the lovely Carlotta Mancini when they were students together at London University, and she'd left him, quite inexplicably, just when—impoverished as he was—he was about to propose marriage.

And now, there was Wendy, a woman of extraordinary attraction who could never quite fill that long-lasting void. His relationship with her was a very strange one, sexual in part and mostly intellectual, full of ups and downs, exciting and frustrating at one and the same time.

"The League of Hawks," Mrs. French said, interrupting his reverie. "We want to know who they are, and what they want to achieve. The murder itself is of secondary importance."

He scowled at her. "You think so? All I'll want to do is find out who murdered Carlotta's father."

"The one will lead to the other."

She handed him an envelope and said, "Your tickets to Rome."

He opened the envelope and stared at the contents. "*Two?*" And Robin Harris said, apologetically, "Wendy is going with you, Quayle. She has an official position, which you don't. She can open doors for you by merely flashing a card."

"When Wendy's content with opening doors," Ian said sourly, "that'll be the day. And does that mean that I'm expected to do what she says? She's my boss?"

Robin Harris smiled. "I would not have put it quite so bluntly. I'm sure you can work it out between you. And you leave tonight. Trails can grow cold very quickly."

"Well, I'll hand over the party to someone down there if anyone's still sober."

"If not," Robin Harris said drily, "it'll be that much easier, won't it?"

"And how right you are."

"We'll stay for a while after you've gone," Mrs. French said, "to keep up the pretense that we're just friends of yours and nothing more."

Ian Quayle held her look. "Do that," he said, "as long as you realize that drunk or sober no one's going to believe you could possibly be a *friend*. These are all nice people. But try it anyway, an exercise in futility."

He could feel the daggers as he led them downstairs, and he said to Eddie Forbes, the model man whom he'd known for some years and rather liked, "Take over the party, Eddie. I have to split. You know where everything is."

Eddie peered at him. "Okay. But what about your bird?"

"Who?"

"Paula."

"Who the hell's Paula?"

"The one with the big boobs, remember? I had this crazy impression she was your date."

"Oh, Paula." He was not in a very good mood, and he said, "Yes, I forgot. Do me a favor, Eddie. Paula's expecting to get thoroughly laid tonight, so substitute for me, will you do that?"

Eddie said nervously, "The twins are going to get mad as hell, Ian."

"Put it down to the demands of our friendship, Eddie. I'm sure they'll understand."

"Like hell they will."

"Goodnight, Eddie. Take care of the bar."

"Goodnight, Ian."

"Lots more stuff in the cellar if you run out."

"For God's sake," Wendy said plaintively, "can we go?"

And Ian Quayle nodded. "All right, let's do that. No one's going to notice that we're not around anymore."

He pulled up short, remembering. "And isn't that just what Mrs. Bloody French said? 'Your guests won't even miss you?' I hate people who are always right, especially if they're women, more or less."

Wendy threw him a look and said tightly, "My bag's already in the back of the Mini."

"Then give me five minutes," Ian said, "to put a few

28

things together."

He went upstairs to his bedroom, quite forgetting that it was occupied. The trio was still there, Martin and Linda and Elise, or was it Wilma? Linda had quite recovered, and was the aggressor now, naked female bodies thrashing in a sort of blind ecstasy together, breast to breast and thigh to thigh.

It was the moment of mutual orgasm when Ian Quayle mumbled, only slightly embarrassed, "Sorry, boys and girls. I need some shirts..."

They still paid him no attention at all. Martin Fox had a glass of cognac, and was dipping his finger into it and rubbing it over Linda's tiny nipples and then fighting his way there to taste it and he murmured, "Remy Martin, I think?"

Ian Quayle sighed, and threw some stuff into his carry-on, took it downstairs and found Wendy Hayworth waiting for him impatiently.

"One more moment," he said. "I have to make a phone call..."

The phone was in the hall, and when, just not prepared to wait any longer, Wendy went there to find him, he was saying into the old-fashioned upright mouthpiece: "...all right, darling, but you will remember to hold back on the tarragon, won't you? It's really very important. 'Bye now, and I love you."

"Okay," he said. "I was just talking to Claudine, we'll be staying with her overnight..."

Claudine.

Claudine Andrassy was Ian Quayle's mother, and she lived in the fashionable Paris suburb of St. Cloud. Retired now, she had once been among the top two or three of the world's greatest ballerinas. In the esoteric circles of balletomania, her name was a diamond, a synonym for the utmost in excellence. Italy's foremost critic had once written: "*Last night I watched*

Claudine Andrassy dance Don Quixote's Kitri, an expression of the most astounding delicacy and sensuous femininity, quite beyond belief. And now, I have nothing else to live for. If I die tomorrow, I will go to Heaven or to Hell a happy man..."

Wendy said quietly, "What a shame, I've always wanted to much to meet her. But we're on Alitalia, it's a direct flight to Rome, no stopover in Paris. On the way home again, perhaps?"

She looked at him strangely. "Your dossier says that when you were just a kid, you rescued Claudine from the Russians in Budapest. I read the whole story, it gave me goose-pimples. What were you then, fifteen?"

Ian Quayle said, almost snarling, "Get your facts right, for Christ's sake, it was a month before my fourteenth birthday." He recovered his good humor at once, and grinned. "That's right, but I was never just a kid, I was born grown up. I remember being breast-fed, can you believe that? I used to scream at my mother: "Enough of this bloody milk, give me some Brie...!""

He was in one of his moods again, one of the good ones that never lasted for long.

They went out into the pouring rain, and he switched on lights and glared at the Mini's dash; and he said, scowling, "Less than a quarter of a tank left, and where the hell am I going to fill up at this time of night?"

But it was no great problem. He had a length of rubber tubing on a four-inch nail in the stable that served as a garage. He found Mrs. French's shiny new Rover 3500 standing there in the moonlit rain. Straight off the showroom floor, she'd had it repainted in custom lacquer, innumerable coats of Old Rose which the darkness helped to conceal. Its filler cap was locked, and he said to Wendy, "Okay, let's see how good you are."

Wendy Hayworth produced her thin stainless steel slivers and went to work, and picked the lock in less than thirty seconds. He stuck his rubber tube in there and sucked on it, and began siphoning fuel into the Mini; and in a few minutes, Wendy said mildly, "Ian, all we need to get to the airport is a couple of gallons..."

Ian grunted. "We're not going to the airport, you know I hate flying. And how would we get around in Rome? Driving a bloody Hertz?"

"Oh."

"If we push her a bit on the way to Dover, we'll just catch the six a.m. Hovercraft."

'Push her a bit', they did.

The tiny toy car hurtled through the hedgerows at better than ninety, and they were chased only once by the ever vigilant cops, and stopped. Wendy produced the little green card she carried, which the officers had never seen before; but after they got on the radio with their H.Q., one of them said gravely, "Seems it's all right, Miss. Just don't try and wreck that thing..."

As they sped on their way, Quayle was in a dark and introspective mood. He said, bitterly, "How come Mrs. Bloody French knows about Carlotta and me?"

She knew that an old wound had been re-opened. "She knows what you have for breakfast," she said, "down to the comic way you eat a fried egg."

He took her up on it at once, very angry now. "There's no one else on God's earth who could have told them about that. Only you."

"Ian, she's my boss! What she wants to know, I have to tell her."

There was a little stony silence, and then Wendy said, "I'm truly sorry she had to be so gross about it. I wanted to warn you in advance, but she wouldn't let me."

"A fucking *bitch*," Ian said furiously.

"Yes, I know it. Would it help to talk about Carlotta?"

"No, it wouldn't help in the least."

31

"Sorry..."

Ten miles of hedgerow flashed by them, and three small villages where he dropped down to a more sedate seventy miles an hour before flooring the pedal again. And he said at last, exasperated, "For Christ's sake! It was yesterday! But it was twenty-one years ago! How in hell can a memory last that long?"

A natural-born romantic, Wendy said with a sigh, "After all these years, you're still in love with her, I like that..."

He grunted. "I don't know. We feast on memories, and there are some women, a very few, who can't be forgotten. Even though they go off and get themselves married..."

He pulled out a handkerchief and blew his nose noisily; and Wendy wouldn't question him anymore.

But twenty miles further on, Ian Quayle said wrathfully, "God dammit, she left me for absolutely no reason at all! I'll never understand what makes women do the things they do, never! I went round to her flat one night, and there she was...*gone*. And I'll never know why."

Wendy knew why; it was all in his dossier, compiled by a dozen nameless clerks in the most secret of all England's secret Intelligence agencies.

But she said nothing. Saying nothing was something Wendy was very good at.

The tiny car sped on through the night.

CHAPTER 3

It was indeed twenty-one years ago.

Only recently out of his teens, Ian Quayle met a girl named Carlotta Mancini, who was studying criminology at the London University, where he himself was worrying about languages and history.

She was his own age, bright, fun-loving, affectionate and really quite beautiful, with dark, somber eyes and tiny wrinkles at the comers of her mouth; she laughed a lot, delighting in almost everything, and she could never, it seemed, stop talking about her father, who was a Major in the Italian Police.

Quayle particularly liked this aspect of her being, because he was devoted to his mother, whose stage-name was Claudine Andrassy, a ballet dancer of enormous competence from Hungary. (His father, the Shakespearean actor Harry Quayle, was a failure in everything).

They met under circumstances that were so ordinary as to be almost comical; she dropped her pile of books, and when he crouched down to help her retrieve them, their eyes met; and he laughed and said, "As a way to meet, it's not really very original, is it? My name's Ian Quayle, languages and history."

His laughter was infectious, and she said, smiling, "Carlotta Mancini, criminology."

"*Criminology*? I didn't even know there was a chair. Isn't

that a very strange subject for a lovely young girl?"

"My father's a copper, in Rome."

The idiom sounded strange in her lightly-accented speech, and he grinned and looked her in the eye and said, "*Mannaggia la miseria, che bellezza...*"

Her English was fluent, but she often wished she had more Italian friends with whom she could speak her mother tongue. And for his part, there just weren't enough people around who knew all the languages he was studying. And so, they always spoke Italian together, and she said to him one day, admiringly, "*Non lo credo*, I don't believe it, but you speak Italian as though you were Milanese-born, no trace of an accent at all..."

They went to the movies together, quite frequently, mostly to the foreign films in the cinemas around Leicester Square: '*Open City*', '*Le Jour Se Leve*', '*Carnet de Bal*', and a re-run of the wonderful old '*La Grande Illusion*'. They'd have supper together at Lyon's Corner House afterwards, and then walk in the relative quiet of the night to her bed-sit on Baker Street for a glass of wine and a game or two of chess while they listened to operatic recordings on her gramophone. They'd have long and earnest discussions of her studies and his, the twin subjects gradually becoming almost as one, history and criminology together. There was always a kiss before he left, and sometimes even a certain amount of hesitant fumbling before he left her for the long walk back to his mother's house in Bloomsbury.

Once in a while, when their chess games dragged on (they were so very well matched) he would sleep over, wrapped up in a blanket on the floor beside her bed, praying that she might slip down in the night and embrace him, yet not daring to go up and try to embrace *her*; he was very young, and she was terribly *vulnerable*...

They became closer and closer, until at last the inevitable

34

moment came.

They were lying on the floor together in front of a gas fire that had to be nourished with shillings once in a while as they listened to Gigli and Maria Caniglia raising 'Tosca' to quite impossible heights of excellence.

The world's greatest tenor had just finished singing:

> '*E lucevan le stelle, the stars were brightly shining...Fragrant, she entered, and fell into my arms...Oh, soft kisses, sweet abandon, as, trembling, I unloosed her veils and disclosed her beauty...*'

Carlotta said calmly, "Why have you never tried to make love to me, Ian?"

He was startled. "What...?"

"I know that you love me. It's true, isn't it?"

The music was soaring under the caress of the steel needle, and his heart was beating furiously.

"Yes, it's true. I love you dearly..."

"Then why? Tell me why."

For a long time he did not answer her, but he said at last, mumbling and unsure of himself, "It's...*because* I love you, Carlotta."

Speaking very quickly, he said, "I want so much to marry you, but how can I, ever? I earn my living, if you can call it that, working on translations for the British Museum. I take home, when I'm lucky, about seven pounds a week, often much less. I won't marry a woman I love and starve her to death."

"I don't necessarily want a husband," Carlotta said steadily. "I just want you to make love with me. Is that so difficult for you?"

It was very hard for him to control his emotions. He said hoarsely, "A virgin, I'm sure you're a virgin."

She held his look. "Yes, of course."

"No, then. No!"

"Why not, Ian?"

He was almost in tears. "Something to do with...I don't know! Desecration, perhaps. Iconoclasm, I don't care what you want to call it. I won't rob you of...of a precious..."

He threw up his arms. "Jesus Christ! How can I explain it, Carlotta? Meet me halfway, for God's sake! Try to understand what I'm trying to say!"

"No, I don't even *want* to consider such foolishness! We love each other, it's all that matters."

To his great despair, she unbuttoned her blouse and slipped it off, and reached behind her to unfasten her bra. Her breasts were small and quite immature, but very provocative. She unbuttoned her skirt and let it fall to the ground and stepped out of it, and there was a moment of hesitation as she hooked her fingers into the elastic of her cotton panties, knowing that she must look quite ridiculous in them, and quickly skinned them away.

She stood over him as he lay there on the floor; the gas fire went out, and he said desperately: "A shilling, I have to put another shilling in the slot..."

But she dropped to her knees beside him, and unbuttoned the top four buttons of his fly, and pulled the pants down over his hips to expose him, fumbling at him, the first time in her young life she had ever seen, much less touched, a penis.

She tried to remember what the girls in her class—far more sophisticated than she was—had told her, trying desperately to reduce their foolish giggles down to pragmatics.

He seemed to know very little more about these things than she did, and it wasn't truly a question of knowledge, but of atavistic instincts. He reached for her little half-lemon breasts and kissed them as he thrust into her, and he was in Heaven, not caring at all about the dreadful things that he knew might happen now. All he could think of was the touch of her wide-spread thighs on his hips and the look of absolute ecstasy in her eyes once the initial pain had passed, leaving its important message.

Later, when he had gone home in a state of miraculous euphoria, Carlotta found a bottle of Lyle's Lemon Soda in the pantry, and swung off the glass-marble top on its heavy wire catch, and shook it till it was almost exploding under her thumb; she used it as a douche, just as the girls in college had told her, hoping against hope that it would work.

For three months, Ian Quayle loved her, two immature children so desperately in love that nothing else mattered for them. And as the time slipped by he knew that there was no one else in the world who mattered to him, no one but Carlotta Mancini.

And then, disaster struck...

He went round to her Baker Street flat one night, and the lugubrious landlady said dismally: "She's gone."

The blood draining from his face, he stared around the empty room. All of Carlotta's personal things had gone with her—the photographs of her family, the framed certificate of her father's *Croce d'Italia* for his services to the Italian Government. The pottery coffee-service from Deruta in a yellow, green and blue dragon design called '*Raffaelesco*'.

All that was left of her was a pile of 78 rpm records on the table, the great Leonard Warren recording of '*Rigoletto*' which he had lent her. They were piled neatly up for him to collect, and they were topped, inexplicably, with a Deruta ashtray, a very beautiful artifact he had given her on her twenty-first birthday, just because it matched her coffee set; there was not even a note.

Was the empty ashtray somehow symbolic? Was it meant to tell him that nothing of their great love was left now?

Not even ashes?

And *why*?

What could have driven her to do this?

* * *

Ian Quayle immersed himself in his studies and tried quite hopelessly to forget her.

For his thesis he wrote an erudite paper on the secret and criminal societies in history, from the Sicarii at the time of Christ to the present day.

'*Sicaria*', he wrote, 'is an ancient Hebrew word meaning 'dagger'; its plural is '*sicariot*'; and Judas Iscariot's name—more correctly Judas Sicariot—meant that whereas every man of fighting age carried a dagger, Judas carried at least two. It means, also, that he was one of the '*Sicarii*, or Dagger-Men, who were members of perhaps the first terrorist organization in history of which there are written records, albeit somewhat skimpy and insufficiently verified.'

He went on (rather abruptly, his professors thought), to the Black Hand of Serbia who were responsible for the murder of the Archduke Ferdinand of Austria which precipitated World War One, and onto the Society of Friends of South-East Asia who were currently concerned with drug-running, a more profitable occupation than mayhem.

He continued with deep thoughts about the Secret Army for the Liberation of Corsica, back to the origins of the Mafia under the Bourbons; and his final arguments were devoted to the rise in modern times of an offshoot of the old-time secret societies—the equally clandestine terrorist groups operating under similar circumstances all over the world.

He had reference to the Hidden Army of Croatia, the Death Squads of Argentina, and to Italy's Red Brigades.

The thesis was quite brilliant, minutely detailed and very thoroughly researched.

And a copy of it fell into rather surprising hands...

CHAPTER 4

He was in one of the tiny bars at the Cheshire Cheese one night, his favorite of all the London Pubs, and he saw that his habitual-corner table was occupied by a couple he'd never seen there before, though there was nothing strange in that.

But the woman was a quite stunning beauty, tall, svelte, roan-haired, and very expensive looking indeed. She wore a tailored suit of light blue worsted that almost exactly matched the startling aquamarine of her eyes; eyes that were rather cold, he thought. *Cold*? No, that wasn't the word. Perhaps it was *cool*.

Her white silk blouse was open at the throat, and from what he could see of it her figure was good. And she was the kind of woman whose age could never be guessed at; thirty? Forty? Perhaps even more? She had the kind of face that would stay that way till she reached her sixties, and then suddenly collapse; it was a face of remarkable beauty, both in nature and in artifact.

The man with her was a little older, also rather distinguished looking, and conservatively dressed; a banker, perhaps, though his tie was Old Etonian. He caught Quayle's eye, a touch of amusement in his dark, thoughtful eyes, and he shuffled over.

He said apologetically, "We've taken your usual place, haven't we? How very thoughtless of us..."

Quayle shook his head. "No..." He looked around; the other tables were full, and the pub was crowded, as usual.

"Do please sit down," the man said, "we'll be leaving very soon now."

"Well..."

"My name's Harris, Robin Harris."

"Quayle," Quayle said, and looked at the woman.

"Mr. Quayle, Mrs. French," Harris said, making introductions. She held out her hand, a long-fingered, very capable sort of hand, and murmured, "How do you do?"

There was no smile, no emotion of any sort, just: "How do you do...?"

The two men chatted, amiably enough, and Mrs. French said not a word, though once in a while, out of the corner of his eye, Quayle caught her looking at him, rather *speculatively*, he fancied. He finished his beer, and Harris rose and said, "It's mild and bitter, I believe?"

He went to the bar and came back with a pint and two more glasses of Scotch, one of them very large indeed. He set the large one down in front of Mrs. French (not even a thank you!) and took up the conversation again.

It started off with nothing of importance—Cassius Clay's fight with Sonny Liston in Miami Beach, the raising of the Bank Rate by the British Government from four to five percent, the trial of Jack Ruby in Dallas...But it seemed to turn to more political matters—the blockade in Cyprus, the evacuation by the Americans of Wheelus Air Force Base in Libya, the talks in Washington between President Johnson and President Macapagal of the Philippines...

It was Harris who was doing most of the talking, and Quayle found he was saying (rather too often,) things like, "Yes, of course," and "Exactly..." and "Well, yes..."

He was also grunting a lot, and he said in desperation, "Are you a Parliamentarian, Mr. Harris? You seem to have access to a great deal of information I haven't seen in the papers, though I'm an avid reader. I'm afraid your name is not known to me. Should it be?"

Harris smiled, a man of infinite charm. "A politician? What a horrifying thought! Although I *am* a Civil Servant, Mr. Quayle. I *do* work for dear Mr. Wilson's Government."

There was hardly a beat; and then: "I console myself with the thought that I am actually working for Her Majesty."

Mrs. French rose abruptly, and Quayle saw, startled, that she had finished both her drinks.

She said imperiously, "My coat, please."

"Of course," Harris said.

He went to the rack and brought back a dark blue, very lightweight suede overcoat, the kind that costs an awful lot of money and would be irreparably ruined if a drop of rain ever fell on it. As he helped her into it, Mrs. French said, not looking at anyone, "Freelance only, not on the staff."

She turned to Quayle: "Goodnight, Mr. Quayle. We'll meet again."

"Mrs. French..." He tried to hide his surprise.

And when she had gone, Harris let out a long sigh and said mildly: "Do you ever have that strange feeling Quayle, that Damocles' sword has dropped. And *missed* you? That's how I always feel when she goes. Could we take a walk? There are some things I'd like to talk to you about, if I may. Along the Embankment, perhaps, it's a splendid night."

A trifle puzzled, Quayle looked at his watch. It was a few minutes to eleven. "No," he said. "I have to get home."

"We really must talk..."

Quayle found the insistence somehow displeasing, and he said, "Some other time, perhaps. Goodnight, Mr. Harris."

As he turned away, Harris said gently, "The performance ends at eleven-forty. Your mother won't be home until well after half-past twelve."

41

Quayle froze.

He turned. "I don't think I like this very much, Mr. Harris. Who are you?"

There was a gentle, even somewhat abashed smile on that thin, aristocratic face. "Will it help," Harris asked, "if I tell you that I am one of the most fervent of Claudine Andrassy's fans? Together with millions of balletomanes far more knowledgeable than I am, I regard her as one of the greatest...No, *the* greatest Prima in the whole history of ballet. I've even followed her to Paris, Zurich, Belgrade, Budapest, just to watch her dance. I *adore* her, Quayle, I'm probably even secretly in hopeless love with her. There! Does that make things better?"

"My question was," Quayle said coldly, "who are you? I'm beginning to hate everything about this meeting. You know just too damn much about me."

"Yes, I do, I admit it. And I apologize for it. An hour of your time, Quayle. *Please?*"

It was the *please* that did it, and thirty minutes later they were leaning together on the wall of the Embankment, staring down into the dark waters of the Thames, listening to the melancholy foghorns, and Harris said, out of nowhere, "That was a damn good thesis you wrote. On terrorism."

Quayle refused to be surprised any more. He said, "It's not supposed to have left the hallowed walls of the University. I don't suppose it's any good asking how you got hold of it?"

"Quite," Harris said gravely, "no good at all."

"And that brings us back to the original question: Who exactly are you? Intelligence, I assume?"

Harris appeared to be shocked. "Intelligence? Good God, no! Wipe that idea from your mind at once, I'd rather die. No, I'm with a thing called CLB, do you know us?"

"No, I don't think I do..."

"The Continental Liaison Board. We worry about what the West German Minister of Agriculture, for example, thinks about his French counterpart. About just which way Constantine, the new King of Greece, will switch his allegiances, a matter of delving into his mind. About how the shooting down of a U.S. jet over East Germany might endanger Western-Soviet relations. All that kind of nonsense. And for an intelligent Governmental appraisal...we need a great deal of high-class *research*, which is something not everyone is good at. You, apparently, are expert at it."

He was talking too much, and too earnestly, and Quayle said, "In any student body, every Tom, Dick, and Harry is a researcher. Why me?"

Harris nodded immediate agreement.

"Tom," he said, "turns to the Encyclopedia Britannica. Dick goes a mite further and collects clippings from the New York Times and Newsweek. Harry looks at *Le Monde* and maybe the *Corriere*, turning to a dictionary every five minutes before coming up with nothing. But the work you did on your paper indicates that you're a natural-born researcher, and that's a very rare breed. You have six languages, *six*! All of them fairly fluent..."

"Fairly fluent my arse," Quayle said coldly. "The six are immaculate. If you add what is loosely called a 'working knowledge,' then the number is nine."

"I don't know how you do it..."

"Only the first three or four are difficult. After that, it's easy."

Robin Harris said abruptly, "What did you think of Mrs. French?"

"Mrs. French?" He was puzzled by the question. "Well, what I thought of her doesn't really matter, does it?"

"Tell me anyway."

"Well...she's gorgeous, isn't she? The word that comes to mind is...*stunning*."

"Yes, she's really quite beautiful. She's also frighteningly competent, perhaps the most competent operative, male or female, the Continental Liaison Board has ever had. And..."

He hesitated. "I sometimes have the idea that it's at least partly because...because she doesn't have the weaknesses that you and I normally associate with...well, with real women."

"*Real* women?"

Robin Harris was covered with confusion. "I'm sure I should never have mentioned it, most ungentlemanly of me, please forget I said that."

"Of course," Ian Quayle said. "But you didn't ambush me here, did you, to discuss Mrs. French's sexual preferences? I can't imagine they're any of your business, certainly none of mine."

Robin Harris sighed. "Of course, forgive me. But I want you to work for us, Quayle, on research, it's very important for us. Your own hours, no nine-to-five nonsense. Strictly freelance."

"Freelance," Quayle said, "Mrs. French's parting words. She's your boss, I assume? I bleed for you."

"No she's not!" Harris said wrathfully. "She's my underling, though I sometimes find it hard to convince myself of that. She's actively engaged in...in *easing* me out of my position of authority, in two years' time she *will* be my boss. In five, she'll head the Department! She clambers up, tooth and nail, she's honestly not a very nice woman. But you'd be working for me, not for her."

Quayle thought about it for a while. Then: "I suppose there'd be some money? I'm not particularly avaricious."

"Yes, we know that too." Harris said softly, "I hate to tell you this, but we know *everything* about you, it's not nice, is it? Right down to the fact that you wear silk pajamas."

"You never know whom you might meet in the middle of the night."

Robin Harris was suddenly very serious. "I'd like very

much for you to go to work for us. The pay's not good, I'm afraid, but it would be a little something extra, a retainer sort of basis. Shall we say...four pounds a week?"

"How about seven?" Quayle said hopefully.

"Well, alright then, five. Mrs. French won't let me go any higher."

"I'm beginning to like Mrs. French less and less. Very well, five it is."

"Agreed, then."

Robin Harris shot out his hand, an old-fashioned gesture, and as Ian Quayle took it, (an old-fashioned sort of man himself), he said clearly, "My own hours, I work at home, on research and nothing else."

"Understood and agreed to."

That very upper-class face was suddenly alive with delight, and Robin Harris said, "In the course of time, God alone knows when, you'll have a case-officer, and I know just the right one for you. Her name's Wendy Hayworth, and she's a lady of very considerable spirit."

"Another Mrs. French?" It was beginning to worry him already.

But Robin Harris shook his head, smiling as though there were some secret there. "No. Nothing like Mrs. French at all. She's honestly the nicest woman in the world, you'll fall in love with her at first sight."

"Not something I do very often, Mr. Harris."

"So...Your first job. Herr Doktor Oberhausen of Austria, Second Secretary to the Ministry of Munitions...His last speech indicated that he was prepared to sell Libya some of their new ground-to-air missiles, the L-16, which, frankly, isn't that good. We don't really believe that the *Herr Doktor* can be so foolish, because Libya is planning on turning them over immediately to the PLO. Look into Oberhausen's background, read every speech he made since he suddenly shot into the forefront of Central

European politics five years ago, tell us what he *really* thinks. Will he? Or won't he? *That's* what we have to know."

"All right. It'll take me a week..."

"You've got a month."

"And where do I find you?"

"You know the Press Club in St. Brides Passage?"

"I can find it."

"The receptionist there is called, believe it or not, Hortense. An interesting lady, in many ways. Just give her the envelope and say it's for Robin."

"In many ways?"

Harris sighed. "Among all the things we know about you, nobody ever thought to type out your preferences for the female figure. Hortense has a bust that just has to be forty-eight disgusting inches, I always like to think she buys her bras from Omar the Tent-Maker. But she's nice...Just give her the envelope."

"All right."

CHAPTER 5

Three weeks later, Quayle went to the Press Club on St. Brides Passage with a bulky Manilla envelope filled with forty-two pages, single-spaced typing, about Herr Doktor Oberhausen's secret desires to arm all the mutually-hostile Arab countries with Austrian arms, and then set them at each other's throat so that the arms supply could be comfortably continuous...

He saw the receptionist sitting at her desk, nice-looking, attractive, sweet. He said to her pleasantly, "Good afternoon. I'm looking for Hortense..."

Her eyes were very bright, her smile quite disarming; she positively beamed. She said happily, "I'm Hortense. And what can I do for you, Mr. Quayle?"

He was disconcerted for only a moment. "You know my name?"

There was no one else in the lobby, and she laughed, tiny white, and almost perfect teeth showing. "Of course, we've been waiting for you, a package for Robin Harris..."

"*We?*"

"*Our* people, Mr. Quayle. Yours, and mine."

His eyes dropped to her bust; thirty-four at the very most, perhaps only thirty-two.

So where was Omar the Tent-maker?

The Manilla envelope was burning his hands. He sort of

waved it at her—how could he possibly hide it?—and said vaguely, "Perhaps I should come back tomorrow..."

It was a singularly foolish remark, and he was very conscious of the fact as he turned away.

"Wait," she said, and he turned back.

There was a gun in her hand.

It was almost the first time in his life that anyone had aimed a gun at him. It was a revolver, though he didn't know what kind, and the barrel was covered with an odd-looking contrivance that he thought must be a silencer. She said, very calmly, "I want that envelope, Mr. Quayle."

"Yes. Well. Of course. I'm not really very expert at arguing with guns..."

He laid the envelope down on the desk with both hands, and knocked the gun sharply to one side. It fired, with a surprisingly soft sound, and he grabbed her wrist in panic, over the desk. He fell to the ground with it, and heard her arm break, heard her sudden scream of pain.

He clambered to his feet and stammered, "I'm...I'm sorry...I really didn't mean to hurt you..."

He stared at the gun on the floor, wondered if he should pick it up; and for what reason? There was copious blood coursing down his forearm and dripping to the carpet, and he realized with a sudden sense of shock that he had been shot. There was no pain at all; he knew that it would come later.

He picked up the envelope, and when he reached the door to the inner office, there was an elderly, grey-haired man there, staring. He said, "Barbara? I heard you shout..."

He looked at Ian Quayle and said, more irritated than angry: "Would you mind telling me what the hell's going on?"

Barbara was lying over the desk, nursing her broken arm and moaning, and Quayle said to the elderly man, "I'm sorry. Temporary help, you never know who they really are, do you? I mean...*guns*? In a Press Club?"

The gray-haired man stared at him as Quayle went out.

And that evening, Robin Harris came to the Bloomsbury home to pick up the research. He said, "What you did at the Press Club, dear boy, was exactly the right thing. Mrs. French is very pleased with you."

Quayle said coldly, "If I knew you better, I would have precisely the right answer to that comment. Lots of four-letter words." He held up his bloodied arm. "She creased my forearm, and the bullet's still in there, I'll probably die of ptomaine poisoning. And it hurts like hell."

"So, you called a doctor, no?"

"Right. No. A bullet-wound, they have to notify the police. I figured that wouldn't be such a good idea. Was I wrong?"

"You were absolutely right, and I admire you for the thought. Do you have ice?"

"Of course I have ice..."

"Then we should both have a rather large Scotch on the rocks?"

"Coming up."

"And a lot more ice cubes, with a towel. We don't want to rush you over to Emergency and have to answer a whole lot of terribly embarrassing questions, do we?"

Quayle sighed, dreading it. "No, I suppose not."

Harris packed the ice over the wound in Quayle's arm and sipped his drink; for an interminable period, they just kind of stared at each other and tried some desultory conversation.

"Who do you think is going to win the cricket match tomorrow," Harris asked. "At Lord's?"

"Who cares...?"

Silence. Then: "Did you listen to Harry Truman's speech to the Senate in America? His eightieth birthday, the first time a former President has addressed a regular session of the Senate. What a grand old man..."

"Yes, indeed," Quayle said politely.

Silence again. Then: "Did you know that the first stage of the Aswan Dam in Egypt has just been completed?"

Quayle said wearily, "Christ, there's nothing in the world I hate more than small talk, Harris."

"Oh, really? Then let's get to work, you should be fairly well frozen by now."

From his hip pocket, Harris took the little pen-knife he always carried, tested its blade with his thumb-nail and found it sharp, and used it skillfully to dig the bullet out of Quayle's forearm.

He held it up and said scornfully, "A two-two, a woman's kind of weapon. You can take a dozen of these in your body and not have to worry too much, so what are you groaning about? You're a weakling, Quayle."

"That may well be," Quayle said. "But I still want to know why my report on Oberhausen was so important. He's really a nobody."

"And we know it. It was a successful effort to flush out the enemy. And could I please have another Scotch? You pour very small drinks, don't you?"

As Quayle up-ended the bottle, Harris said, musing, "I really have to admire you, in spite of everything. Do you know who it was you disarmed? Just *whose* gun-arm you broke over the edge of her desk?"

"Barbara something or other, that's the name I heard..."

"Barbara my arse," Robin Harris said. "She's Ilse Eckhardt, West Germany's number three on their list of most-wanted terrorists, one of the most deadly women in the world today. And yet...you disarmed her! I can't begin to believe it! I wouldn't even want to send a ten-man Commando from Special Services to tangle with her! How did you do it, Quayle?"

"Oh, I suppose," Ian Quayle said modestly, "just a case of masculine superiority..."

"Or else she recognized you as a nothing, and therefore relaxed her guard."

"That might be true too."

"Try it again sometime when she escapes from prison, as she will...we'll see how you make out the second time around."

"And I'm working," Quayle said sourly, "for a purely innocuous organization called the Continental Liaison Board. That just has to be a cover for *something*. What is it, MI5?"

"No," Harris said. He sighed. "Well, with your talents you'll find out sooner or later, I suppose. We're not MI5, they're a bunch of nitwits, and we don't like them very much. They're counterespionage, and not very good at it. We're MI*Six*, but don't ever let Mrs. French know I told you. She'd have my guts for garters. Can I trust your discretion?"

"If you thought you couldn't," Quayle said tartly, "you'd never have admitted it."

"A secret. Just between the two of us."

"Plus people like Ilse Eckhardt."

"Well," Harris said apologetically, "that was very unfortunate, I admit."

Unfortunate? Quayle was very put out. He'd been hired to do research, and here he was faced with life-threatening situations and he hated it. Moreover, his arm was giving him hell.

He went to the bathroom and doused the wound with cologne, the only disinfectant he had; and that hurt like hell, too.

Now the foolish little Mini-Cooper was hurtling towards the south coast at ninety miles an hour and was never going to make it to the Hovercraft in time.

Ian Quayle floored the pedal, came out of a distant reverie, and said to Wendy, hating his need for comfort from her, "Can we talk about Carlotta?"

51

There'd been mile after furious mile of silence, but Wendy was a very understanding sort of woman. "Of course."

Ian sighed. "The night before she left me, we were listening together to the Cetra-Soria recording of *Boheme*. All the great singers, Maria Caniglia, Ebe Stignani, Carlo Badioli and Guiseppe Taddei, with the incomparable Luigi Infantino...I remember that when Mimi died, and Rudolfo screamed: *Why do you look at me like that?* Carlotta burst into tears, she was a very emotional character. We made love together, and all I could think of was I have to get a new needle for that damned gramophone...Does that make me a number one idiot?"

"No, I don't think so..."

They hit the ramp at the precise moment when the flag was being run up and the stevedores were beginning to wheel it away. Ian Quayle put his thumb on the horn and floored the pedal, and leaped the Mini over ten feet of open water, to land with a terrible thud on the deck.

He got out and said to the startled attendant, growling,

"If I broke a back axle there, I'm going to sue you..." and led Wendy off to the bar for something to drink.

Comfortably ensconced with a large cognac on the plastic sofa, Ian Quayle said to Wendy, "The League of Hawks, I know I've read of them, somewhere, a long time ago. God dammit, my memory's not what it used to be." He glared at her, nursing his drink. "You know what research is about, don't you?"

She nodded. "I should do, by now."

"You don't really have to know anything about anything, you just know where to look it up."

Her mind was on other matters. "Did you know that I was there that night? When your mother had her accident?"

"No," he said, surprised. "You were?"

"We were home on leave from Washington, and my father took me to the Sadler's Wells to see her dance. I *cried*...Jesus, how I cried! I thought the standing ovation would never stop, and there wasn't a dry eye in the house, people were openly weeping, as I was too..."

Wendy was in tears again at the thought, and she dried her eyes and said, "The next day, the Press...it was outlined in funeral black, they said: "Claudine Andrassy will never dance again..."

"And she was dancing again a year later," Ian said heavily. "She just knew she could never be a Prima again. You'll meet her soon. You'll love her."

For the first time, Wendy Hayworth was about to meet a woman who had become a legend in her own time; one of the greatest ballerinas in history.

Claudine Andrassy, *Prima Assoluta*, now retired.

CHAPTER 6

At the age of sixty-two, Claudine was fabulous.

She was tall and slender and straight-backed, and very lithe indeed, with long dark hair piled now on top of her head, and the most enchanting grey-green eyes; there were tiny wrinkles at the sides of her rather full mouth, as though she smiled very often, which was true, true in spite of a life that had not always treated her kindly.

There'd been the problems with her late husband Harry Quayle, who could possibly have been England's foremost Shakespearean actor if he'd only stayed away from the bottle.

During her lonely nights, Claudine still lay awake and heard that magnificent voice intoning, so strongly that the theatre seemed to be reverberating with its forcefulness:

'Now is the winter of our discontent
Made glorious summer by this sun of York;
And all the clouds that loured upon our house
In the deep ocean buried.
Now are our brows bound...'

And then the awful stumbling:

'Bound with...bound...with victorious, yes,

54

victorious wreaths...'

How often had he played Richard? A thousand times, perhaps.

But he went on (and Claudine was standing in the wings, growing paler by the moment):

> *'Therefore, our sometime sister, now our Queen,*
> *The Imperial jointress to this warlike state,*
> *Have we, as 'twere with a defeated joy,*
> *With one auspicious and one dropping eye...'*

Claudine was in tears, and the stage manager was in hysterics, screaming. "Jesus fucking Christ, he's done it again! We got us a Claudius in the middle of Richard, get that curtain down! Down curtain, down...!"

But Harry Quayle found his way through it, and that magnificent, resonant voice flooded the auditorium:

> *'This Island's mine, by Sycorax my mother,*
> *Which Thou takest from me...!'*

The audience was booing now, and there were hands dragging the great Harry Quayle back into the wings. Claudine took him gently into her arms, and she whispered, "It's all over, Harry darling. It's going to be all right, let's go home..."

Life was not easy for her...

There'd been that terrifying business in Budapest, where she had gone to find her father.

"*Sick,*" they had said, and the sickness had turned out to be three machine-gun bullets in his stomach.

The Russians were in control, the Hungarians were

fighting back in a useless battle. Their leader, one Pal Melater, had raised the white flag of surrender to put a stop to the awful slaughter, and the Russians had accepted it.

But once he crossed the street under that white flag, Pal Melater had been arrested, whisked over the border into Romania for the sake of protocol, and there, executed.

Claudine had been foolish enough to protest the slow death of her father, and in her interview with a certain Russian Colonel Malakov, she had been raped.

There was no overt violence in the rape, none at all.

Malakov had said, quite simply, "I am a balletomane myself, dear Madame Andrassy, I have long admired your work, and yes, admired your great beauty too." And then—the clincher: "My artillery is trained on the school across the street, filled now with your so-called 'freedom fighters' and a number of frightened children too. And I give you a choice; either you sleep with me tonight...Or, at dawn, I will order the guns to open fire. And would you perhaps care for a glass of wine?"

What could she do?

That had been when her very young son, Ian, had maneuvered his way into war-stricken Hungary, had found her, and had told her, (hiding his own fears), "We're going home now, Mama, it's all arranged. Just don't let the border guards know who you really are. And I'm sorry to tell you, but Father is dead, our plane crashed in Austria..."

The great Harry Quayle *dead*? It was hard to take. Their marriage had never been a bed of roses, but still...

And finally, there was the famous accident where that goddam defector, high on stuff he really ought not to have been sniffing, had dropped her, a dreadful fall that had cracked her kneecap in two to put an end to her career as a Prima.

She really had very little to smile about...

* * *

She was dressed now in a very casual gown of silk in a strange almond-green shade; it seemed to be wrapped quite carelessly around her flawless body and tied loosely at the waist, a Bill Blass original from America that had cost her a fortune and showed every last penny of its price.

She embraced her son and kissed him on both cheeks, and she whispered, "My darling, how very good to see you again..."

Her eyes went to Wendy, somehow veiled, and Ian Quayle said, "And this is Wendy Hayworth, Mother, she works with me. My mother, Claudine Andrassy."

Wendy took the outstretched hand, and was very emotional. "All I can say, I suppose, is how nice to meet with you. But I'm crazy about ballet, and perhaps that says a great deal more."

"How very sweet of you..."

"As we say in the States, the greatest."

"You're American? I would never have guessed it."

"No. My father is Sir Richard Hayworth, the Ambassador. I've spent most of my adult life in Washington. But I came home a few years ago to fend for myself, to find my own way of life, you know what I mean? So now I'm working with Ian, and I love it. And I'm talking too much, aren't I?"

"Dinner's at eight," Claudine said. "We have lobster *Thermidor*. You like lobster?'

"I adore it," Wendy said, and Claudine laughed, those little wrinkles at the corners of her mouth deepening.

"Yes, I know," she said. "When Ian called, he said: "Hold the tarragon..." That's what I did."

A little later, at dinner, Claudine said to her son, "What are you doing in Paris, darling? There just has to be a motive of some sort, you never made an unmotivated motivation in your whole life..."

"A thing called the League of Hawks," Quayle said, dunking his garlic bread in the sauce. "I have to know everything about them. I thought that you might perhaps take time out and research for me. They're French, I'm convinced. I seem to remember they go a long way back, perhaps to Napoleon the Third or even earlier."

He frowned. "I just can't remember! In the early seventeen-nineties, try there. England and Russia were at war with France, and somewhere in there was a League of Hawks or Owls, I'm sure of it. Can you do this for me?"

"The Musée Nationale," Claudine said, "the natural place to begin."

"Yes, I'd say so...It really would be a very great help."

"And you?"

"I'm off to Rome. A little problem arose there."

The word 'little' was wrong, and from the look on his face, Claudine was instantly aware of it. She said gently, "It is a dangerous problem, darling?"

"No, I don't think so."

He fiddled with his fork for a moment, and said, "This is honestly the best *Thermidor* I ever had in my life..."

With no change at all in his voice, he went on: "Twenty-something years ago, do you remember a girl named Carlotta?"

"Of course," Claudine said at once. "Carlotta Mancini, I remember her very well. We were living in the Bloomsbury house then. You used to walk all the way home from her place on Baker Street, and you always arrived very tired, and with a strange sort of light in your eyes that told me all kinds of things you couldn't even begin to understand in those days. You brought her home just once, I remember, and I thought—and hoped—that it was the prelude to a proposal of marriage."

"Yes, that's the way it was," Ian said. "But before I could propose, I needed a few pounds a week more."

"A shame. She was a sweet and innocent child, and far too good for you. You should have married her, while you had the chance."

"I know it."

"And now?"

"Carlotta's father has been murdered. General Mancini. They blew his car up."

"*They?*"

"The League of Hawks, Mother. That's why I'd like you to find out about them for me. I owe it to Carlotta—to find out who killed her father."

There was a certain tone to his voice, and Claudine said, only slightly surprised, "Ian, after all this time, you can't still be in love with her..."

"No, of course not." He looked at Wendy and saw her examining her fingernails, and said stubbornly, "Yes, perhaps I am. After all these years, yes, I still think of her with something more than affection...And I don't give a damn who knows it."

It could have been an awkward moment, but the silence was broken by a ring at the door. The maid went to answer it, and when she came back, she said, wide-eyed, "A Police Inspector, Madame, Inspector Pleyer. But he talks...he talks like a *gentleman*, so I showed him into the library. I do hope that wasn't wrong of me..."

"It was absolutely correct, Cecile," Madame Andrassy said.

There were little lines of humor around her mouth as she turned back to her guests. "Let's take our liqueur there, let us find out what it can possibly be that can bring a *gentlemanly* police officer into my home. A little excitement to liven up my rather dull existence..."

The library was a splendid room, wall-to-wall bookshelves on three sides crammed with works in Hungarian, French, English, German and Latin, the fourth made up entirely of glass, overlooking the famous rooftops of Paris.

Inspector Pleyer was standing there, a thin, wiry, tightly knit man in surprisingly elegant civilian clothes. He took

Claudine's proffered hand, brushed it with his lips and murmured, "May I first say, Madame Andrassy, that this is an honor that a simple policeman would never even dream of. Unhappily, I know little of ballet, but your great reputation has filtered down even to *hoi polloi* such as myself."

He was a very down-to-earth sort of man, and he came at once to the point. "The reason for this intrusion, Madame, is that I must ask you to draw your curtains, the drapes over the windows. Open as they are, I regret to inform you that they invite a danger we would all wish to avoid. There is a gunman out there, a man with a high-powered rifle. I have a squad looking for him...So far, they have not been successful. The curtains, please."

"Yes, of course. Cecile?"

The maid drew the drapes, wondering with her peasant thoughts if the mysterious gunman out there would seize the opportunity to put a bullet into her heart as she did so.

Claudine said curiously, "And would you tell me, Inspector, just why your potential assassin should concern himself with us?"

Inspector Pleyer betrayed himself with a quick glance at Ian Quayle. But he shrugged deprecatingly, and said, "I am merely obeying the orders of my superiors, Madame. And with your permission, I will leave you now. Just keep those windows covered."

"But before you go...will you take a glass of cognac with us?"

The Inspector inclined his head. "That is most gracious of you, Madame Andrassy, but I am on duty. It might be...very serious duty."

He reached for her hand and bowed over it again. "And may I say once more, Madame...a very great privilege."

When he had gone, Claudine turned to her son and said, accusingly, "So! Is someone searching for you already? To kill you? Is that what it's come down to? Already?"

Quayle said, worrying about it, "There's an enemy out there somewhere, Mother, an enemy we know nothing about, as yet. But every move he makes tells us a little something more about him. We may have to let him get closer, to see him more clearly."

Wendy said tightly, "That's a very dangerous philosophy, Ian. Don't ever think like that."

Quayle said stubbornly, "We may have to let him get very close indeed. Look him straight in the eyes and try to decipher what he's up to."

Midnight came, and the grandfather clock in the hallway—a fine old Thomas Tompion from the Seventeenth Century—chimed the hour. Wendy had gone to the powder room to fix her face, and Claudine said, smiling her secret smile, "I'm not sure what your relationship with Wendy is, you gave me no hint at all. So I've put you in separate rooms. But there's a connecting door, you won't have to pad barefoot through interminable corridors all night long."

There was a little pause. Then: "She's in love with you, isn't she? I'm not so sure how you feel about her."

Quayle sighed. "You're a very perceptive woman, aren't you?"

"When it comes to my son's happiness...yes, I am."

"Well...she's in love with me only *sometimes*. I suppose that goes for me too. Does that make sense to you?"

"But of course, darling! Do you normally sleep together?"

He laughed suddenly. "You know, I have the feeling that you're probably the only mother in the world who can get away with a question like that! Perhaps that's one of the reasons I love you so much."

"Do you sleep with her?"

For a moment he did not answer her. He said at last, "Not

normally, no. Just...once in a while. And always for the wrong reasons."

It was an explanation that Claudine could understand perfectly well.

Ian Quayle was restless that night, and the mattress of the big four-poster bed was a little soft for his comfort. He awoke in the early hours of the morning, and opened the French windows in the darkness and went out onto the rooftop in his pajamas.

He lit a cigarette, and a shadow detached itself from the brickwork of the chimneys and stood beside him; it was Inspector Pleyer, and he said quietly, "Nothing but the silence of the Paris night, Mr. Quayle. It's a very romantic silence, isn't it? I'm sure he's gone, but we are still watching."

"And I'm glad of it. Do you know who he might be?"

"No. They tell me nothing."

"But it wasn't just...a neighbor's report, was it?"

The Inspector hesitated. But the aura of the night was conducive to confidence, and he said slowly, "No. That faceless entity we call '*They*' told me: 'Madame Andrassy's apartment, watch it carefully tonight, there may be murder attempted.' And so, I placed my men..."

His anger was rising, and he said, "Why would anyone want to harm a woman who is so greatly loved and respected, one of the greatest ballerinas in history?"

He peered at Quayle, and said tightly, "Is it possible that you are his target, *M'sieur*?"

"Perhaps," Quayle said. "Goodnight, Inspector."

He went back to his room, and tossed and turned on the too-soft bed. He thought about the lovely Carlotta, and became cognac-emotional about her. Would she ever overcome the tragedy of her father's murder? He remembered how close knit the family was.

Would her tears ever cease?

He thought of her only as she had been then, twenty-one

years ago; and at this moment it was a purely physical image, that of a slender young girl of dark, intriguing beauty, roused very easily to heights of passion because of their love for each other.

Would she really have changed that much over the years?

The spark of an old love was flaming strongly...

He remembered one exciting night when, for her pleasure, he recited the Song of Solomon to her as he played with her:

'Behold, thou are fair, my love...thous has doves' eyes...thy lips are like a thread of scarlet...thy two breasts are like two young roes that are twins...'

He twisted and turned in a kind of torment, and in a little while he arose and went to the communicating door that led to Wendy's room.

He knocked, hesitantly.

He heard her voice, low, controlled, expectant: "It's not locked, Ian. Come on in."

CHAPTER 7

Wendy Hayworth, age 29, British born, brought up in Washington D.C., youngest daughter of an aristocratic and highly respected family of British landed gentry. Attractive, imaginative, ambitious, dedicated, sometimes fool-hardy, and stubborn as hell.

Correction: *extremely* attractive.

She'd had a god-awful interview with Mrs. French in the secret office in St. James' Street, where the brass plaque on the door said *DEPUTY DIRECTOR*.

And nobody went to Mrs. French's offices to discuss anything; they went there to listen.

Not even looking up from the dossier she was leafing through, Mrs. French said casually, "It's unusual for a woman of your remarkable good-looks at the age of twenty-nine, not to be married. Does it mean anything the Board should know about?"

"No," Wendy said coldly. "It does not."

Mrs. French looked up only briefly, and leafed through the file again; but she somehow gave the impression that she already knew everything that was written there.

"Four years," she said dispassionately, "you were living with one Wilfred Slocombe-Brent in Soho. I never realized that some people actually live in Soho, particularly with lovers named Wilfred..."

Wendy's mouth was dry, and she was very angry, but Mrs. French went on: "Then, for a year and a half, there was that mad affair with Lord Stephen Horley, right under the nose of Lady Horley."

Wendy froze and said nothing.

"And I find it interesting," Mrs. French said, "that from Lord Horley you flew into the arms of..." (a glance at the dossier again here), "a woman named Cecile Deschamps. But that only lasted for two months. What happened?"

"We took a house in Kensington Gardens together, because neither of us could afford it alone. It didn't work out."

"Are you a natural-born lesbian, Miss Hayworth?"

"No! I am not! And if that's what you called me here for..."

"I called you here on more important matters. You met Ian Quayle, I think?"

Wendy was startled by the sudden change in the conversation's direction. "Yes, I've met him several times."

"A thumb-nail sketch then. What do you think of him?"

It was a time to get even, and Wendy said, "You're hung up on sex, aren't you? Well, I think he's a charming man. I think he'd probably be very good in bed. There, does that satisfy you?"

Mrs. French would not be fazed. "I want you to *monitor* Ian Quayle," she said. "I want to know everything he thinks about, everything. I have a feeling he's field material, something that's very hard to come by these days. So, get close to him. And you will accept whatever intimacies might be required of you."

Wendy Hayworth stared. "Are you suggesting...?"

"No."

There was a thin smile on Mrs. French's handsome face. "I suggest nothing. I'm giving you an order. If you can suffer poor Lord Horley's pathetic blandishments...then Ian Quayle's should be perfectly acceptable to you. You might even enjoy them. That will be all, Miss Hayworth."

Wendy went slowly to the door, and when she opened it, the full realization of what had happened struck her. She turned back in a restrained fury, and said, "You're trying to turn me into some kind of a whore, aren't you?"

"No," Mrs. bloody French said drily. "I just want to make your established lifestyle work for us. Good day, Miss Hayworth."

The first time she seduced Ian Quayle, the realization of what she was doing was quite horrible for her, because he was so gentle and considerate with her. The second time, and the third, were less so. And at last, at strike five, was it? She inevitably fell head over heels in love with him.

And she dared not ever admit it, even to herself.

It was only six in the morning, but Claudine was as beautifully groomed and lovely as she had ever been, her hair tumbling down over her shoulders now, almost to her waist, carefully brushed and shining nicely; she looked adorable.

She said, fussing around, "You'll want to stop somewhere to eat, I've had a picnic basket prepared..."

Wendy said, "May I use the phone, Madame Andrassy. To call Rome?"

"Of course, darling. It's on the desk there."

Wendy looked at Ian. "And what time do we arrive?"

"It's one thousand and twenty-two miles," Quayle said. "No speed limits on the Continent, thank God, we'll hit a hundred, a hundred and ten most of the way...Say an average of eighty, given a few towns to pass through...we'll be there by nine."

Wendy dialed, and the call came through very quickly.

"Leo?" she said. "Wendy. Nine o'clock tonight." She

listened for a moment in silence, and then: "Yes, do that. Security, amber. Goodbye, Leo."

Their farewells were highly emotional, and Claudine said, "Tomorrow I'll be all day at the National Museum, about your League of Hawks. And where will I find you?"

"In Rome," Wendy said. "The number is highly confidential, 84-17-32."

"I'll call you."

She embraced Wendy, a certain affinity building up between the two of them.

"In Rome," Claudine said, "I'll see you soon. Perhaps with a few answers."

"I can't begin to tell you, Madame Andrassy..."

"Claudine, Wendy."

"Claudine...what a great pleasure."

"Look after Ian for me. You're so much more competent, I feel, than he is. And he's heading for trouble, isn't he?"

"Perhaps. Together, we'll manage."

Driving like a controlled maniac, Quayle passed through Fontainbleau, Nevers, and Lyons, seldom taking his foot off the pedal. He took the Rhone route to avoid most of the mountains, and by one o'clock they were still on Route N7 and just outside Nice. They stopped at a scenic roadside viewpoint for a picnic lunch, and Quayle said mildly,

"You phoned Rome from Paris, shouldn't I know about that?"

"A man named Leo," Wendy said, "our top agent in Italy. He has a safehouse for us to stay in, on the Via Appia Antica, you know it?"

"Of course. Rome's most historic road. And one of the most delightful."

"He'll be there to meet us, and you'll like him."

"I will?"

"He comes from Naples, highly emotional, a true *Napolitano*. But very, very bright. Yes, you'll get on famously together."

"Just as long as he doesn't feed us with Napolitan food. If there's a bloody great wash-basin filled with *Pasta 'sciutta Napolitana* waiting for us, I'll scream."

"Then gargle. You might have to do just that."

They were in the mountains of the French-Italian border, and behind them, even though the foolish little soapbox of a Mini was holding a steady ninety miles an hour on the winding, dangerous mountain road, a low slung and quite ancient Ferrari was creeping up on them.

Quayle looked up into the mirror and said, admiringly, "My God, look at that. That's the old Super-America, but a convertible; they made only a handful of them. Four-point nine liters, you won't believe the savage performance..."

As though to echo his words, the Ferrari suddenly leaped forward like a wild beast; it scraped the Mini-Cooper and knocked it ten feet to the side of the highway, and Quayle screamed, "Christ! We've got a drunk on our hands...!"

He braked ferociously, but the Ferrari had almost stopped, and was already behind him again. It surged forward with monstrous power, and side-swiped the little Mini again, and Ian Quayle muttered, "All right, he wants to play silly buggers..."

He floored the pedal, and watched the needle swing over to a hundred and twenty, and he said, muttering: "God dammit, he's got forty miles an hour more than I have..."

Wendy was swiveled round in her seat, watching as the Ferrari animal pounced, and she screamed, "Ian...He's going to tip us over the cliff...!"

The curves in the mountain road were frightening, and the sea was monstrously far below them, the waves pounding on the rocks down there. Quayle did some very fancy heel-and-toe driving as the long red streak of immaculate bodywork hurtled alongside him.

He was on the very edge of the cliff as he saw the driver's heavily-bearded face, grinning wildly. He waited till he saw the Ferrari's front Pirellis begin their turn, and he slammed on everything...Even at better than ninety miles an hour, the lightweight toy car screamed to a full stop in less than two hundred feet. He saw the Ferrari rip off his left front fender, saw the driver wrestling in sudden shock with the wheel, knowing he'd over-steered.

He saw the lovely old car surge out over the top of the cliff, saw it twisting over and over in midair like a seagull with a broken wing, saw it crash to the rocks down there and explode in the fury of a twenty-gallon tank...

He stumbled out of the Mini, badly shaken. And beside him, trying to control her emotions, Wendy said, "He was trying to kill us, Ian..."

"Balls," he said roughly. "A drunk."

"No. I saw his face. There was murder on his mind."

Ian stared down at the flaming wreck. "One of the great cars of history," he said. "They're not supposed to finish up like that."

He stalked back and found the ripped-off front fender, and tossed it into the back. "We'll get it fixed in Rome," he said.

He was very silent as they continued on their way; and Wendy knew he was trying to hide his emotions; she said nothing.

And a few moments before nine o'clock, they pulled up at the address on the Via Appia Antica that Wendy had given him.

CHAPTER 8

It was a fine old villa, quite small, set back from the road in a dense stand of pines in this most ancient of Rome's ancient streets, very square and squat, two-storied and painted a mellow ochre.

And Leo was there to meet them.

He was in his fifties, an effusive and overwhelming sort of man from Naples; and his knowledge of the English language was remarkable.

He said, beaming, "Everything is ready, Signor Quayle, hot water on the stove...I have assumed that after so long and tiring a journey you would want baths...And will you tell me what happened to your car? One of our truck drivers, no doubt? They are all maniacs."

"Not a truck," Ian Quayle said. "A Ferrari."

He told Leo of the circumstances, and the Italian's soulful eyes were veiled, like the eyes of a cocker spaniel in heat.

He said softly: "And you were far too busy taking evasive action, *senz' altro*, to have noticed the number plate?"

"Well, yes, I'm afraid so. All I could see was this bloody great Ferrari coming at me time and time again."

He felt somehow guilty, but Wendy said, "Italian license plates, the number was FJ-13-76."

"Ah, thank you, I will make the check."

70

Ian looked at her and said nothing, and Leo went on, quite ignoring more important matters. "And I have a very satisfying dinner for you, I cooked it myself. *Pasta 'sciutta Napolitana*, the best pasta in the whole of *Mezzogiorno*."

Ian sighed. "And how much do you know about this General Mancini affair, Mr....Signor...?"

"Just Leo," Leo said. "I find it wiser never to use my family name." He beamed. "Just like the young ladies who take over our streets after dark. And I know everything that is known to anybody about the murder of a very good man. General Mancini was head of a top-secret department dealing with terrorism, reporting only to the Minister of Justice himself."

"And where can I find his daughter Carlotta?" Quayle asked. "And how soon? I used to know her once, many years ago, and I'd like to offer my condolences."

Leo threw a quick look at Wendy and met only a blank stare. He said, "The family has, how you say, gone into seclusion. It might take a long time to find out even where they are."

"Well, give it high priority, will you do that for me? A personal favor?"

"Of course."

"And our starting point is probably the bomb that blew up the General's car. Do we know what sort of bomb it was? They told me the Red Brigades claimed responsibility, and they normally use simple dynamite or gelignite. Is this the case here?"

"No sir." Leo shook his head. "This was a much more sophisticated bomb. It was made with polynitroanthesine, do you know it?"

"Yes, I do."

He thought about it for a moment, searching the recesses of his memory. "The enzymes reach two thousand degrees Fahrenheit within, I think, one-point eight seconds of detonation. It must have incinerated everything, instantly."

"All the police could find was charred remains up on the roof-tops together with the ashes of his all-important briefcase."

"Which contained...what?"

"The General," Leo said, "had compiled a dossier on a very secret organization called The League of Hawks. Almost nothing seems to be known about them, but he was taking his paper to an emergency meeting of the Cabinet, and I prefer to assume that he was killed because his investigation would have exposed them to the world at large. Which would mean that he was killed by this nebulous League."

"Then why should the Red Brigades claim the credit?"

Leo shrugged expressively. "If anyone even farts in Rome, the Red Brigade is liable to say: 'We did it.' Breaking wind is anti-social behavior, they like to take the credit for it. And at this point, I feel I must tell you that very, very few people even know that the General's department exists. Much less who heads it."

There was a little silence, and then Ian said gently, "Go on, Leo. I'm sure there's a punch line there somewhere."

"Yes, there is. It means a high-level leak. And in my own opinion...that leak is in London."

Quayle stared. "Oh my God. Can you be sure?"

"No."

"But have you any idea who it might be?"

"No."

"The remotest possible idea? A suspicion even?"

"No. And I might be wrong."

"Have you told London about this?"

"No, of course not. I might be voicing my suspicions to quite the wrong party."

"You report to Mrs. French, I take it?"

"Yes."

"You think it's she?"

"No."

"Robin Harris?"

"No."

"Then who, for God's sake!"

Leo sighed. "I must repeat, Mr. Quayle, I have no idea at all who it might be. I just...*know*. There's a double agent working out of the London office."

"Oh Jesus. Well, let's leave that problem for the moment. Was anything left of the General's papers, anything that could be reconstructed? There's some pretty sophisticated equipment available."

"Nothing, I'm afraid. Your word, Mr. Quayle... incinerated. All the police could gather together was a pile of ashes, a few arms and legs burned to cinders."

There was an infinitesimal pause, and then: "And three charred skulls."

Ian scowled. "Three? The General, his chauffeur...Who was the passenger? Is it possible that the passenger was the real target? A Minister, perhaps?"

"No, Mr. Quayle, it was not a Minister."

There was that desperate look from Leo to Wendy again, the same stubborn rejection from her.

And now, Ian knew...

He felt his blood suddenly running cold, and he shouted, "Who was the passenger, Leo?"

Leo produced a large handkerchief and blew his nose loudly; there were emotional Italianate tears in those unhappy eyes.

"I'm sorry," he whispered, "but you have to know. The passenger was his daughter Carlotta, he was dropping her off somewhere. At the...at the dressmaker's..."

Quayle was in shock, the memories of her crowding his mind...

She was crouched over a pile of scattered books as he looked into her eyes and said, "Not a very original way to meet..."

She lay beside him on the carpet in front of that godawful gas fire as they listened to Paisiello's 'Barber,' whispering; "Surely one of the best recordings in history..." at which moment that damned fire had gone out, its shillings exhausted.

He saw her standing above him, unbuttoning her blouse and whispering, "It's honestly time for you to take me, Ian, truly it is..."

There was Carlotta lying beneath him, gasping with the pain of his inexpert and quite furious assault, and at last the quiet contentment in which they both knew that they were lovers now, for always...

He was hardly aware that the sound he heard was a low, soft moan that came from his own throat.

He tried to mumble, "Excuse me..." but the words just would not come. He left the room and went outside, and leaned on the iron gate to watch the infrequent cars speed past the villa.

In a little while, he was conscious that Wendy was beside him. She reached for his hand, and said quietly, "I can't tell you how sorry Ian..."

His voice was flat and dull. "You knew, didn't you?"

"Yes."

"And you didn't think to tell me earlier? I had to find out...like this?"

"Back at the cottage, I wanted to tell you. She said no."

"*She*? You mean...Mrs. French?"

"Mrs. French. She insisted that you not know till you were here, 'in position' she called it. Something to do with...with pushing you a little harder once you got here. It's the way her mind works."

"The fucking *bitch*."

"Yes. That's exactly what she is, a fucking bitch. I'm so sorry..."

He wouldn't let her off the hook. "And you do

everything," he said, "don't you, that Mrs. fucking French tells you to?"

"Yes."

The instant admission startled him. "Then tell me why?" he said.

"All right, I will."

Wendy took a long deep breath. "It's because...in spite of her failings, she's probably the best brain we've ever had in a department I work for and am devoted to. Okay, rightly or wrongly, I *believe* in what we're doing in CLB. And she's so good at it...it terrifies me sometimes. I hate her guts as much as you do, perhaps more. But she's the best we've ever had."

"And just might be a double agent."

"No. I don't believe that. It makes no sense at all, she's too ambitious to fool around with low-grade stuff like that."

He wanted to be nasty, and he said tightly, "The first time we made love, do you remember?"

There were warning signals flashing, but Wendy nodded. "Yes, of course I do. In your London flat."

"She'd told you to take me to bed, isn't that true? Jesus Christ, you think I didn't suspect it? You lay there like a side of mutton."

Wendy stifled her anger, not without difficulty. "That's not a very nice thing to say, Ian Quayle."

"I'm sorry, I got carried away. But the second time, down in the cottage, you remember that too? The third time? The fourth? It wasn't just duty any more, was it? Unless you faked it better than I give you credit for."

"You unconscionable *shit*...I" She too was getting carried away. She said furiously, "And while we're talking about sides of mutton...you're not exactly God's gift to women, in bed. Did you ever stop to think about that? Bang-bang-bang, and that's it. Go to Hell, Ian Quayle."

He would say nothing more, even though he was

seething, and in a little while Wendy left him, already sorry for the confrontation and hoping that he might be too.

She knew his secret pains; but how could she hope to share them with him?

Later, he lay on his back under the goose-down comforter in the darkness, dry-eyed and staring out at nothing. The lovely Roman moon threw an oblique beam across the bed. It was a London moon, striking through the open windows of the Baker Street bed-sit, and he could almost hear Titta Ruffo's extraordinary voice echoing:

'*Come to the window, my treasure,*
Come and console my weeping...
You whose mouth is sweeter than honey...'

Carlotta's hands were touching him, exciting him beyond endurance, and that damned fire plopped and went out as he rolled over onto her.

A Deruta ashtray, in satisfying shades of yellow, green, and blue, with dragons all over it...And a pile of 78rpms. Was there nothing more left of her?

That glorious, vibrant body nothing more than a mess of ashes now...?

The door to his bedroom opened silently, and a beam of light cut through the secret darkness.

Wendy was standing there, and backlit, her hair was framed in a halo; her negligee was almost non-existent, her long legs and even the curve of her breast also lit from behind her, a breast that was very full and yet firm, a breast that any woman could be immensely proud of, a breast that any man would worship as he feasted on it.

She said hesitantly, her voice a zephyr, "I'm so sorry we quarreled, Ian. We're very close, you and I. We shouldn't quarrel, ever."

"I know it. Forgive me."

She stood there, not moving.

She whispered, "If I can somehow make it easier for you...?"

He turned over onto his stomach and buried his face in the pillow, trying to stifle the tears.

"Goodnight, Wendy," he said. "Sleep tight."

The door closed; the light was cut off; there was only darkness left.

CHAPTER 9

Ian Quayle was a man possessed, just as Mrs. French, back home in London had wanted him to be. He was driving himself with an obstinate kind of fury that he found very hard to contain.

The officer in charge of the investigation, Leo had told him, was one Police Captain Arrigo. And he sat in the Captain's sparsely-furnished office, now, and waited; discourses with the Italian Police were almost always a matter of waiting.

Arrigo was putting the finishing touches to his manicure as he sat at his battered plastic desk, on which there was a framed photograph of the late Benito Mussolini (small enough to be slipped quickly into a drawer if the wrong people came calling), a much larger photograph of his wife, (a plump and dreary woman in her forties) with their four children, all girls; and a framed color photograph, carefully cut from the weekly magazine Panorama, in which he himself was physically wrestling with a terrorist who was trying to evade arrest.

The photograph (he had a dozen more copies of it at home) was one of his most prized possessions; the terrorist's Baretta pistol was only an inch or two under the Captain's jaw as he fought for control of it.

He was immensely elegant, in his early sixties, and had long been resigned to the fact that he'd never make

Commandante, even after almost forty years of service; he just spoke out too clearly about the things that he thought were wrong.

He was tall and willowy, and always worried about his personal appearance, spending hours every morning with a pair of nail scissors, clipping unsightly hairs from his ears and his nostrils, and setting his still-abundant grey hair just so, running a comb through it a dozen times till it was exactly right...

He threw down his emery board, and said: "There is a lady in your department, Mr. Quayle...A Miss Wendy Hayworth. I saw her only fleetingly, but may I be permitted to say—a lady of the most remarkable quality?"

"Oh really? Yes, she's alright, I suppose."

"A very beautiful lady, I'm sure you'll agree."

"Ah...Yes. I've noticed..."

"And she's blessed with a certain...stateliness."

"Stateliness?"

Arrigo patted his hairdo. "She carries with her the strong authority of your London office, with whom my superiors are always pleased to co-operate. She chose not to talk with me, nor even with my Colonel. She went straight to the Minister of Justice himself. And I find that truly remarkable."

"Oh? How so?"

"*Nobody* ever talks with our current Minister of Justice, Mr. Quayle. His office is really quite sacrosanct; it's far easier to arrange an interview with the Pope. And yet...she did it. And as a result, I have direct orders from the Minister himself, who never before even knew of my existence, to help you in any way I can. Would you care for a glass of Strega?"

Surprised, Quayle looked unobtrusively at his watch, it was shortly after ten o'clock in the morning, but he said, "Well, that would be most acceptable, Captain."

Arrigo slid open a drawer and found an old-fashioned taxi-horn, a black-rubber bulb and an aesthetically satisfying twist of tarnished brass opening up at its end into a funnel. He squeezed the bulb twice, *wurp-wurp*, and the door from the outer office opened almost instantly.

A frightened young girl was there, almost visibly trembling with the fear that something might be wrong, and the Captain said to her, using the '*tu*' that was reserved for people of inferior station in life, "We will have two glasses of Strega. Wash the glasses first."

She bobbed up and down. "*Si, signor Capitano, subito...*"

She scurried out, and came back in no time at all with two glasses and a half bottle of Strega on an enameled tin tray overprinted with the Cinzano logo. Earnestly she polished the glasses with her handkerchief, just to show how serious a matter this was. But Arrigo himself did the pouring, and found a pencil to make the mark on the label for where the level was...

He raised his glass and said, "Your very good health, Mr. Quayle. And would it be asking too much...if you were to mention to His Excellency the Minister how well you were received in my office...?"

"The next time I have the pleasure of the Minister's company for dinner," Quayle said gravely, "I'm sure the matter will come up. Now...the General's report on the League of Hawks was 'Eyes Only', a rather foolish characterization. But it means, does it not, that there's not a copy filed away somewhere?"

Arrigo nodded. "That is absolutely correct, no copies anywhere."

"But someone must have typed it up for him."

"Yes, how very understanding of you. It was prepared for him by his personal assistant, a woman named Renata Dominici. A very *personal* personal assistant."

"Which means...? That she's his mistress?"

"Yes. She's really a very attractive young woman. A little plump, perhaps, but in the whole history of Italian sexuality, adipose deposit has never ever been considered a detriment."

"Er...yes, I suppose so. Then this is the lady I have to talk to next. She will undoubtedly remember a great deal of what she typed."

"I'm sure of it." Arrigo sipped his Strega. "Unfortunately, she seems to have disappeared."

"Disappeared?"

"She's undoubtedly aware of the fact that whoever killed the General for what he had written about this mysterious League of Hawks...must know that she still holds at least the essence of it in her mind. She will, therefore, be understandably frightened that they'll be looking for her. And so...she's *gone*. Where to, God alone knows. And unhappily, God is very seldom on the side of the Police Department, he prefers not to confide in us. I'd like to find her myself, there are many questions I have to ask her."

"Unless, of course, she's already been killed. Her name, again?"

"Renata Dominici."

There was a little silence, and then, Ian Quayle said steadily, "And I want to see what's left of the bodies. Even if it's only ashes." It was hard for him to control his voice; "I want...I want to see the...the residue."

Arrigo was a fool in many ways, but he was not entirely insensitive; he felt the hair curling on the back of his neck.

"They told me, Mr. Quayle," he said carefully, "that your interest in this affair transcends the borders of the official and has very personal overtones. Is it true?"

"You put it rather crassly," Quayle said. "But that is correct. Carlotta Mancini was once a very dear friend."

"Then may I dissuade you from any endeavor that will only cause you pain?"

"The bodies," Quayle said stubbornly.

"There are no bodies, *signore*. Only pieces of charcoal.

Charred remains, nothing more."

"You have your orders, I believe? From the Minister himself?"

Arrigo, reluctantly, rose to his feet. "Very well then, if you insist on torturing yourself."

They drove round to the Morgue together, in silence.

It was a cold grey basement room, and the old man in charge, his cuffs and his collar frayed, opened a steel drawer for them. It wouldn't roll out properly, and he swore and thumped at it with his fist. "*Disgraziati loro*," he said. "Sometimes they just don't want to be seen..."

The drawer contained a large cardboard box that was over-printed with the words: *Birra Dreher, Trieste*, a container that had once been filled with four dozen bottles of beer. It was filled now with charcoal, twisted limbs and bits and pieces...

Ian Quayle stared at them, and Captain Arrigo, watching him, had the terrible impression that he was...*searing* the sight of them into his mind.

He said, knowing that there was something here he was not capable of handling, "Please, Mr. Quayle, it will not help at all, I promise you..."

He tried to slide the drawer shut, but it jammed at the halfway mark, and he shouted to the old man, "*Mannaggia la miseria...!*"

The old man took it from him, and worked it back and forth and slid it home. He said mildly, "It has to be jiggled, like a toilet, you know? Just jiggle it, and it will work."

Quayle wanted to vomit, but he bit his tongue and held it back; and an hour later, he was back at the safehouse on the Via Appia Antica.

He said to Leo, not trying to mask his impatience, "A woman named Renata Dominici, Leo. She's in hiding, and I want her found. I want her found *immediately*. I want her found *yesterday*."

Leo sighed, his soulful *Napolitan* eyes veiled. He said, mildly reproaching, "Renata Dominici, the General's mistress. We are not sleeping, Mr. Quayle. We've been looking for her for some time now. We've almost found her."

"*Almost*? God dammit, how can you *almost* find anyone? Either you find her, or you don't!"

"No, that is not quite true."

Wendy was there, sitting quietly in a corner with needle and thread, a picture of domesticity as she raised the hem of one of her skirts; it seemed very important for her, but she murmured, "Tell him, Leo. Show him those lousy snapshots of yours."

Leo dug into his pocket and produced a packet of photographs. He laid them out on the table and said apologetically, "They're not very good, I'm afraid, but then...they weren't taken by my people."

"Oh? Then by whom?"

Ian Quayle stared at them, three shots, dreadfully out of focus, of a woman on a wrought-iron balcony.

In the first, she was leaning over and looking down on the street, in the second, a very tight shot of her face, there were hands reaching in to grab her, very strong-looking hands; and in the third, the angle wider again, a man, his face half-turned away, was dragging her back out of the sunlight and into the darkness of the room.

"Renata Dominici," Leo said. "Not very good photography, but there's no doubt about it at all."

"And who took them, if not your people?"

Leo smiled thinly, and sighed. "How I wish I could answer that. But I cannot." He said blandly, "Someone stole them from the Police Department, Mr. Quayle, I can't think who it could have been..."

"The Police Department! Then they know where she is?"

"No. It's a very sad tale, I'm afraid. At around noon yesterday, four armed men tried to kidnap one of our magistrates, Mr. Justice Pezzimento, on Via Nazionale. The attempt failed, and two of them were shot and killed by his bodyguards. These three photographs were in the pocket of one of those men, who is believed to be a member of the Red Brigades."

"Go on," Quayle said drily. "I can't wait to hear the end of this."

"Very well. It is known to the underworld that...that our *opposition* is looking for Renata Dominici and offering a very handsome reward to anyone who finds her. It may also be known, I fear, that we were looking for her too, and again, a substantial payment could be hoped for. The Police too, want to know where she is. No reward, but a professional criminal could legitimately expect all kinds of charges against him to be dropped if he were to turn her in. So..."

Leo was getting carried away with his theorizing, and as Quayle waited patiently, he went on. "What we have here is a three-way market for news of a woman who ought, by now, to be dead. The enemy, the Police, and *us*, are all searching for her. Notice, if you will, that the shots are very, very close. Just a woman, and a man, an iron balcony, one of hundreds of thousands all over the city. No street signs visible, no apartment numbers, no identifiable restaurants. To me, this means only one thing."

"That the photographer wanted to prove he'd found her, but was holding out for the money, for the quid pro quo."

"Exactly..."

The phone rang, and Leo said, "Excuse me..."

He went to answer it, and listened, and said at last, "That's in Trastevere? How long to set up some interference in case we need it? Two or three trucks, at least a dozen men...? All right, we'll be in a foolish little English car, painted red, a box on wheels..."

84

Wendy, intent on her sewing, said quietly, "Well, thank God, at last we're getting somewhere. Or are we? Is it all going to be screwed up, now that we have something to go on?"

Leo came back, smiling smugly, and he took the third photograph and said, "You see the man there? He's reaching for Renata to drag her back from public view, and that speaks very well for him. And now...he's been identified for me. His name is Bartolomeo Sassi, an ex-cop who was fired by guess who?"

Ian Quayle stared. "Not the General?"

"Yes. And may I round it all off nicely for you?"

"I wish to God you would, Leo."

"Renata Dominici was a secretary at Police Headquarters. The General set his sights on her very soon after his wife died. But Renata had a boyfriend on the force, Bartolomeo Sassi. Well..." He sighed. "Was there not one of your English poets who wrote: '*Alas the love of women, a lovely and fearful thing...?*'"

"I'm still waiting, Leo."

"Lord Byron," Leo said, and Quayle flared. "For God's sake, will you stop fart-arsing around and tell me about the photographs!"

Leo was crest-fallen. "Yes, of course. The General wanted the lovely Renata, but it was obviously necessary to get rid of Bartolomeo. And so, regrettably, Bartolomeo was framed on a bribery charge, and summarily dismissed. Renata was persuaded the charge was true, realized that she had been in love with the wrong man, and practically fell into the General's arms."

"And now...she's gone to find safety with her ex-lover."

"Yes."

Wendy murmured, "It opens a can of peas for us, Leo."

"No," Leo said. "'You're thinking that this might, after all, have been a *crime passionelle*. That Bartolomeo killed the General to get her back."

Ian Quayle grunted. "It's a very distinct possibility."

Leo shook his head. "Except for one thing."

"Which is?"

"A question of character, Mr. Quayle. Bartolomeo's the kind of man, very violent, who could easily kill in the heat of passion. Defending, for example, someone he loves, he wouldn't think twice about it. But...the cold precision and calculation required for manufacturing a highly sophisticated bomb—which he's not capable of anyway—for working out the time and place, for rigging it and waiting for the explosion...No, I have painted a picture of someone other than Bartolomeo Sassi. The enemy is still your original League of Hawks. I'm convinced of it. Working, perhaps, for reasons of their own, with the Red Brigades."

"Well...I'll accept that."

Ian picked up the first of the photographs and stared at it. An attractive woman in her early thirties, a little plump, with interesting eyes and even out of focus an air of quite potent sexuality about her.

He said tightly, "We can't assume that no one else has copies of these. It means we have to find her pretty damn fast, before they do."

"We've done so already, Mr. Quayle," Leo said smugly. "That phone call...Bartolomeo Sassi lives in Apartment 14, Number 82, Piazza Mastai, in Trastevere."

"For God's sake!" Quayle said. "You wait all this time to tell me? Don't you realize every second counts? *They* may have identified the apartment too."

Leo looked at his watch. "In thirty minutes," he said, "there will be a dozen of my men on the street outside the apartment. We wait for them to get into position, because...you're right. Yes! They just might be watching, waiting for the opportune moment to slip in and take her too."

Quayle rose to his feet. "I'll be back," he said abruptly,

"with Renata Dominici."

When he reached the door, Leo said sharply, "Wait! I'm coming with you!"

Quayle turned. "No." he said coldly, "I'm looking for the people who murdered Carlotta, it's not just an assignment any more. It's become personal, and I'll handle it myself. Stay here, Leo, I'll be back in an hour or so."

"Bartolomeo," Leo said, urging, "Is known as a very violent man. He won't accept you at face value, he'll assume that you're one of *them*! Please, you'll need help..."

"And you're wasting valuable time. Stay here."

"Please...?"

And Wendy echoed the comment. "Take it easy, Ian. You're letting your emotions overcome your common sense."

He was furious with her. "I am not! Renata is the link we're looking for, and if she has any brains at all she'll know that I'm on her side. I *have* to talk with her!"

He turned to Leo. "Stay here! I want you on the end of a telephone if it gets to be rough. Stay here!"

He was gone.

Leo looked at Wendy and raised his expressive arms shoulder high. "What can we do with him?" he said, and Wendy shook her head.

"There's *nothing* we can do with him, nothing at all. When Ian Quayle gets an idea into that stubborn mind of his...farewell all sense or logic. We just have to roll with it."

Wendy Hayworth set aside her stitching, and said, "So pour me a drink, Leo, for Christ's sake."

CHAPTER 10

It was just around midnight when Ian Quayle arrived, in the little Mini, in Trastevere's Piazza Mastai.

This was one of Rome's older quarters, pleasantly cluttered with apartment houses cheek-by-jowl, four, five, and six stories high, with stone and wrought-iron balconies, the street lamps dropping their tree-filtered light everywhere.

He found number eighty-two and drove past it, searching for a parking space; there were too many tourists here in their rented cars, dining and drinking in the nearby restaurants.

On his second pass, a pick-up truck that was parked almost directly outside the building started up, and the driver leaned out and said stolidly, "*Me ne vado, signore*, I'm leaving..."

"*Two or three trucks*," Leo had said, "*at least a dozen men...*"

One of his silent helpers, then? Or just a casual trucker? Or one of the enemy? The pick-up was an old Lancia, crudely repainted in an appalling shade of mustard yellow, and the driver was elderly, grizzled grey-bearded.

Ian Quayle found himself looking into passing faces as he parked, and he wondered if he were perhaps beginning to suffer from some sort of paranoia, with all the world against him; a young man sitting on a wooden chair under a tree and staring out at nothing; an apparent drunk leaning against a doorway; two burly men playing backgammon at a cafe's corner table on the sidewalk; three others, businessmen with briefcases tucked under their arms whispering together...

He climbed the dark stairway, half-expecting some shadow to emerge from deeper shadow and resolve itself into a mortal threat.

He found apartment number fourteen on the third floor, rang the bell and waited, standing carefully exactly where he could be clearly seen through the tiny glass peephole.

He waited, and rang again, and then waited some more and rang a third time, and in a little while a deep and sonorous voice answered him from beyond the heavy door. "*Chi e?* Who is it?"

"My name is fan Quayle," Quayle said amiably. "And if you are Mr. Bartolomeo Sassi...then we have to talk on a very urgent matter."

There was a long pause, and then: "Concerning what?"

"The safety of Miss Renata Dominici," Quayle said.

The silence was longer now, broken, Quayle thought, by the muted sound of running feet in there, and then the voice came back again. "There is no one of that name here. Go away."

"Not till I've spoken with you. Will you please open up? I feel like an asshole trying to talk to you through a closed door."

There was the sound of a lock, a bolt being drawn, and the door opened a matter of some eight inches, stopped by a firmly-planted foot on the other side.

Quayle saw a short and very muscular young man with very angry eyes, thick-set, tousle-haired, tough-looking. And there was a pistol in his hand, a Beretta .32, aimed at his stomach. But those dark eyes were searching the corridor, and he said, "Are you alone?"

Quayle nodded. "Yes, I am."

"I'm going to open the door for you. If anyone else

rushes in..." He gestured with the automatic: "Right between the eyes."

"There's no one with me," Quayle said wearily, "can I come in?"

A muscular hand reached out and dragged him in, and the door was shut behind them; there was the business with the locks, and then Bartolomeo turned back to him and said tightly, looking him up and down, "You speak Italian like a *Milanese*; but those clothes came from England, we learn to see the difference here. And yet, you are not a tourist..."

"No, I'm not. I'm from an organization that is concerned with the lady's safety."

"An *organization*...Yes, I know it. From the League! I've been expecting you...!"

The gun was aimed at his head, and in a split second of sheer panic Ian Quayle saw the crazed light in those angry eyes, fancied he saw the finger tightening on the trigger.

He could not be sure, but dismay took over and he yelled uncontrollably and knocked the weapon to the side.

It fired, whether by design or accident he would never know, and he grabbed at the gun-arm and wrestled for control of it.

They fell to the ground together and fought for a moment; the Italian was younger, and stronger by far, but when the pistol fired again he lay deathly still and there was blood at the side of his head.

Quayle knelt beside the silent body and whispered, "Oh, Jesus Christ..."

He felt for the pulse and the heart and found them still beating, and forced on himself the reminder of what he had come here for.

There was only one other room in the apartment, the bedroom, and it was locked. Quayle put his foot up against the lock and thrust hard, throwing himself off balance and falling to the ground. He picked himself up and tried again, wondering where all those stories came from about how easily a door could be battered down in this fashion.

At the fifth or sixth attempt, the door gave way, and the chair that had been wedged under its handle was in broken remnants on the floor.

In the light of the bedside lamp, she was doubled up on top of the comforter, a youngish woman dressed in a blue nylon slip, her arms wrapped around herself, and a look of the most abject terror in her eyes that broke his heart; the message in those eyes was: *The end has come now...*

How could he even begin to tell her?

He said, trying, and speaking very quickly, "Renata, I am not an enemy, I'm a friend. You're in danger, and have to get you out of here, *now*, every moment counts, will you come with me..."

Her voice was a whisper. "I heard shots, it means..."

"No, it doesn't mean anything of the sort, there was an accident. Come."

She would not move, and he reached for her, suddenly more conscious than ever of the passage of time, that paranoia intruding again.

He said, "Oh, for Christ's sake! There's no time to explain! Come!"

He grabbed her by the arm; and suddenly, her nails were raking down his face, drawing blood. She screamed, "No..." and fought with him.

With most unfeminine force, she reached down and grabbed at his balls, a monstrous grip, and heaved on them. He yelled out his pain and hit her in the stomach, pulling the punch because she was a woman; and he realized at once that his restraint was a mistake, and he hit her again, much harder.

She recovered quickly, and tried to choke the life out of him, and he shouted, "Jesus, doesn't anyone in this house understand *anything*?"

He grabbed a wrist and twisted her arm up behind her back, and slipped his other hand up in the crook of her elbow to grab a handful of hair. Now, he had her, and he forced her bodily into the other room.

She stared down in shock at Bartolomeo's unconscious body and started screaming again, and broke away from him to drop to her knees and wail in fine Italian hysteria, picking up that tousled head and clutching at it like a madwoman, weaving back and forth and moaning, "*Amore, amore mio*, my love, my love, what have they done to you...?"

Ian went to the phone and dialed the safehouse on Via Appia Antica, and Leo's voice was never more welcome.

He said, "Thank God you called, Mr. Quayle. Are you all right?"

"Yes, I'm fine. But Bartoloemo's been hurt. Get a doctor over here fast, Leo."

"I'll arrange it...But the lady?"

"If I can stop her screaming, we'll be onto the street and into the Mini within two minutes."

"No! Stay away from your car!"

"Oh?"

Leo's voice was very calm. "You're surrounded, Mr. Quayle, by all kinds of undesirables. I've just received word from Giancarlo."

"Giancarlo?"

"He drives a yellow Lancia pick-up, an elderly man with an untidy gray beard, one of my best men. I'm afraid I have to admit that you were right..."

"I frequently am, Leo."

"It seems there were indeed copies of those photographs. And both the police and the Red Brigades—working, we can be sure, for the League—have identified that balcony. They're massed on the street below you. You have two enemies to worry

92

about, both of them competent."

"Stay away from my car, you said..."

"There's a Kalashnikov machine-pistol trained on it, waiting for Renata to appear. Run, instead, to a yellow Lancia pick-up, Giancarlo has been advised, he'll bring you back here."

Quayle worried. "I can't leave my Mini on the street all night, someone's going to rip it off!"

Leo said excitedly, "Mr. Quayle! The possible theft of your foolish little automobile is of absolutely no importance! *Mannaggia la miseria*, your lives are in great danger now, can't you understand? I have just had a call from Mrs. French in London, asking for a progress report. It seems, though I cannot think why, that she is concerned about your personal safety. I told her that you were in good hands, and I do not wish to be obliged tomorrow morning to call her with the sad news of your death. Forget your *disgraziato* motorcar. I'll have it picked up later, when the danger is past. If it's still there."

"You're a great guy, Leo."

"I know it. Now, look for a yellow Lancia pick-up. The driver's name is Giancarlo..."

"With a grizzly gray beard, I spotted him already."

"Good. He's the only hope you have now, Mr. Quayle."

"All right, we'll be home in half an hour."

He put down the phone and looked at Renata, still weeping and wailing. He said sourly, "The kind of brains your Bartolomeo has, I doubt if even a forty-five could damage them. He'll be all right, there's a doctor on his way. Come, let's get the hell out of here..."

He reached for her arm and pulled her up, and she went with him reluctantly, still moaning.

He said, "Oh, shut up, for Christ's sake! We may have problems on the street, we need all our wits now..."

They went down the dark stairway together, and when they reached the steps he took her arm and ran with her to the darkness under a hazel tree...He saw the Mini parked there and wondered about it...Across the street there was the yellow-painted Lancia pick-up.

His eyes were everywhere, and he whispered, "The pick-up there...."

Suddenly, a burst of machine-pistol fire smashed into the portico that was sheltering them, the fire from the Kalashnikovs that were the favorite weapon of the Brigades. It was answered almost at once by the more controlled fire of the police, lying in ambush.

Quayle grabbed her and shouted: "Come on...!"

He reached the pick-up with her, and the door was flung open for him. A hand reached down to help her up, and then Quayle was beside her and shouting, "Get out of here, for Christ's sake!"

Behind them, the firing went on, an enormous burst of sound crashing through the stillness of the night as the cops and the Brigades shot it out.

The driver said, grinning broadly, "This is no place for Christians, Mr. Quayle, is it? So...let us leave it instantly."

He turned into Viale Trastevere and headed south; and when they hit the railway line and had to turn east or west, he said cheerfully, "We turn east, and it'll take us nowhere. Has it occurred to you that to get to the Via Appia Antica from Trastevere is almost impossible?"

The driver was a bright and excessively amiable young man in his late twenties, dressed in jeans and a sweat shirt with the imprint of the Los Angeles Dodgers, a status symbol of some sort. He was clean-shaven, with dark curly hair; his biceps bulged ferociously.

"*Giancarlo,*" Leo had said, "*an elderly man with a long grey beard, one of the best...*" And what had happened to him?

"And your name," Quayle said. "Leo tells me it's Giancarlo?"

He nodded happily. "That's right, Giancarlo."

Quayle said nothing.

They came to a *semaphoro*, a red light, and when they pulled to a stop, Quayle carefully arranged his fist, curling the second knuckle up...He drove it suddenly into the driver's throat, finding the unprepared Adam's Apple instantly and with great force.

There was a dreadful choking sound, and the doubling up of an enemy body; Quayle leaned across him and opened the driver's door and shoved him out onto the deserted street. He scooted over and took the wheel, and roared off through the still-red light.

Renata stared at him in shock. "Why?" she asked, and Quayle answered her briefly, "Trust me. He's one of the people you were frightened of."

He swung north on Via Ostiense, and he muttered, "But he was right, you can't get there from here..."

He came to the piazza and swung south-east again on Viale Marco Polo. His way was blocked by the Arco di Vero, and he swore and turned north again, then east to Adreatina till he could make his final right on Appia Antica and relish the pine-trees there.

"Thank God," he said, "we're almost home."

Wendy and Leo were waiting anxiously for him, and Quayle said, a trifle smugly, "You may remember I told you I'd bring Renata Dominici here. And this is she."

Making the introductions, he said, "Wendy Hayworth, my associate, and, er...Leo. Also an associate."

Her voice was dulled with her pain. "And Bartolomeo...is dead."

"No," Quayle said firmly, "there's a doctor on his way there now, if he's not already there. A bullet creased his skull, but that man's skull, I suspect, is practically Cro-Magnon, it could stand up to the blast from a howitzer. There's a great deal to be said, after all, for the Neanderthal intelligence, it was encased in bone two inches thick."

Renata stared at him, and hated him. She said clearly, "Bartolomeo was one of the sweetest, kindest men in the whole world. And you killed him..."

"Balls," Quayle said.

He turned to Leo. "Leo, why don't you get on the phone to that apartment and find out what's happening? It just has to be crawling with cops right now."

"No one below the rank of Colonel of Police," Leo said pompously, "knows of my authority. In the Trastevere apartment, the man in charge will be a Sergeant."

"Leo," Ian Quayle said plaintively, "don't give me a bad time."

"And we don't even know the number."

"It's 37-34-61."

Leo sighed. "Very well."

He picked up the phone and dialed, and in a moment, he said, "The Sergeant in charge, please. This is signor Respucci, Senior Editor on Panorama Magazine." There was a long pause, and then Leo said, "If I may know your name, Sergeant? We may want to mention it in our next issue..."

A long pause, and then "Sergeant Corena? No, it's a matter of policy for my magazine that we only refer to the police in the most flattering terms possible...We stand for an old-fashioned concept, law and order...Can you tell me what happened in that apartment this night...?"

There was a silence that went on forever, and then:

"Yes, I know how to spell Corena, Sergeant...We might need a photograph of you...We'll be in touch..."

He put down the phone at last and turned to Quayle.

"Well," he said, "the news in an almond-shell. No, a

walnut-shell, how do you say it?"

"Go on, Leo..."

"Bartolomeo is still alive, and recovering fast. A .32 bullet went through his left bicep, came out, and slightly damaged his head. It practically bounced off him. As you say, a Cro-Magon skull...In a few days he'll be as right as rain. Meanwhile, he's been arrested for possession of an unlicensed .32 Beretta automatic. He's already in the hospital ward of the prison."

"But he's recovering?"

"Yes, he is indeed. Has it ever occurred to you that the lower the intelligence, the more resilient the animal is?"

"Oh, shut up, Leo," Quayle said.

He turned to Renata. In her nylon slip, she was curled up on the sofa, almost in the fetal position. He said gently, "You heard that? He's all right, not gravely hurt."

"But you tried to kill him, didn't you?"

"No, I didn't."

"And he'll live? Truly?"

"Yes, truly."

"Then...could I please have something to wear?"

It came out of the blue; he'd been aware of her semi-nudity, but hadn't quite realized that she might be too. He said: "Wendy...?"

Wendy looked at those full breasts and said, trying not to make it sound too unkind, "Well, I don't have anything that will fit her. I'll talk to the cook..."

She left the room, and Ian said somberly, "I wish you'd accept that we're on your side."

She hesitated. "Perhaps I do. If you were really the people I thought you were, at first...I think I'd be dead already."

Quayle switched tracks. "I assume that Bartolomeo is your lover?"

"Yes."

"Are you in love with him?"

"Yes."

"And he with you?"

"Yes."

"True love?"

"Yes."

"On both sides?"

"Yes."

"Till death us do part! All that jazz?"

She was angry now, and she said, restraining that anger, "At your age, Mr. Quayle, you may not understand exactly what it is that binds the younger people together. Yes, I'm in love with Bartolomeo Sassi, and he's in love with me."

"At *my age*? Jesus Christ, how old do you think I am?"

Not waiting a moment for her reply, he went on: "Tell me about your affair with General Mancini."

"He was an incident in my life, nothing more than that."

Quayle turned to Leo. "Can we spring Bartolomeo?" he asked.

"*Spring* him?"

"Get him released, and bring him here."

"We can try," Leo said. "I know a lawyer..."

"Whatever he asks," Quayle said. "But I want Bartolomeo Sassi released. I want him here by this time tomorrow. Can I count on it?"

"Well, I suppose so. This lawyer friend knows the right palms to oil."

"We say '*grease*.' So grease his palm too, I don't want to just sit around waiting."

The phone rang, and Leo picked it up. A mite surprised, he said, "London, Mr. Quayle, for you..."

Ian Quayle took it, and there was Robin Harris on the line, saying affably, "We honestly don't want to look over your shoulder, dear boy, but...we were wondering if you perhaps had some progress to report...?"

Quayle wasn't exactly in the best of moods, and he said tartly, "I'm just taking in the sights of this splendid city, and eating too much damned pasta. I'm sure Mrs. Bloody French initiated this call, so kindly tell her that when I have something to report...then I will report it."

"And *that*," Robin Harris said, pained, "was a quite unnecessarily acerbic remark, Mr. Quayle."

Quayle grunted. "Sorry," he said, meaning it. "I just damn nearly got killed. It's not something I'm accustomed to yet. I suppose it has to grow on you. I'll be in touch."

He put down the phone as Wendy came back and held up a cotton print dress in a size ten with scarlet roses and green vines all over it, and Renata stared at it coldly.

"No," she said, "I would not wish to be seen dead in that."

"Suit yourself," Ian Quayle said. "You probably look better half-naked, anyway, then covered over with a flowery mural. Make yourself comfortable. Because now...we are going to *talk*."

CHAPTER 11

It was two o'clock in the morning, and Renata was tired, hungry, and thirsty.

She was still a little apprehensive about just who these people were; Leo, a *Napolitano* and therefore suspect; the strange Englishwoman who called herself Wendy and just sat there altering a dress but taking in, she was sure, every word that was said.

And most of all, Ian Quayle, who seemed to be in charge of everything; and who the hell was he?

She sipped the very large Aquavite Quayle had given her, and said slowly, wracking her memory, "I typed up the *dossier* in my own apartment, where the General had seen fit to give me an escort, two policemen...And yes, it was all about an organization called '*La Lega delle Falcone*,' the League of Hawks. It wasn't operating only here in Italy, but all over the world, and they're concerned, it seems, with espionage."

"'Concerned'," Ian Quayle murmured. "Can you be more explicit?"

"It seems they buy and sell secrets, from everybody. And they're headed by a man whose code-name is '*Bacca*', nobody knows who he is."

She took a long drink from her glass, and felt her head reeling. "Bacca," she said, "a code-name. Only...there was one reference to him as '*Bacca Maggese*', I don't know if it means anything to you. And...he had associates in high places, the General said to me: 'Underline the phrase: *Associates in high places*, I want it known that he has friends who can help him, even at cabinet level, it's very important'."

"Did the General know where this man Bacca might come from: Is he Italian? Presumably he is, if he has friends in Government."

"That's a bad deduction, Ian," Wendy said mildly, and he nodded. "Yes, I suppose it is. I'm reaching..."

He turned back to Renata. "A description of any sort?"

"No."

"Age? Whereabouts? Habits?"

"Nothing. Really, the report was more concerned with the League than it was with him personally, and I can remember thinking how terribly dangerous they seemed to be."

"For example...?"

"They kill a lot of people. But they don't do it themselves. They use the Red Brigades as their assassins, in exchange for contributions."

"Ah..." Quayle nodded. "Yes, it's all beginning to make sense. And the League must have a Headquarters. Where, Renata? *Where*?"

"The General thought it might be in the north, but he wasn't sure. He was fairly sure, though, that their last auction was held in Florence. There were all kinds of people..."

"Wait, wait!' Quayle said. "Their *auction*?"

"Yes. That's how they sell their secrets. And could I please have another drink?"

As Leo poured, she said, "Last July there were apparently a whole lot of people arriving in Florence from all over the world who might have been just ordinary tourists, but weren't."

"Meaning?"

"Intelligence agents. From Russia, China, France,

Germany—from all over. Some of them were even *persona non grata* in Italy. But the General suggested that by the time they'd been identified and ordered out of the country, they would already have achieved what they came here for."

"Names," Quayle said urgently. "Can you remember any names?"

"Well..." Renata was no longer sipping her acquavite, but gulping it. She sighed. "There's something I imagine you don't understand..."

"Which is?"

"If you're a skilled typist, as I am, you don't necessarily know what it is you're typing."

"You don't?"

Wendy nodded. "That's true, Ian. You're concentrating on form rather than on content. Many's the time I've typed up thirty pages or so without even being conscious of what it was all about. Just knowing, instead, that there wasn't a single typo anywhere. Immaculate spacing, and no errors."

"Well, that's a great help, I must say."

"Madame Ging-Sen from China," Renata said suddenly. "Yes, I remember her name because the General laughed about her, said she'd been wandering around town in most uncharacteristic costume. She arrived here in unisex grey, and promptly became, for a day or two at least, a lady of high fashion. The General found it quite touching, as I did too. There was a Russian named Rastopovitch, I think, and representatives from both East and West Germany, though I can't remember their names..."

Ian Quayle frowned. "Both East and West?"

She nodded, and gulped some more of her drink; her voice was slurring now. "Yes, both...both of them. There was a Pakistani, a Saudi Arabian, and that...that unshaven lout from the PLO, what's his...his name?"

Wendy stared. "Arafat? Arafat was there too?"

"Yes. And a Venez...Venezuelan who, who..."

She took a long, deep breath. "The General said everybody present was scared to death of him. And there was a Frenchman there named Claude...Claude I-don't-know-what who bought...bought a West German disposition of something-or-other for three million dollars. Could I get some sleep now...?"

"No," Ian Quayle said. "We've only just started."

The questioning went on; and by four o'clock Quayle had drawn a great deal of information from her, not all of it relevant. She was good and drunk now, and Quayle said, "Do me a favor, Wendy? Put her to bed?"

"A large bowl of Leo's spaghetti," Wendy said reprovingly, "would have kept her sober."

"Yes, I'm sure of it," Quayle said. "It has to have some virtue...And she wouldn't have talked quite so easily. Let her sleep it off now."

The light of early-morning Rome was quite incredible, an artist's dream.

The sun came up, impossibly red, and sent its warming rays through the pine trees, awakening a slumbering earth. And at a knock at Ian Quayle's door he turned over onto his back and murmured, "Come in, Wendy..."

But it was Leo, apologetic for the early intrusion, not sure that Quayle would be alone and worrying about it. He was already fully dressed, and shaven, and nicely polished, with Givenchy cologne seeping out of every pore...

He said, "A call from Paris, Mr. Quayle, during the night. Your mother is on Air France Flight 32, it arrives at Ciampino Airport at seven fifteen, I was sure you'd want to meet her."

Within ten minutes, the Mini, rescued from Trastevere with hardly more than a dozen bullet-holes in it, was racing down Via Portense to Fiumincino and the airport, and Ian

Quayle's heart was beating wildly; even after so short a time, a reunion with Claudine was a momentous event.

He threw his arms around her and held her close; and how fragile she was becoming these days, all skin and bones...! But looking very elegant indeed in slacks of dark blue cotton and a safari jacket in a lighter shade of the same color, very suitable for Paris and Rome.

He raced back with her to the safehouse, and en route she said, "The League of Hawks...Darling, I know *everything* about them now. And really, they're quite alarming people."

He pushed the pedal to the floor to overtake an Alfa Spider that was crawling along at a mere ninety.

He said, smiling, "Let me ask you to hold it, Mother, till Wendy can sit in on it too."

"All right. But you were correct...they go back a very long way..."

In twenty minutes they were back at the safehouse on Appia Antica, and Quayle said, "This is Leo, Mother, he chooses to have no other name. My mother, Claudine Andrassy."

Leo was highly emotional, as always. He took her hand and kissed it, and said earnestly, "An admirer, Madame Andrassy, for...for some years now. I saw you dance in Milano, and in Venezia, Rome, Florence...and that wonderful night in Ascoli Piceno where all night long they just wouldn't let you leave the stage."

"Ah yes...I remember it well, it was just before...my accident. I was at my best then."

She sighed. "The old days. They're gone forever, Leo, aren't they?"

He was suddenly beaming, a very happy man. He said, "Breakfast! I have arranged for a very *British* breakfast, bacon and eggs and grilled lambs' kidneys..."

As they ate together, Claudine said, "The year, Ian, was 1792. The War of the Second Coalition, England and Russia were trying to drive the French out of Germany, the Netherlands, Italy and Switzerland, all of which countries were fairly crawling with French troops on the rampage. At this time, in England, a certain Lord Alfred Mayberry organized a spy network for the Coalition. In those days, spying was in its infancy, of course, but Lord Mayberry apparently brought the art to a state of very high efficiency. To head this new department, he chose his son, Captain Archibald Mayberry. And now, now comes the juicy bit...Archibald was a womanizer *par excellence*, and one of his mistresses was a ravishing London beauty of French extraction who just happened to be a French spy herself."

Hanging on to her words, Ian was earnestly separating the white from the yolks of his two fried eggs, meticulously making sure that the yolks were left untarnished by the white, slicing it away in minute little pieces.

He said, "In the seventeen-hundreds, spying must have been very easy. The wars were between armies only, civilians were free to come and go as they pleased."

"Exactly. Well...Archibald was a very bright man, as all the Mayberrys seem to be, and he soon found out what his lovely mistress was up to. But instead of turning her in to the authorities—she was far too beautiful to face a firing-squad—he allowed her, instead, to pay off his gambling debts, in exchange for certain military information. In other words, darling, with that one deal, he became a double agent."

She said, delightedly, "In 1799 there was a letter from Joseph Fouché, widely regarded as the father of modern espionage, to Buonaparte, describing the growth of what Lord Mayberry was calling 'The League of Owls.' *Owls*, you notice, not Hawks. One of Mayberry's schemes led to another, and he quickly discovered that the Dutch, for example, were prepared to pay highly for news of what the Turks were up to, that the Turks would pay equally well simply for the information that the Dutch *did* know what they were up to."

She spread a piece of grilled kidney with her fork. "Am I making it clear for you? That's the way they continued, they never looked back, they just made millions. They became, really, quite a force in world affairs, but they burrowed deeper and deeper into the ground, as they had to, until, today, almost no one's even heard of them."

Quayle was staring at egg number one, just the yolk left. He found an infinitesimal piece of the white still clinging to it, and removed it surgically. Both Claudine and Wendy had seen all this nonsense before, but Leo had not; and Leo's eyes were boggling as he wondered what would happen now.

"Control of the League," Claudine said, "passed from father to son, from one Lord Mayberry to the next incumbent of the title."

"And the League's change of name?" Quayle asked.

"Ambrose Mayberry," Claudine said, "in World War One. He had a sardonic sense of humor, a characteristic of the Mayberry family. He decided that his League was not peering myopically into the darkness like owls, but *hawking* what they learned, selling their secrets to the highest bidder. And so...he changed the name to the League of Hawks."

"Cute," Wendy said. "And now?"

"Now? We're getting there."

Ian Quayle slid his fork very carefully under his egg yolk, quite denuded now of its virginal white, and placed it carefully in his mouth.

For a moment, he held it there, and then, he pressed it with his tongue against the roof of his mouth and broke it; and as it drenched down, his look of the purest delight was positively beatific.

"Mayberry," he said, the first indication that he'd been listening. "May Berry. Berry in Italian is *Bacca*. And May is *Maggese*. Our search is almost over. *Bacca Maggese* is our quarry, and all we have to do now is locate Lord Mayberry. And

106

we're home free. Simple, isn't it?"

The phone rang, and Leo was there at once.

"*Pronto*," he said, and listened, frowning.

"Thank you," he said at last, "you are a good friend, Captain. And your wife has a birthday coming up soon, I believe? I have a little present for her which I hope will please her...Yes, it will be delivered to your house tomorrow morning."

He came back to the table and said smugly, very satisfied with himself, "Thaddeus Norton, an Englishman living in Villa delle Rose, just outside Florence. He's a dealer in very high-class antiques."

"Well," Ian Quayle said sardonically, "that's the most exciting news I've had all day! Who the hell is Thaddeus Norton? First of all, I don't believe the name, there's never been a Tom, Dick, or Harry in history called Thaddeus."

"Italian plates," Leo said, "license number FJ-13-76, the Ferrari that tried to drop you off the cliff. The driver was a nobody, employed by the car's owner, a wealthy expatriate Englishman living at the Villa delle Rose, just outside Florence. His name is Thaddeus Norton."

Quayle was fussing with his second egg, and he said, grumbling, "So all of a sudden we've got a Thaddeus Norton intruding. Why? Who the hell is he?"

"The Consulate," Claudine said. "If he's English and living in Italy, they'll have a record of him. It might be helpful..."

"No," Wendy said, "I can go one better than that. The Consulate will have his name and address and not much more, but at the Embassy...The British Ambassador here is Sir Michael Farrar, an old family friend from way back, ever since I was a child. He used to bounce me up and down on his knee, an exercise I always suspected had sexual overtones. These days, they call it child molestation."

"Oh, shut up," Quayle said amiably. "Just call him, there's a dear girl."

"Keep your shirt on."

She went to the phone and dialed, and after a few moments of hectic argument with an overzealous voice at the other end, she said patiently, "Just tell him it's Wendy Hayworth, will you? I promise you he'll talk to me. I also promise you that if you don't put me through, and he finds out, as he will, he'll send you to bed without your fucking supper."

The disembodied voice was female ice. "If you'd kindly hold one moment..." And then Sir Michael came on, bright and breezy and delighted to hear from her.

She told him what it was all about, and said carefully, "We just might be wasting our time, Michael. But if we're *not*...then there'll be a cross-reference in the Intelligence file. And if there is...that's the stuff we need."

"Well, if there's anything at all," Sir Michael said, "I can have an extract of it for you in a couple of hours. That'll be damn nearly lunchtime, so why don't you come round about noon? I always have my lunch sent up to the office, we'll have it early...And if there's nothing...Well, at least we can talk about the old days for a while."

"All right."

"How's your father? I hear the poor devil's in Washington, he must hate it. He nearly got Paris, did you know that?"

"Yes, I know..."

"Missed it by a hair's breadth, rotten luck. Give me that name again."

"Thaddeus Norton."

"Got it. See you soon, darling."

When she put down the phone, there was the slightest smile on her face. "He's such a nice man," she said. "He's got to be nearly seventy now, and he's never yet learned to keep his hands to himself." She shrugged.

"Well, it's a good cause, I suppose."

When she had gone, Quayle went upstairs to check on Renata.

He knocked lightly, and when there was no answer he opened the door quietly and found her fast asleep, lying naked on top of the big brass-knobbed bed. It was stuffy in the room, and he opened a window and went back to stare down at her for a moment, realizing for the first time what an attractive woman she was, in an animal sort of way. To his astonishment, she opened her eyes briefly and looked at him before closing them again, making no other movement of any sort.

He leaned down and pulled the sheet up over her, and he said quietly, "Sleep, Renata, there's nothing to get up for now. No more danger at all, you're perfectly safe here."

She did not answer. Was she asleep again?

Or had she, indeed, even woken up at all?

Wendy was back in very good time, looking a trifle disheveled, but excited nonetheless. She waved an envelope at them, and said, "I suppose it's axiomatic that the long shots are the ones that pay off the best, isn't it?"

"It is indeed," Quayle said politely. "What have you got for us?"

"The jackpot. And that Michael Farrar...! The first thing he said to me was: 'My, how you've grown', and guess where his eyes were riveted, the lecherous old sonofabitch."

"Wendy..."

"Okay..."

As they sat with her, she picked up the first sheet and said, "The Commercial file. Thaddeus Norton is a rather classy dealer in antiques. His store in Florence is only open by appointment, which is regarded here as an ultimate status symbol. About two sales a month, but it's usually a Ming vase of museum quality costing several hundred thousand dollars. He does all right. And frankly, the commercial stuff is rather dull. He came to Italy as a young man, twenty-three years old, in 1955, and bought the Villa delle Rose in Florence, where he's lived ever since..."

"So he's now fifty years old," Quayle said, and she nodded. "How very clever of you. He makes a lot of money...He gives a great deal to various charities...He's highly respected everywhere and regarded as an English *gentilhuomo* of high caliber. Now..."

She shuffled through the pages. "Can we talk for a moment about the Mayberry family?"

"Oh?" He made no attempt to hide the sarcasm. "You have something on the man we're really interested in too? I'm so glad."

"Shut up, Ian, and listen, for Christ's sake. Okay, 1947, two years after the end of World War Two in Europe. I wasn't born then, but I'm sure you remember it."

He said plaintively, "Wendy, in 1947, I was a babe in arms, so can we continue?"

"Oh. Well. In 1947, Lord Paul Mayberry was arrested in England on charges of treason. Specifically, he was charged with selling the precise disposition of America's 1st, 4th, and 29th Infantry Divisions to Admiral Canaris, the Head of Germany's Secret Service. Canaris, of course, was a double agent working for the British, as we all know, and he blew the whistle on Lord Paul, for reasons of his own. After an interminable trial, Lord Paul Mayberry was found guilty, and he was *hanged*. A few years later, his young son, not willing, presumably, to put up any longer with the stigma attached to a father hanged for treason, changed his name and left the country."

Quayle stared. "Changed his name...?"

"And in 1955," Wendy said, "Thaddeus Norton arrived in Italy, and bought the Villa delle Rose. He's a Mayberry, Ian. The latest of the Mayberrys."

He took a long, deep breath. "Well!" he said at last. "Well! So we found *Bacca Maggese*."

He scowled. "And now, what the hell happens next?"

"What we do next," Wendy said, "is exercise a great deal of caution."

She held up another sheet of paper. "There was an elder Mayberry son, whose name was Luke. He was the natural heir to a vast family fortune. But he was killed in a traffic accident."

Quayle held her look. "Go on," he said.

"One year before the new 'Thaddeus Norton' fled the country, Luke's car was forced off the road and went over a cliff. I think the police term is modus operandi. It was the same operating procedure that nearly killed us, Ian, with the Ferrari."

Quayle sighed and thought about it. He said at last, "We have to take the bull by the horns, we have no other option."

"Dangerous, Ian," Wendy said. "Deadly dangerous."

Claudine was silent, a hand at her throat, her lovely eyes veiled. But Leo was already at the cupboard where the telephone books were kept, and he leafed through the pages and said, "You're right, Mr. Quayle. There are no other options."

He found the entry, and read, "Thaddeus Norton, Antiquarian. Residence: 33-0-15."

Quayle picked up the phone and dialed, and had to dial again and again; but eventually a female voice came through, a strong Sicilian accent: "Mr. Norton's residence, pronto."

"Mr. Norton, please."

"Who's calling, please?"

"My name is Ian Quayle."

"And may I know what it's about, Mr. Quayle? I'm Mr. Norton's personal assistant."

"Tell him," Quayle said, "it's about *Bacca*."

There was only the slightest pause. "*Bacca*? I don't think I understand."

"*Bacca Maggese*," Quayle said, and the answer came

back at once: "I'll have to put you on hold, Mr. Quayle, while I see if he's home."

"If he's not home," Quayle said, "just tell him I'll drop in on him with the Hundred-and-First Airborne Division, all right?"

"If you'll hold, Mr. Quayle, please..."

She was very cool, and in a moment there was a long, long chuckle at the other end, followed by an amused and very amiable voice.

"Ian Quayle, by all that's holy! This is Thaddeus Norton. I wondered how long it would take you to find me! Allow me to congratulate you. Record time!"

"Wait a minute," Quayle said, a trifle confused. "You know me?"

"Well, of course, dear boy. You don't think we're fools, do you? And you want to talk, is that a fair assumption?"

"Well, yes."

"Good. I find that absolutely exciting. And it so happens that I'm having a party tonight. You're in Rome, I believe? It'll take you less than three hours in your little bomb of a car, so why don't you come and join us? You'll bring Miss Hayworth with you, of course, we're all just dying to meet her. She has a formidable reputation, did you know that? Yes, I suppose you must. You'll be here...by what? Seven o'clock, I imagine. Splendid! All kinds of delightful and interesting people will be here. And you'll stay the night, of course."

The other end clicked with an air of finality. Quayle put down the phone, and said, still in shock, "For God's sake! He *knows* about us!"

Wendy would not meet his eyes. "Yes," she said, "and I'm not surprised. Ever since that accident with the Ferrari...It meant they were expecting us, Ian."

He thought about it for a long time, and then: "That double agent in London?"

"Almost certainly."

"Well, isn't that bloody marvelous? Pack a bag, Wendy, something exciting. We're going to have dinner tonight with a multi-millionaire antiquarian, isn't that nice?"

He embraced his mother, and said, "We'll be back some time tomorrow. Take care of Renata for me. And Leo...Leo will take care of *you*."

Claudine was worried, enormously. "Be careful, Ian."

"The only true quality I have," he said lightly, "is a high regard for my well-being."

She would not be mollified. "Do you have a gun of some sort?"

"No. I never carry a gun."

"I'll worry about you, darling."

"Don't. I'm the most resilient man you ever met. *Au voir, Mama.*"

They went to the Mini, and drove the 170 miles to Florence at breakneck speed, the needle resting, for most of the time, on its maximum of a hundred and twenty.

Once, when the car very nearly turned over on a sharp bend in the road, Wendy laid a hand on his thigh and said: "Careful, Ian. There's time."

"What, we have time?" he said harshly. "We're going to meet with the man who had Carlotta murdered."

She fell silent.

CHAPTER 12

The beautiful villa was way out of town, set in some three acres of spectacular gardens, shaded with trees and heavy shrubbery in gorgeous (and carefully calculated) disarray.

It was large and very old, three stories high with a steeply sloping tile roof almost everywhere, carved stone archways all over the place, and an air about it of decadent splendor; three hundred years ago, it had been the home of the orgy-loving Prelate Cardinal Giuseppe Crequi di Gonzaga.

And its current owner, one Lord Mayberry who had given up his title to become Thaddeus Norton, was a delight.

In his fifties, he was ramrod-straight and athletic, and terribly Upper Class, absolutely convinced that God's prime contribution to Western culture was the English gentleman, a group of which he himself was a solid epitome.

He spoke rich and fluent Italian with the eloquence of a Tuscan poet, and he was devastation with the ladies. His face was as lean as his body, his nose was aristocratically aquiline, his forehead was high and wide, and his jaw firm. His dark hazel eyes very, very penetrating indeed.

But for one thing, he was almost a caricature of a comic-strip hero; but comic-strip heroes were seldom dangerous...

* * *

He was on the huge main lawn when they met, dressed in pale gray wool slacks and a yellow cashmere sweater. He had an old-fashioned wooden bow in his hand and a quiver of arrows at his shoulder; there was a series of targets set up on bales of straw at fifty paces distant.

He bowed over Wendy's hand, brushing it with his lips. "I cannot tell you," he said, "what a great pleasure this is for me. To meet so beautiful a lady on such a beautiful evening..."

He shook hands with Quayle, a hearty, gung-ho handshake, and held out the bow. "A seventy-five pound pull, Mr. Quayle. Would you like to try it? I understand you're an amateur toxophilist."

"You do? Well, isn't that interesting?" Ian Quayle scowled. "It so happens that when I was a kid I bought myself a bow and some arrows and fooled around for a couple of years. So if your Intelligence puts me down as a toxophilist...someone ought to get fired."

"Ah, yes, that's our major trouble in this business, isn't it? Ninety percent of our intelligence is either grossly distorted, or completely false. A question of separating the wheat from the chaff, that's what we always have to do. And it's a wearisome occupation, isn't it?"

There was a gesture with the bow again. "Try it, the kind of bow I'm sure you never ever held in your hand. The old English long-bow, Mr. Quayle, and this one is roughly eight hundred years old, back to the time when King Richard the Lion Heart insisted that every honest English peasant carry a bow at all times, the germ of a citizens' army. They didn't *cut* them to shape in those days, they *scraped* them, from the finest yew available in the forests of Surrey and Sussex and Kent. And did you know? The wood of the yew, though long dead, has a life of its own. Feed it properly with weekly rubbings of neats'-foot oil—and your bow will last forever. And there's great satisfaction in the touch of it, something you'll never get from the plastic and pulley abortions they make today. Try it, Quayle."

Ian Quayle took the bow and hefted it, and found that indefinable satisfaction at once. Eight hundred years old, for God's sake? Had it seen service, perhaps, in Jerusalem?

He fitted a shaft to the string, sighted on the target, and pulled back; reaching his nose with the string was sheer purgatory, and he muttered, "Seventy-five pounds? It's going to give me a hernia..."

But he tensed his muscles, and at last felt his thumb brushing the corner of his mouth. He held it for a second and let fly, and saw the arrow embed itself in the blue, very close to the red.

"Bravo!" Mayberry shouted. "Your first shot with a strange bow, and a five! That's very creditable indeed...!"

He took back the bow, and sent the four remaining shafts from his quiver with incredible speed into the gold.

He said mildly, "I wonder if we can take that as a measure of our relative competence, Quayle? What do you think? And shall we go into the house?"

As they walked together up the brick-paved path, he said earnestly, "I really have very few talents, Quayle. But one of them is my aptitude with weapons, of every kind."

"And in that category," Quayle said sarcastically, "do you include four-point-nine liter Ferrari Europas?"

"Oh *that*..."

Mayberry sighed. "One of the best of my cars, I truly mourned its loss. It was supposed to be the end of you both."

He turned to Wendy and said, all gallantry, "But now that I've met you, Miss Hayworth, I'm glad it didn't work out. I can't bear to think of you in the bottom of a chasm, burning to death."

He smiled. "You see, I'm truly a very *nice* sort of fellow. I *grow* on people."

"Yes," Ian Quayle said, "I'm sure of it. And when can we get to talk?"

Mayberry gestured vaguely. "In the course of time," he said. "You'd like to freshen up, wouldn't you? The other guests will be arriving within the hour, so..."

They were already in the house, and a young Italian girl was standing there, waiting for them. She was scarcely out of her teens, very small and slight, and looking like hell. She wore jeans and a tank top, and glasses with lenses as thick as the bottom of beer bottles; her untidy hair looked like it hadn't been washed in years; there was a tight and angry look in her eyes, the dark, wild eyes of a fanatic.

Mayberry said cheerfully, "This is Bianca, my...personal assistant. She makes sure that nobody gets close to me who shouldn't. She'll show you to your rooms. Shall we say...in an hour or so, down here?"

Without another word, he turned and stalked out. And the cute little doll Bianca, who somehow gave the impression that she would be more at home commanding a tank, looked them both up and down, very disapprovingly, and turned looked them both up and down, very disapprovingly, and turned on her heel and said, "*Di qua*, this way..."

She took them upstairs, and showed them into two splendid bedrooms, high-ceilinged, beautifully paneled, and separated by a joint bathroom as large as a playing field, and with inter-communicating doors. The beds were huge four-posters, 17th century; the floors were of marble covered with exquisite rugs, the windows very large and looking down on the rose gardens. And there was a bottle of cognac, too...

The girl stared at Quayle, and in this setting of the greatest luxury her grubby, too-careless appearance was an anachronism and an affront to the ancient past and all it stood for.

She said nastily, "My name is Bianca, remember it. Because if you've come here to make trouble...it's me you'll have to answer to. Mr. Norton thinks you're harmless, and that makes you a very lucky man. But I *don't*. And that makes you as unfortunate as an enemy can be. I like to make sure that our enemies remember me well. In their nightmares."

She turned on her heel and was gone, and Quayle grunted. "Cute little harpy, isn't she? Well, the hell with her."

He wandered from one room to the other, through the bathroom with its sunken bath and acres of snow-white bath sheets folded over the warmers. He said, "Will you shower first, or shall I?

Wendy hid the touch of dismay that swept over her; it was the kind of occasion when they'd be showering together.

But she knew. And how could she compete with the ghost of a twenty-year-old passion? Carlotta was still on his mind, she was sure. And, somehow, she could not hold it against him; it meant permanence and loyalty and everlasting love, and as a woman she could readily understand this; it even gave her a certain comfort.

Nonetheless, as she soaped her breasts and her loins, she wished very fervently that they were his hands and not her own that were moving over her body.

She watched him shower as she dried herself, and tried not to be hurt by his lack of tumescence. She said, sitting on the edge of the bath and forcing herself to speak of more mundane matters, "That goddam fanatic Bianca...can you believe that her threats were almost a relief?"

"Oh? How come?"

"Because Mayberry Norton is just too damn friendly. And as phony as a tin sovereign. Under all that excess of charm, he's a very dangerous man."

"Yes, I know it."

Ian Quayle wrapped a bath-sheet around his waist and went to the window of the bedroom; Wendy followed him, like a little pet poodle.

He pulled back the drapes and looked out over the garden

to the big wrought-iron gates. Cars were arriving now, and there were three guards prowling there, and he said mildly, "I wonder what would happen if we got in the Mini and just drove off? A test, so to speak?"

"We don't have to test them," Wendy said impatiently.

"He doesn't keep three Cro-Magnon sub-humans at his front gate for nothing. With guns tucked under their sweaty armpits."

"Ah, you noticed the guns."

"I'm not blind. They'd turn us back with stock phrases they've been taught."

He sighed. "Yes, you're probably right. Purely an academic question, anyway. And what are you wearing tonight?"

"I brought my white cocktail dress, the one you like so much, and a pant-suit, a sort of beige. What do you think?"

"I think I should have brought a dinner jacket, but I didn't."

"That's a very helpful comment."

"The cocktail-dress."

"Good."

Within the hour, they were ready; and as they stood together at the ornate balustrade that overlooked the *gran' salone* where the buffet had been set out, they saw that a dozen or more of the other guests had already arrived.

Ian Quayle could only stare...

There were faces there that he knew, from carefully compiled dossiers etched into his mind; and he whispered, "I don't believe it! The tall man in the rather ill-fitting tuxedo, at the bar there, you know who he is?"

Wendy nodded. "Yes, I do. Hans Richter, East Germany's number one spy."

"Right. And the man talking to the girl in the red dress? You know him too?"

Wendy followed his look. "No, I don't think I do..."

"He's Conrad Weiss-Histermann," Quayle said, "the number two or three man in West German Intelligence. So what are they doing here together? Jesus, they're mortal enemies! And there's General Enrico Diaz of Chile, perhaps the most dangerous man in the whole of South America...And Madame Ging-Sen of China, you know her?"

He indicated a slim and quite lovely Chinese woman, wearing a peacock-blue silk dress that hugged her body and was slit up the thigh damn near to her non-existent waist.

She was sipping a glass of Champagne, and almost as if she knew with some strange sixth sense that she was being watched, she looked up to the balustrade and held Ian's eyes with hers for a moment.

He murmured, "Christ, she's really a stunning beauty when she's dressed to kill, isn't she?"

Wendy said coldly: "She is? And no, I don't know her."

"Head of China's Bureau Seven," Quayle said. "The cover-name for their External Security. Oh, this promises to be a very interesting evening..."

"Let's not forget one question," Wendy said.

"Which is...?"

"The why? Why did he invite us here? I don't like unanswerable questions."

"There's an answer," Ian Quayle said. "So let's go down there and find it."

CHAPTER 13

Lord Mayberry, now known as Thaddeus Norton, was waiting for them at the bottom of the winding staircase, the very essence of goodwill to all men. He was immaculately dressed in a thousand-dollar dinner-suit of midnight blue cashmere, and he said, beaming, "Miss Hayworth, Mr. Quayle, my very dear friends...Come and meet some marvelous and quite important people..."

He took Wendy's arm and guided them through the crowd, swelling now with the arrival of more and still more chauffeur-driven cars, pausing here and there to make the introductions:

"May I present Colonel Jean-Pierre Moulins, from Paris? Miss Wendy Hayworth and Mr. Ian Quayle from London..."

The plump little Colonel took Wendy's hand and bowed over it, and murmured, "A great pleasure, Miss Hayworth. And may I say how happy I am to see your organization's representative here at last, after all these years? Mr. Quayle..." He shook hands. "I do hope you're not going to outbid me on the Saudi matter?"

"Er, no," Quayle said. "We're not too interested in the Saudis at the moment," and they moved on.

"Captain Vasili Vicek from Bulgaria, General Rastopovitch from Russia. Miss Wendy Hayworth and Mr. Ian

121

Quayle."

Moving on interminably: "Fraulein Elisabet Kraus from Austria, Brigadier Farsi from Iran, Madame Ming Chu'an from Taiwan, Captain Pastroudis from Greece, Colonel Benedetti from Corsica..." It seemed that the introductions would never come to an end.

White-gloved waiters were flitting by, filling glasses, and waitresses in neat gray uniforms were carrying trays of the most excellent canapes around.

There were rolled slices of smoked ham wrapped around little dollops of Chevres cheese, slices of rare roast beef encasing a mixture of hard-boiled egg and anchovy, Beluga caviar on tiny squares of garlic toast, prawns fastened to rounds of cucumber with toothpicks, little pieces of crab's legs dusted with grated orange-rind, tiny cherry tomatoes cut almost through and the pockets stuffed with very thin slices of quails' eggs, minute squares of scaloppini topped with paper-thin lemon slices on which were pitted green olives powdered with ground ginger...

For the heartier eaters, there were four legs of roast lamb, already expertly carved, one of them with a heavy infusion of garlic and anchovies, another drenched in Madeira; and six standing roasts of prime rib, some of them rare and others almost raw...

There were dishes of vegetables—potatoes Anna, braised celery, artichoke hearts cooked in chicken bouillon, Chinese peas stir-fried very briefly, a kohlrabi remoulade, slivers of celery-root in a fantastic white sauce that had a touch of cognac in there somewhere...

It was a very *satisfying* party.

The men were almost all in dinner-jacket or white tie, and the ladies were fit to kill, a great number of originals in evidence—Givenchy, McFadden, St. Laurent, Jean Paul Gautier, Oldfield, and Issey Myake.

They were in silks and satins, and cotton gauze and fine

lace; and almost every one of them wore the kind of dress that would drive a virile man to distraction...

Ian Quayle found himself, though none of his own doing, next to Madame Ging-Sen, and her large, dark, slanted bedroom eyes were holding his with no Oriental inscrutability at all.

He somehow felt that the time might have come for a little of the cards-on-the-table bit.

He raised his glass of champagne to her, and said, "Madame Ging-Sen, I believe? My name's Ian Quayle. And may I say...I have a photograph of you at home in London."

"Oh?" She was laughing. "In your bedroom, I hope?"

"It's not that kind of photograph, unhappily. It was taken, I believe, six months ago, in Peking. You're wearing a gray unisex uniform with a railway engineer's cap. It's all honestly not very flattering. So may I say how much your gown becomes you?"

"Ah...If my own people could see me now! They'd probably sentence me to twenty years in Outer Mongolia! But it might even be worth it. To feel like a woman, instead of...just a comrade."

She sipped her drink and watched him, and thought what a handsome man he was. In his early forties, she guessed, just the right age. She fingered the dress, made from the thinnest and most expensive silk, and she murmured: "I arrived here in my gray uniform, but I went to a place called Madame Flora's, and I said: 'Dress me as a woman of high fashion, I have money.' This is what the salesgirl sold me. Does it really become me?"

Quayle said gravely, "It is exquisite, Madame Ging-Sen...Yes, it becomes you."

"It cost me almost all of my travelling expenses, which I had husbanded very carefully. Of course, I have more funds for the actual purchases. And will you bid against me on the Korean matter?"

"The Korean matter? Er, no. I think not."

"Good. If you do not, I will be happy to show my gratitude to you."

"Oh really? Yes, that's quite splendid. I mean..." Ian Quayle found he had suddenly acquired a certain incoherence. "Er, yes, if I'd ever harbored such an intention, it would, er, well, er, be easy enough to, er, reconsider, I'm absolutely convinced of that."

Wendy rescued him, coming to him, glass in hand, and saying brightly, "I just had a delightful conversation with Senor Contreras, from Venezuela. He's really a most charming man."

Madame Ging-Sen murmured, "Excuse me," and wandered off to talk with Colonel Rastopovitch. Wendy said darkly, "Lay off that slant-eyed Jezebel, or I'll throw you to Bianca."

"Just polite conversation," Ian said, "and who's Contreras? Do I know him?"

"Over there." She indicated. "That horrible-looking dark stuff in his glass is Coca-Cola, he tells me it's all he ever drinks. Well, all kinds of people have all kinds of odd quirks, don't they? But really, apart from that he's very bright."

Quayle followed her look, and saw a man of medium height, a little overweight, neatly dressed in a dark blue, double-breasted suit with a white shirt and a dark red tie. His hair was dark, of medium length, and very thick, and he wore a moustache of the kind that drapes over the corner of the mouth, a wide hairless gap under his nose separating the two segments of it. His brows were dark and heavy, his eyes almost black and filled with a kind of wary intelligence. His lips were quite full and very red, but altogether there was an air of enormous competence about him.

Quayle said, "*Señor Contreras*?"

"Yes. From Venezuela."

"No," Quayle said. "From Venezuela, yes. But his name's not Contreras. You don't recognize him?"

She blinked at him. "Should I"

"Most emphatically, yes! He seems to have put on a little weight, it always changes the shape of a man's face. But that is Ilich Ramirez Sánchez."

Wendy gasped. "*Carlos*?"

"Carlos the Jackal, yes. Without a doubt, the world's number one terrorist, wanted for murder in almost every country in Europe. And what's he doing here, I wonder?"

"Oh my God..."

"And you found him...*charming*?"

"Yes."

Wendy sighed. "I found Mayberry charming too, didn't I? Does it mean that my standards are all screwed up?"

And then, suddenly, Mayberry/Norton was there, glass in hand. He said quietly: "The party is going marvelously well, Quayle, wouldn't you say?"

"I'd say so indeed," Quayle said politely. "You're the perfect host, Mayberry."

"Not Mayberry, please. Norton."

"Yes, of course."

"And you wanted to talk. Why don't we sneak away? Nobody's going to miss us. The Armor Room might be a good place."

'*Nobody will miss you, Mr. Quayle,*' Mrs. Bloody French had said at that other party, back home in the quiet confines of the Surrey cottage.

As he led Quayle away, Wendy said, "Wait! Shouldn't I be in on this too?"

"You'll forgive me, Miss Hayworth," their host said blandly. "This is just between the two of us, man talk. Why don't you circulate, and add your womanly attributes to a party that might easily become very dull without us? I'm sure your underling will give you a full report on what transpires between us."

"'Underling'?" Quayle said testily. "I'm supposed to object to that term, right? And tell you who's really in charge here? The hell with you, Mayberry, we're a team. So lead on."

He turned to Wendy. "Do like the man says, darling. Circulate. Go and talk to Carlos the Jackal, find out what he wants with the League of bloody Hawks, it should be very interesting. But be careful, don't let him cut your bloody throat."

Mayberry led the way down to the cellar, a high-vaulted room or arched brickwork, faintly lit. There were suits of armor lining the walls, and a shadow was stirring in a corner, somehow threatening.

Mayberry switched on the main lights, and the shadow was Bianca, still dressed in her jeans and tank top. She seemed to melt away from the glare of the lights as they picked up the shining suits of armor, some of them dating back to the twelfth Century.

Mayberry touched one of them, his hand lingering on a breast-plate, and he said sighing, "Norton, Mayberry...It's at moments like these that I regret changing my name. The Mayberrys' were once Norman, did you know that? And this is the suit of armor my ancestor Tancred wore when he fought against King Henry the Sixth in what is today Italy."

There was the briefest pause, and then he went on. "I come from a very long line of aristocrats, Quayle. Soldiers of distinction, every one of them. Men who changed the course of history, as I am doing now."

"And making millions while you do it..."

"Of course! Expertise of my quality doesn't come cheap. I deal in the world's most potent weapon—the Intelligence *secret*. And when a secret becomes known to both opposing sides—it promptly loses its potency as a weapon. In my own way, Quayle," he said sardonically, "I'm disarming the world. And isn't that a noble effort?"

"You're all screwed-up, Mayberry. Screwed up to hell

and gone."

"No. I am Lord Mayberry, an upper-echelon executive of aristocratic lineage. And you are Ian Quayle, a man of no consequence at all, a grossly under-paid researcher for England's MI6. You came here to find out about a man code-named *Bacca*. So will you tell me how you found me so quickly? If you don't...I'll have Bianca question you, and I promise you in all sincerity, you'll be talking your head off in about two minutes."

"Yes," Quayle said sourly, "you've got yourself a real doozie there, haven't you? But I've got nothing to hide. I'm more than happy to talk, if you'll talk too."

"So tell me how you found me."

"A man called Joseph Fouché."

"*Fouché*?" Mayberry stared. "Joseph Fouché died two hundred years ago."

Ian Quayle nodded. "Some years after the League of Owls—Hawks—was founded. He wrote a lot of letters to King Louis. The French are very good at this kind of thing, all through the years they kept up their surveillance, long after Joseph Fouché was dead and buried. Bureaucrats taking over from him, that kind of jazz. For me it was a matter of research, pure and simple. Research is something I'm very good at. And where do we go from here?"

"Where we go from here," Mayberry said equably, "is to your sudden demise if I decide you're a threat to me. Another one of my cars over the edge of a cliff, perhaps the Porsche, a good car but I really don't use it very much."

"Balls," Quayle said. "You just can't afford to knock me off."

"Oh, but I can," Mayberry said. "I have protection in very high places. The man who pulls the strings in the Ministry of Justice is a dear personal friend of mine, and a king-maker. Just a Deputy, but the Minister himself doesn't make a move without his approval."

"I'm not thinking in terms of legalities."

"Really? Than what *are* you thinking of?" There was a strange look in his eyes, and he said slowly, "I suspect you're up to something, Quayle. And whatever it is...I don't think I'm going to like it very much."

"Oh, but you will," Ian Quayle said. "I promise you...you *will*. If only because there's a great deal of money, I think, involved in what we have to talk about."

He was conscious that Mayberry was ready to just let him talk now, and he thought, *Well, and why not...?*

He went on, sure he was well on track now. "You made the point yourself. *Grossly underpaid*, you said and you were right. You want to know what my take-home pay is? It's around a hundred quid a week. Just about what I imagine you pay for one of your silk shirts. I've been living at that kind of level for too damn long, and I've come to the conclusion that it's time to call it quits."

Mayberry was watching him like one of his own hawks, and there was a long silence. At last, he said quietly, "I take it that you're thinking of becoming a double agent, is that it? Which would mean working in your London office for me..."

"Are you crazy?" Ian Quayle shook his head vehemently. "No, that sort of caper is too damn dangerous—for too little money."

"The money would be very considerable, Quayle."

"I'm sure it would be. And what the hell could I do with it in London? Buy myself a Rolls Royce? Start dining every night at Mirabelle? Live the way you live? How long, do you think, before I'd have a number of sticky questions to answer if my life style went overnight up there where I want it?"

Mayberry agreed. "Yes, you do have a point there. So, what is your alternative?"

Ian Quayle said carefully, "I'd like to enjoy your hospitality for a while, a couple of weeks, say, maybe more. And every day I'd sit down with a tape-recorder and answer questions for you, wouldn't that be nice?"

The long silence again, and then: "We could, of course, merely apply...persuasion, instead."

"No, it wouldn't work, Mayberry. Oh, sure, I'd talk my head off once you started your bloody torture. But you'd never be sure, would you? You'd always have to worry that with my dying gasp I'd be feeding you stuff that might be harmful to you. Without my *willing* cooperation...you can never be sure. Don't you agree?"

"Yes, I think I do."

"That's why I've kept my price at a reasonable level. To make it worth your while as well as mine."

"And the price is...?"

"Five million dollars," Ian Quayle said. "I want it deposited, irrevocably, in a Swiss bank of my choosing before I even sit down in front of your tape recorder. Once I have the proof that the money's there for me...I'm all yours, for however long it takes. Five million's very little for you. For me...It'll keep me in great luxury in, perhaps, Rio de Janeiro, for the rest of my life." He paused, and then said stubbornly: "I've been sixteen years with MI6, Mayberry. Sixteen years! Every word I have to say will be worth its weight in gold to you. And all it's going to cost you is a lousy five million dollars. If I were less chicken I'd have asked for fifty."

For a very long time, Mayberry/Norton thought about it, the practiced wheels turning over in his mind; was this a genuine defection?

Or just a trick?

But what did he have to lose at this point? He said smoothly, "So give me a sample, Quayle. At no cost to me."

"For free? Well...A little tidbit then."

Ian Quayle thought for a moment. "You know, of course, that France is supplying nuclear fuel to Pakistan?"

"I've heard rumors," Mayberry said blandly.

"There's a *massive* sale coming up, very hush-hush indeed. It's going to be flown to Karachi, by a French Air Force plane, quite soon now."

Mayberry nodded. "Yes, that sort of information could perhaps be useful to me. But only if you know the date and the flight plan."

"I know that, and a lot more." He said flatly, "The Israelis are going to hijack it."

Mayberry's eyebrows shot up. "*Do what?*"

"They've found out who the pilot will be, one Captain Wilson. They're standing by to kidnap his wife and his two kids. He'll be told to fake engine trouble over the Mediterranean, and go for a forced landing in Israel's Negev, or else."

He was aware of Mayberry's excitement, and he shrugged.

"I don't really know," he said, "what you'd like to do with Intelligence of that nature, but if I were in your shoes...I'm sure Libya would pay handsomely for it with petro-dollars. They might like to send up a squadron of their S22s and shoot that plane down. Alternatively, they might want to hijack it themselves, if they're up to it. We all know how desperately Colonel Ghadaffi wants to make himself a nuclear weapon."

There was not a word of truth in the whole story; but he was quite sure that Mayberry was buying it.

Out of the shadows, Bianca said furiously, "Lies! Lies, nothing but lies! Don't trust him, signor Norton!"

"Be quiet," Mayberry said again. "I want to think about this..."

"Deceit!" she screamed. "He's fooling you...!" and he answered, more sharply: "*Quiet!*"

It was an order to a dog: '*Sit...Lie down...! Quiet...!*' and she fell silent at last.

"Well then, think about it," Quayle said tartly. "I've also

got a lot of ordinary but quite useful stuff at my fingertips. Like the day-to-day disposition of the American Sixth Fleet in the Mediterranean, Turkey's contingency plans for the seizure of the whole of Cyprus...And did you know that the Cubans are wondering how they can establish a presence in Papa'ete the moment Tahiti gains full independence? I know the date and place of the meeting between Malta and Russia to work out the details of the new Russian submarine base in Malta's Valetta to replace the one they lost in Albania's Valona, their long-cherished dream of a home base in the Mediterranean."

He went on, pushing it. "I know the plans that King Hassan of Morocco has vis-a-vis the Polissario guerrillas, and who really cares? But I also know the French plans for a new uprising in Chad—the plutonium deposits up there on the disputed border, I'm sure you know how important they are. No? And for the moment, at least, need I say more? You need me, Mayberry. You really need me. And Wendy Hayworth comes with me, all the way."

Mayberry was staring at him, completely hooked, and Quayle said plaintively, "But do you mind if we break off this discussion? It's getting to be very one-sided, and you've got a very interesting party going on up there."

He turned away and began to mount the stone stairway. He heard Bianca's voice behind him, filled with venom. "Nothing but lies! I know it...!"

Then Mayberry's answering voice before the door closed behind him. "Don't worry about it, Bianca. Quayle and I are on the same wavelength, it's enough for the moment. And if I find out that he's trying to trick me...Then I promise you, you shall have him..."

When he had gone, the cute little Bianca said, more quietly now, "This Ian Quayle is a very dangerous man, signor Norton. He has to be terminated, and the sooner the better."

"And terminate all that priceless information too? No!

He's a nobody!"

He was musing, a thought coming to him, and Bianca said furiously, "Strip him and strap him down, and give me a razorblade! In four or five hours I'll have everything he knows down on tape!"

"No. I have the glimmerings of a far more profitable idea. And you really are a little savage, aren't you?"

"Yes," she answered clearly, "and you ought to thank God that I am."

"Weapons," Mayberry said abruptly. "Any problems this evening?"

Bianca glowered. "Yes. Madame Ging-Sen was concealing one of the new Chinese Y47 .18 pistols at her inner thigh. They're made entirely of plastic and just don't show up on the scanners."

"Then change the scanners, dammit! Update them!"

"Of course, it's already in the works."

She smiled thinly. "And Carlos the Jackal, I beg his pardon, senor Contreras...Can you believe it? He had a switchblade in his boot."

"Any problem? That's a man we mustn't offend unless we have to."

"I just told him I'd take it from him if he didn't hand it over. And castrate him with it. He handed it over. And the new scanners are twelve thousand dollars apiece, is that okay?"

"Change them all, our security has to be immaculate at all times."

A thought occurred to him. "If the scanners didn't detect Madame Ging-Sen's pistol...?"

"A matter of human sensibility taking over from the electronics that have superseded it," Bianca said sourly. "That damned Chinese woman's dress is skin-tight, too skintight. And I spotted it."

"Good. Tell me about *last* month."

"Three guns, two knives. Security is improving. But I still want the new scanners. I also want an updating of the Barras-Massena System, it hasn't been tested, even, for far too long."

Mayberry said, startled, "The B.M. System? Bianca, we are never, ever, going to use that!"

She said coldly: "Then why do we have it, signor Norton?"

He was furious. "Because you sweet-talked me into installing it! *Porco Dio*, it cost me seven hundred thousand dollars! And what did it do on its test? It incinerated a couple of cows is what it did!"

"Actually," Bianca said mildly, "the number of cows was seven."

"Wandering around my *salone* and defecating all over my marble floor! They deserved to die!"

"And we couldn't even eat them," Bianca said caustically. "They got themselves boiled from the inside out. That's no way to cook a steak."

CHAPTER 14

Wendy was nowhere to be found, and for a while Ian Quayle worried about her. He wandered around the crowded room, sipping champagne and skewering prawns, chatting half-heartedly here and there...He found General Rastopovitch a bloody bore, was more interested in Madame Ming Chu'an from Taiwan, a quiet and introspective woman dressed very fetchingly in oyster-colored silk.

He spoke for a while with Greece's Captain Pastroudis, a pale-faced young man who seemed somehow out of place here...With the plump little Colonel Moulins of France, who was bright and articulate and who filled him in, rapidly and fully, on the situation in Central Africa.

And most of all, he chatted with Madame Ging-Sen from Peking, whom he found to be a lady of the most extraordinary charm and sensuality.

"And when you leave here," she asked, mocking him, "will your remembrance of me be as I am now? Or as you saw me in that dreadful photograph you spoke of?"

"Neither," Ian Quayle said. "In my imaginings, I'm a step ahead of you. I'll remember you in my imagination without the trappings of such trivia as peacock-blue silk gowns or drab grey uniforms."

"Well, really, Mr. Quayle..."

She was almost fluttering her eyelids at him, and yet...he had the feeling, backed by no reason that was apparent, that she was a very shrewd woman.

And then Mayberry was there, smiling, and he said, "It's terribly rude of me, Quayle, isn't it, to have been watching you for the last half hour? But I saw your eyes darting from corner to corner, questing, searching, and a trifle worried. Are you perhaps wondering where Miss Hayworth might be?"

Quayle nodded. "That's exactly what I was wondering," he said. *A lie; he had spotted something very strange...*

Mayberry laughed. "Well, let me put your mind at rest. We don't have her confined in a dungeon, being squeezed into an Iron Maiden, if that's what you're worried about. She's out in the grounds with a new-found friend, touring the garden. And he's telling her all about the moonlit roses."

"Oh."

"'*Oh*' is not really a very suitable answer," Mayberry said. "You're supposed to ask me who the new-found friend is."

"Very well. Who's the new-found friend?"

"Senor Contreras, from Venezuela."

Quayle's blood froze.

"Contreras?" he said. "I know him by a different name."

"Well of course," Mayberry said evenly. "I was quite sure you'd recognize him. Carlos the Jackal."

"Possibly," Quayle said tightly, "the most dangerous man on the face of the earth."

Mayberry agreed at once. "Yes," he said, "I think you're right. But not *here*."

"*Here...?*"

"Within the hallowed confines of my Villa. It's a convention we've all adhered to for some years now. Mutual enemies everywhere, but once they pass through my front gates, all enmities are set aside, for as long as they stay here. We have representatives here from East and West Germany who, outside these walls, would kill each other on sight. North and South Korea are both here...Madame Ging-Sen of China, in whom, I've noticed, you have a certain interest...She's chatting amiably at this moment with Madame Ming Chu-an of Taiwan, even though she was the brain behind that recent attempt on the Taiwan lady's life, which failed horribly. But in this Villa, we are all friends, for a short and limited time, in the name of the great God Mammon, sometimes called Profit. So don't worry about your Miss Hayworth. Carlos has no reason at all to harm her, and if he were to...he'd know that he would not leave the Villa alive, the penalty for breaking our long-established rules are swift and ruthless. So, why don't you have some more champagne?"

Quayle drank, and soaked it all up insufficiently with a plateful of the best canapes he had ever tasted. And at two o'clock in the morning, he went to bed, a little woozy with too much of everything.

He slept fitfully, and he awoke at a sound in his room, and said, "Wendy? I was worried about you. Come on in..."

He stared bleary-eyed at the illuminated dial of the bedside clock: 2.12.

And then the light went on, and it was not Wendy at all but the cute little Bianca. She held a silenced 9mm Baretta trained on him, and her other hand was on the light switch.

She kicked the door shut behind her, and advanced on him like a prowling animal, and he stumbled out of the bed and stood up, conscious in spite of everything that a man didn't look his best in the pajama tops he liked to sleep in.

He said, stammering, "Now, wait a minute..."

He broke off, realizing what a foolish remark it was; *wait? For what?*

Bianca's maniac eyes under those beer-bottle glasses were on fire, and she said, "I haven't come to kill you, Quayle, which is what I really ought to do. But, just to warn you."

Her gun dropped down to knee-level, and Quayle knew

instantly what it meant—the shattered knee-cap, the most painful wound there is. It was the hallmark of the Red Brigades, taught to them by the teenage monsters of the Irish Republican Army.

He saw the pistol aimed, saw her finger tightening on the trigger...

He screamed out his rage and his fear, and hurled himself under the shot she fired.

He rolled against her legs and brought her to the ground. He reached for her gun-arm and grabbed the wrist and held it high, and smashed his other fist to her jaw.

It was inexpertly aimed, and the blow—with all his weight behind it and very powerful—went to the side of her head, a little below the ear. The gun fell from her hand, and she dropped back, quite unconscious.

Behind him, as he stared down at her, the intercommunicating door of the bathroom opened, and Wendy was there.

"A shot?" she whispered, looking at Bianca's unconscious body. "Is she dead?"

"I *hit* her," Quayle said. "A little slip of a girl, and I punched her on the side of the head and knocked her out!"

In a sudden access of fury, he picked up the Baretta and hurled it out through the open window, out there into the famous rose garden somewhere, and Wendy whispered, "She was trying to kill you?"

He was on his knees beside Bianca's body.

"No," he said, "to maim me, what she called a warning."

"Ian," Wendy said urgently, "let's get out of here, *now*! While we can."

Quayle was recovering his composure, and he said stubbornly, "No. For the first time ever, we hold the advantage. Do you know where Mayberry's room is?"

"Yes. It's the last room on the right at the end of the corridor."

"Stay here."

"No. I'm coming with you."

"Very well."

Ian Quayle put on a robe, and they went together out into the passageway, past surly, heavily armed guards who, for the most part, merely scowled at them.

Till they came to the door at the end.

The guard there held his Uzi at the port across his body and said sternly, "*No, non si entra*, Mr. Norton is sleeping, you may not disturb him."

"You want to bet on that?" Ian Quayle said tartly.

"I'm the guest of honor in this house, and if you turn my body into a sieve with your damned machine-pistol...Mr. Norton is going to use your guts for suspenders to hold up his pants, so stand aside."

He hammered briefly on the door and threw it open, then groped for a light switch and found it. And in the sudden brightness Mayberry, startled, sat up and automatically pulled the sheet up over the naked woman who was with him; Fraulein Elisabet Kraus from Austria.

But he was very fast on the recovery...

"Quayle!" he said, positively delighted. "And Miss Hayworth! How very nice to see you! Would you care to join us?"

"God damn your eyes," Quayle said furiously. "Your bloody bodyguard just tried to maim me."

Mayberry smiled. "Bianca?"

"Who else?"

"Well, isn't that interesting? What happened? I see she didn't succeed, and I find that interesting too."

"She went for my knee-cap, and if I hadn't guessed before, doesn't that put her in the camp of the Red Brigades?"

"I told you that was a shot," Fraulein Kraus murmured, but Mayberry paid her no attention at all and he went on: "She thinks you're a terribly dangerous man, Quayle, but I don't. I'll give her a good talking-to, it won't happen again."

"It won't be necessary," Wendy said coldly. "We're leaving. Now."

"You can't do that, you know..."

"You mean we're prisoners?"

"Let's say guards at my gates are Red Brigades too."

"And that," Quayle said angrily, "is about the most fatuous comment I've heard in years. A great number of people know exactly where we are, and if we don't return to Rome in a reasonable time..."

He broke off, Mayberry, smiling gently, was shaking his head. "No, that's not true," he said. "A number of people know that you *set out* for Florence, with the intention of visiting the Villa delle Rose. But did anyone see you actually drive through my gates? Except my own people? We're very isolated here, Quayle, and believe me, if anyone had seen you actually arrive...those gates would never have been opened. So, you see, quite apart from the fact that I have all the high-level protection in the world, and that no one knows you're here, I can hold you for as long as I like. So why don't you stay and enjoy yourselves? Besides, I'd dearly like you to come to the auction tomorrow. Go back to bed, sleep in for a while tomorrow, and you'll have no more problems with Bianca. She tends to get a little out of hand once in a while in the interests of my own personal safety, bless her murderous little heart. I'll have a word with her tomorrow, and you have my promise of absolute safety. The word of an English gentleman."

"Let's go back a bit in that fatuous speech," Wendy said. "'The auction'? I take it you're not selling off your priceless Ming Dynasty ceramics?"

Mayberry chuckled. "Not that kind of auction at all, you and I all know, don't we? We're selling off a few secrets."

He turned back to Ian. "And if you truly want to sell

139

some of yours, then we'll put them on the block too, and won't that be nice for you? You get seven and a half percent, that means..."

He was smiling, an affable and kindly man. "It means that on Day One of your defection, you get to make an enormous amount of money. Positively *enormous*. Are you sure you won't join us, both of you? It could be amusing."

Quayle turned on his heel and stalked to the door. "Goodnight, Mayberry," he said. "See you tomorrow."

They found their way back through the maze of marble-floored corridors, tall and narrow, with plaster friezes everywhere, little cherubim and seraphim smiling down on them from the pools of yellow light the lamps cast.

And Wendy was strangely silent...

But when they reached his room, Bianca was still there on the floor, still quite unconscious.

There was a moment of alarm, and Quayle dropped to one knee beside her and felt for her heartbeat and found it strong.

"Get your hands off her boobs," Wendy said. "Or do you get a kick out of fondling unconscious female bodies?"

Ian Quayle ignored it. He said glumly, "The first time in my life, I think, that I ever hit a woman. Not very gallant, is it?"

"I shouldn't worry about that too much," Wendy said tartly. "If she'd tried that on me, I'd have broken both her arms."

"The question now is...what the hell do we do with her?"

"Tip her over the balcony into the rose garden."

"We're three stories up..."

"Four would have been better, but three's enough..."

Quayle sighed, and Wendy said, "Okay then, just leave her here, she'll come round in time. You'd better spend the rest of the night in my room."

"All right. I'll do that, if I may."

He sat on the edge of her bed in his robe as she poured him a very large drink, and he said, "You were out there in the garden, with Carlos of all people! What could you hope to find out from him, for Christ's sake?"

"Nothing," she said calmly. "I was looking for a different kind of information. I just felt I couldn't wander around out there without a suitable escort, one of *them*. And actually, he's a very bright and charming man."

"Charming?"

"On the surface, of course."

"How many people do you think he has personally killed?"

"Only God and Carlos himself can know the answer to that. And there's a strong possibility that Carlos lost count a long time ago."

"And you still say he's charming."

"He was my reason for being out there," Wendy said patiently. "I wanted a look at the walls. They're ten feet high, topped with broken glass, and there's a light every twenty yards all the way around. A small gatehouse, three guards at the gate. I heard a car driving slowly around the perimeter outside the walls, and when it passed the gate, I saw that it had no lights. It won't be easy to get out of here, I'm afraid, although night-time might offer a better chance than broad daylight. And isn't there something more serious we have to talk about?"

For a long time, he was silent, knowing exactly what was on her mind. He said at last, "Yes, we do, love. The reason why we *don't* try to escape now."

"Go on, I'm all ears. I'd particularly like to know what Mayberry meant when he referred to what he called '*Day One of your defection.*' What the hell was that all about?"

"I'm on the verge of penetrating the League of Hawks," Quayle said.

Wendy stared. "You're...*what*?"

"I told Mayberry I was ready to defect. And he fell for it hook, line and sinker."

"Ian, you're mad! You think this man is a fool?"

"No, I don't, I'm well aware of his intelligence. I'm aware of his greed too, and so...I dreamed up some phony MI6 'secrets' for him, as samples of the stuff I was prepared to sell him. And I promise you, he bought it all, fell for it completely. He'll be auctioning off some of those so-called secrets tomorrow. It's going to make me one of *them*."

"Mad!" Wendy said. "A maniac! Ian, you are *not* a field officer...."

"I am now. Mrs. French made me one."

"But you don't know the ropes!" She was in despair. "Ian! No competent field officer would ever try a stupid trick like that! It's pure suicide! And we don't spend all that time, trouble, and yes, money, on training field officers just to get them killed off the moment they make fools of themselves! You don't *have* the training! You're a beginner, an amateur!"

She calmed down a little. "And you've just made the most godawful mistake a beginner can make—you're underestimating the competence of the opposition. And if you'll take my advice..."

He interrupted her angrily. "I don't need it, I know what has to be done now!"

But he too calmed down, and he went on more rationally, knowing that it would not be easy. "I want to pursue the matter of the murders, and I want to find out about the League. Both those aims absolutely require that somehow I get close to Mayberry."

"You don't *know* that he killed Carlotta..."

"Agreed. But I suspect it. And if and when that suspicion becomes a conviction—then I know what I'll have to do."

"I don't even want to hear about that. But let me make a point—the *psychology* of the opposition, which is always important. Mayberry knows about you, and he knows about me. That means that he knows...about *us*."

142

"Well, that's a startling deduction."

Wendy Hayworth said patiently, "Listen to me, Ian, for Christ's sake! He knows that we're more than just partners, and he's not likely to believe that you'd throw me over quite so readily. Didn't he even raise the point?"

"No, he didn't."

"Well, I find that very strange."

"He didn't raise it for a good reason. That's exactly what I expected him to do, so I got there first. I told him you were in this with me all the way."

"Oh my God..."

He grunted. "Well, I was quite sure that once you knew how I was sticking my neck out, you wouldn't want to run off and let me perish without at least holding my hand."

"That's great, just great! And now I'm part of an operation I would have vetoed the moment it was suggested! And there's no way out of it unless we get the hell out of here tonight!"

"Which you yourself said would not be possible."

"Yes, that's true, isn't it? And all this started because you fell in love with a girl a hundred years ago! Carlotta! Who probably forgot you the moment she left you! Whose only sensible thought must have been: *Good riddance*."

Ian Quayle thought about it, and then said coldly, "I think that with the solitary exception of Mrs. bloody French, you are probably the most unpleasant woman I've ever met. Goodnight."

She knew she'd hurt him badly. "Ian, wait...!"

"No. I'd rather sleep in my own bed, thank you very much, even with an unconscious female on the floor beside me, it might be interesting, at that."

He gulped down his cognac and stalked out in high dudgeon, just a little bit smashed. And when he reached his room, he found that the manic Bianca was no longer there.

"So much the better," he said to the world at large, and

stripped off his clothes. He lay down on the bed to fall into a restless semi-sleep, thinking about his Carlotta, thinking that perhaps Wendy was right after all.

Had that monstrous murder really clouded his judgement? He could not be sure. Had it been engineered by Mayberry? Or the Red Brigades acting on their own? After all, General Mancini had been head of the anti-terrorist authority, and he was the Brigades' enemy just as much as he was the League's.

There was a pressing need to be *sure*.

In a little while he heard the soft opening of the door in the darkness, felt the movement of the bed as Wendy climbed in and stretched her naked body beside him.

Her head was very close to his, and she whispered almost inaudibly, "We were very, very foolish, Ian."

He sighed. "Yes, I know. We fight too much, don't we?"

"Not that."

"What then?"

"It should have occurred to me at once, but it didn't. Our rooms are almost certainly bugged."

Ian shook his head. "No, I thought about that too. But there just wasn't time. It took us only three hours to get here, and bugging a room isn't just a question of hiding a microphone under the bed, not these days, it takes a very long time. Floorboards to be removed to conceal the wiring, micro-mikes to be skillfully hidden where even a careful search won't find them...No, he just didn't have the time."

He kissed her and found her breast with his lips. "No, don't worry about that. Just worry about *us*..."

Ian Quayle was not a Field Officer, or he'd have known better. And neither was Wendy Hayworth, she was a Case Officer, her duties confined to collating the reports of various operatives risking their lives out there some place, with very little knowledge of what field work was actually like.

In the rough and dangerous business of field espionage, these two were babes in the woods.

For years now, the beautiful villa had been so well wired for sound that it was, in itself, a huge stereo system.

Ministers and other high Government officials often stayed here to enjoy the hedonistic luxury that Mr. Thaddeus Norton, antiquarian, offered them in his lovely old villa.

Often, they brought their own secret mistresses, but if they did not, then an accommodating Mr. Norton always had a sufficiency of elegant and gorgeous female 'guests' who just happened to be dropping by for a drink, some of Italy's highest priced hookers, well-trained enough (by Mayberry personally) to pass as ladies of established nobility.

There was always *Contessa This*, and *Duchess That*, and even, when the occasion demanded the highest possible quality, a *Principessa The-Other*.

And the constantly mounting stores of tapes from their bedrooms were what Lord Mayberry, commonly known as Mr. Thaddeus Norton, liked to call his *'protection'*.

Down in one of the basement rooms, Bianca peered myopically at the rev-counter of the big Teac reel-to-reel.

She said to one of the assistants who manned the computers twenty-four hours a day, "One hundred and five to twelve hundred and seven. I want the transcription for Mr. Norton."

"*Si, signorina.*" The man gestured to one of the girls there, and she nodded and slipped on the earphones.

"And now," the cute little Bianca said, "perhaps he'll listen to me. Give me Room Nine."

The operator threw a switch. "Colonel Moulins," he said, "I've checked before, he's alone."

The speakers registered only heavy breathing, and Bianca said, "Room Seven..."

More switches, and there was Colonel Rostopovich's voice, heavy with an excess of vodka and speaking in Russian: "...and permit me to say, my darling, that your thighs are made from the purest ivory."

And then a female voice, in heavily-accented Russian: "Sweetheart, the nice things you say! I find it just marvelous that *butchers* can fall back on poetry when the need arises..."

"Who's that?" Bianca asked sharply, and the operator shook his head. 'I'm not sure, *signorina...*"

"Then put her on Voice-Track, idiot!"

"Of course."

The operator touched buttons, and on the computer the serrated lines were forming, finally to meet each other and hold; they switched to the legend: *VOICE 182, Elsa Adren, Bulgarian, age 42, fourth in command of Bulgaria's Secret Service, known as BRASIK. Strengths: A high erudition on European politics, fluency in languages (8), and a presence that incites confidences. Weaknesses: Subject is an alcoholic and a nymphomaniac, and her addiction to these twin stimuli has traditionally been put to good use by her mentors in the KBG, under whose close supervision she works. She is also believed to be next in line for the Directorship of BRASIK after the death of the present incumbent, Alexis Zankoff, who is 82 years old and in very poor health. She was born in Vidin, on the Romanian border, of peasant stock, studied Political Science at...*

"Room Four," Bianca said, and at the touch of two buttons the screen went black and the speakers took over with Wendy's anguished voice: "Mad! A maniac! Ian, you are not a Field Officer!"

Then Ian Quayle's voice: "I am now. Mrs. French made me one..."

Bianca touched the reverse button, and as the tape

whirled she said: "*Bene, bene*...I want a transcript of everything they say from the moment they entered the room until they fall asleep. Then, hold them on auxiliary in case they wake up and start talking again."

Her eyes were wild, her emotions extreme, and she said, "*Signor disgraziato* Quayle has just signed his own death warrant, together with that upper-class whore Wendy Hayworth. Bring the transcripts to me directly."

The girl with the earphones was readying her pad for the shorthand.

CHAPTER 15

They slept late; and at ten in the morning, a maid was there with a silver tray on which there were two large bowls of cappuccino coffee, a wicker basket of hot rolls, two silver dishes of butter (one sweet and the other salted) a pot of honey, and three different kinds of marmalade.

She sat the tray down on the bedside table and said cheerfully, "*Buon giorno signor, signora*, it's a beautiful day again..."

She pulled back the heavy drapes and let the sunlight flood into the charming room, and said, "If you need more coffee, or anything else, the bell-rope is right beside the bed. Would you like your breakfast on the veranda, perhaps?"

Quayle yawned hugely, and scratched at his scalp. Casually, he pulled the sheet up over Wendy's naked limbs, and he nodded. "Yes, please. I think that would be very rewarding."

"There's jasmine all over the balcony, and at this time of the day..."

She moved the tray to the veranda table, and left them to their devices, and Wendy said, downcast, "I'm sorry about last night, Ian. I said some rather cruel things, didn't I? You must know that I didn't really mean them."

"And I did too. I'm sorry."

"It's just that...you make me so goddam mad sometimes."

He grunted and changed the subject. "Try some of this wild strawberry jam, it's fantastic."

He broke off a piece of warm bread for her, and buttered it heavily, and spread the jam over it, and popped it into her mouth. "Friends again?"

She reached for his hand. "Ian...you'll never really understand how deeply I'm in love with you, will you?"

"Sometimes," he said. "As I'm in love with you. Sometimes. And just as deeply, if not more so."

"It's not enough, is it?"

"No, I don't think it is," Ian said. "We really have to do something about that, one day. We both have to make a solemn affirmation—no more fighting."

"And then," Wendy said, "all the *spark* would go from our relationship."

The day passed slowly.

A late lunch came, buffet-style, all the guests helping themselves as they saw fit; and in the late afternoon, Mayberry found Wendy and Quayle wandering alone around the rose garden, admiring the spectacular blooms.

He took over at once, an amateur gardener of some consequence and an expert rosarian, and he said, producing a pen-knife from his hip pocket, "This is a Zepherine Drouhin, perhaps the most appealing of all the Bourbon roses."

He cut a mauve-pink bloom and gave it to Wendy with a courtly little gesture. "Smell it," he said, "the true Bourbon perfume, nothing quite like it in our artificial world..."

At seven o'clock, lights were flashing on and off everywhere in the twilight, to warn the guests that the auction was about to begin. Accompanied by Mayberry, Quayle and Wendy went to the *Gran' Salotto*, and Quayle murmured: "The moment I've been waiting for all this time! Is it really going to be worthwhile for me?"

"Hundreds of thousands of pounds." Mayberry said

emphatically.

Quayle appeared to be on edge. "I hope so," he said. "We have a very hush-hush department for this kind of thing, a department that seeks out defectors and quietly eliminates them. It's supposed to be awfully efficient, though nobody knows much about it except that...well, for what I'm doing now, they track people down to the ends of the earth, and just knock them off."

"MI26," Mayberry said cheerfully, "we know all about them, and they're not really very efficient at all."

He shrugged. "They never got to Burgess in time, did they? Nor Kim Philby. They never knew about Blount till the papers published his story."

"MI26? So that's what it's called! The fellows at the office just called it 'The Death Watch.'"

"Ha! Someone there has a sense of humor! You know who the Death Watch beetle is? That's her code-name, *Beetle*. Your Mrs. French runs MI26."

"Oh my God..."

It was a genuine surprise, and Quayle tucked the information away at the back of his mind. "Research," he murmured, "sometimes originates in the least expected places."

Mayberry turned to Wendy. "And you, Miss Hayworth," he asked. "You're really prepared to go along with Quayle on this thing?"

"Absolutely," she said at once. "Ian tells me there's a very great deal of money involved."

Mayberry nodded, and he was smiling broadly. "It all depends, of course, on what you can give me to sell."

He clapped Quayle on the back and said genially, "Once you've seen how we operate...we'll sit down at a tape recorder, all three of us, for a few days perhaps. And then...the next session, a very big one. That's when you're really going to make your killing..."

* * *

Even half-prepared as he was, Ian Quayle could not believe the atmosphere of the forthcoming auction.

It was being held in the *Gran' Salotto* of the villa, a large room of immaculate proportions, its terracotta and white walls draped with tapestries. Its high ceiling was ornately carved and gilded, and its floor, partly covered with priceless carpets, was of polished red-brown marble of the variety called Moroccan Red Flame, sawn with the bed and one of the rarest marbles in the world.

An enormous carved oak cabinet served as a bar, filled with bottles of champagne and liquor, its upper shelves shining with crystal glasses. White-gloved waiters were serving drinks, and half a dozen waitresses in black dresses and tiny white aprons, moved among the guests with trays of canapés.

Some thirty high-backed Venetian chairs in heavy oak and blue velour had been set up in lines, and in one corner a dais had been placed, an ancient oak podium on it. And close by, there was an ordinary school blackboard on which one of the staff was copying, from a typed sheet of paper, a list of the evening's offers. Quayle, intensely interested, was watching him:

1) Russia-Pakistan analysis.

2) Expected coup in Turkey.

3) Forthcoming change in American Sixth Fleet armament.

4) South Korea's duplicity to forthcoming talks with the North.

5) Imminent incursion of Syria into Iraq.

6) Blue-prints of West Germany's new *'Draufganger'* missile.

7) Details of Libya's *'Bokra'* Revolutionary Group.

8) Details of East German spy ring in Hamburg.

And so the list went on. But Quayle was looking now at faces, and he said to Mayberry (seeking to assure himself of something he already knew), "Some of the people here have been at each other's throats for years. And they're all drinking together like the best of friends."

Mayberry nodded. "Friends? Yes, that's what they are as long as they are my guests. Though 'friendly rivals' might be a better term. A house rule, no enmity here, and no weapons of any kind except in the hands of my staff."

"You can't be sure of that," Quayle said, pressing.

"For all you know, I might have a gun strapped to my ankle at this very moment, I haven't been searched once..."

"That's not quite true," Mayberry said, smiling. "Scanners, everywhere. This place is an architectural computer."

He laughed shortly. "When you arrived, you were carrying a pen-knife in your hip pocket, a handful of coins, a bunch of keys, and a Zippo cigarette lighter. Miss Hayworth worried us for a while because of her metal ballpoint. But we decided it was too slim to contain Mace or cyanide gas. And why do I tell you these things? Because you're one of us now, and isn't that nice?"

He snapped his fingers at a passing waiter, and said courteously, "Champagne, Miss Hayworth?"

Wendy nodded, a little preoccupied. "Please."

"Quayle?"

Ian Quayle sighed, knowing exactly what it was that had so disturbed Wendy. "In view of the forthcoming excitement," he said, "I think I'd prefer cognac."

As the waiter hurried off, a dark and swarthy man came to them, very worried, and he said to Mayberry, "The coup in Turkey, Mr. Norton. I am surely the only potential buyer here with any interest in that at all. But I must know what I'm getting for my money."

"Mehmet Pasha," Mayberry said, making the introductions, "Miss Hayworth and Mr. Quayle."

The Turk bowed stiffly, and as Mayberry took his arm

and led him away, he was saying gently, "The coup is being financed by...another country, Pasha. And they will try their damndest to outbid you. So kindly don't haggle with me before the auction even begins. This is not the Middle East, you know..."

Wendy was almost trembling. She whispered, "An architectural computer, he said. You know what that means, don't you?"

Ian nodded. He said tightly, "Every room in the house bugged, without a doubt. Last night...I gave the whole thing away."

"*We* gave it away. And what the hell do we do now?"

"There's an easy answer to that," Quayle said bitterly.

"There's *nothing* we can do, nothing at all except play it by ear."

And then...

He was standing close to the wall, and a tiny flash of reflected light in a tapestry beside him caught his eye. It was gone almost instantly, but appeared again when he moved his head ever so slightly, and what the hell could it be?

He had an instinct, an intuition, and somehow felt that he should not be seen staring at it too obviously. He was very cautious now as he sipped his drink and sort of casually looked over the walls and found more of them. They were all around the room, hardly much larger than the head of a pin.

They were alone now, with the hubbub of conversation all around them, and he whispered to Wendy, "Tiny pieces of broken glass set into the walls all over, and I can't think what they're for. I spotted a couple of them once before and wondered about them. But, Christ, now that I know what to look for...the whole blasted room is covered with them."

Her voice was a zephyr. "Yes, I've noticed them too. But it's not just glass, Ian. It's *cut* glass, maybe crystal. Maybe even sapphire, maybe even industrial diamonds."

"Don't look for them too obviously."

"You think I'm crazy?"

She was smiling broadly as she looked over the assembled guests, and she said loudly, "What a lovely party, isn't it? And this champagne really is the greatest."

There was a circumspect silence for a moment, and then she whispered, "You like the decor here?"

He was startled. "It's fantastic..."

She turned away, and her lips were hardly moving. "Just one thing out of kilter."

"Oh? What's that?"

"The painting of Tancred. Over the light-switch by the door."

"What's wrong with it? Mayberry claims Tancred as one of his ancestors."

"Then why is it so small? Every other painting in the room is ten times its size. And *Tancred*? The most important of them all, given a mere eight-by-ten instead of the fifty-by-seventy of the others?"

A short and stubby Arab in traditional dress came to them, his keffieh wrapped around his head. He was wearing sunglasses, the Third World indication of quality, and he shot out a hand to Quayle and said, that perpetual smile fixed in place, "I believe that you are Mr. Ian Quayle. And I, as I am sure you must know, am Yasser Arafat. Will you not introduce me to this charming lady?" His English was not bad, though heavily accented.

Ian Quayle said mechanically, "Mr. Arafat, Miss Hayworth..."

The Arab bowed over her hand: "I am delighted to meet with you, Miss Hayworth. And is the famous MI6 bidding against me on the plans for the Israeli incursion into Jordan? We have so little money, and this is something I really must know about. Your abstention from the bidding could mean for you the blessing of the whole Arab world."

Ian Quayle said amiably, "We don't need to bid for those plans, Mr. Arafat. We instigated them. So we know them, down to the last detail."

Arafat was in shock. He wormed himself awkwardly away, and Ian Quayle returned to the matter in hand. "The portrait of Tancred," he whispered.

"It's too small," Wendy said, "and it's extruded an inch or so from the wall, it means it's on a hinge. There's a box underneath it. So...what's in the box!"

"The switch for the cameras."

There were four unobtrusive camera lenses there, one in each upper corner of the room. But Wendy shook her head. "No. The cameras will be on remote control from another room some place, without a doubt."

Ian Quayle sighed. "Mysteries, mysteries. We'll have to solve them somehow, won't we? And meanwhile...there's just no way out of here."

He looked at the salotto's only two doors; three husky waiters were standing at each of them, their arms folded to conceal the bulges under their white dinner jackets that their shoulder-holsters made.

But a bell sounded now, and Mayberry was at the podium. He waited till the guests had all taken their seats, and then held up a box of folders. "A mixed bag tonight," he said cheerfully, "as you'll see on the board there."

He forced a little joke: "We all know, don't we, about the disposition of the American Sixth Fleet, the world's worst-kept secret! But there are some new details on the changes in their armament that might be worth half a million or so, I don't expect too much for that. But the Russia-Pakistan papers are very, very interesting indeed, detailing what the Politburo calls 'Securing the Border' but which really amounts to an invasion—and we have the date—to a depth of from six to forty kilometers along seventy-two percent, roughly, of the frontier. It's a massive assault, and I'll not take less than five million for these papers. We even have the number of tanks, and their type, that will head the first thrust."

He smiled thinly. "Colonel Rastopovitch will be interested in that, I'm sure, if only because we have the name—and the signature—of the Russian Colonel who sold it to us. And, of course, the Pakistanis might wish to prepare themselves in the sure knowledge that America will reimburse them when the time comes."

He sipped his champagne and went on. "The Libyan papers, I'm sure, will fetch more than you might expect, because they contain not only the Bokra Group's plans for overthrowing the present government, but also their well-thought-out ideas concerning a subsequent invasion of the Sudan to bring the Libyan people quickly to their side. And let me make a point here; whoever buys this item will almost certainly be able to double his or her outlay overnight by reselling it to the damned Americans."

There was some polite anti-American applause from certain members of the congregation, and Mayberry continued: "And on the subject of our American friends—everyone here knows how much they would like to establish, with or without military force, a chain of airfields in the Middle East."

He looked down on Sheikh Mustafa bin Afusa of Bahrein, and said amiably, "*All* of the OPEC countries should be interested in this; we have their contingency plans for their first move in this direction, which is...an airborne landing in Bahrein, which is to become their staging-area."

In the front row of the seated guests, Sheikh Mustafa stared up at him. He whispered, "My country...a staging-area?"

"Specifically, Sheikh Mustafa, the airport of Ad-Dowah. But raise the price of your crude by another fifty cents a barrel, and you'll be able to pay, what? Five? Ten? Even twenty million for this knowledge? Think about it, my dear fellow. We have no objections to oil money. In fact, we thrive on it."

Ian Quayle fingered his empty glass and muttered, "Christ, I need another drink, I don't believe this..."

He rose to his feet, and at once there was a huge and very powerful hand on his shoulder, quite gently pushing him back again.

He looked up and saw a giant of a man standing over him, blue-eyed, blond-haired, lantern-jawed and smiling. "Please, Mr. Quayle," the sepulchral voice said, "you want something? I am Sven, your bodyguard."

Quayle sat and sighed. "All I wanted," he said plaintively, "was another cognac."

The giant looked at Wendy. "Miss Hayworth?"

Wendy shook her head. "No, nothing, thank you, Mr. Sven."

"Not *Mister* Sven. Just Sven. I am a servant."

A waiter had come hurrying to his signal, and Sven said, "A double Augier Freres for Mr. Quayle, at once. No, make that a triple."

Mayberry was touching the board with the tip of his pointer, and he said slowly, "Frankly, I don't know what this item might be worth. But there's a Czech defector in West Berlin who's been very close, for some years now, to the KGB. It seems that he probably knows the names of very many East German spies in West Germany, but he's, well, reluctant to talk very much, he's holding out for more money. Certain people here might like to get to him before he strikes his bargain. And we know where he has been hidden and under what security arrangements. Colonel Rastopovitch of course will be interested, but others might be too. I'm starting the bidding at a mere half million, but he might be worth a great deal more."

Ian Quayle took the drink the waiter brought him, and sipped it, and he said glumly, "Well at least they pour good drinks here, damn their bloody eyes..."

But now, Mayberry had raised his voice, and he was deadly serious.

"And we begin the auction," he said clearly, "with an item the like of which has never been offered here before. I have an extraordinary object for sale tonight."

There was a murmur running through the assemblage, and Wendy took Ian's hand in hers and held it tightly; he could sense her fear.

"We have with us tonight," Mayberry went on, "a gentleman and a lady some of you have already met. For those of you who have not, may I present Mr. Ian Quayle and Miss Wendy Hayworth."

"Oh shit," Wendy said, knowledgeable as always, "here it comes."

Mayberry smiled across the room at them, and said happily: "Would you both take a bow, please?"

He began clapping, and the guests automatically followed him, none of them quite sure what the approbation was about.

As Quayle rose and half-bowed awkwardly, wondering what the hell was going on, Wendy said caustically, "Sit down, for Christ's sake, you goddam idiot! We're being sold, can't you understand that?"

And the guests were quickly enlightened...

Mayberry said, "Mr. Quayle has been working for England's MI6 for sixteen years. Sixteen years! Can you imagine the vast scope of the knowledge he has accumulated in that time? Just a hired hand, working on research, but nonetheless...And Miss Wendy Hayworth, who comes with him, two for the price of one, has been a Case Officer with them for less time but far, far closer to their inner workings. She's probably even more valuable than he is. And I am putting them both on the auction block. With certain perhaps unusual conditions, which permit me to explain."

Mayberry/Norton looked over the expectant faces below him, and he said clearly, "These are the conditions; the highest bidder has them for one month—until the time of the next auction. During those four weeks, the normal physical persuasion may be used, of course. But if recourse to mind-altering drugs should become necessary, they will be used with discretion. Because...at the end of that limited period, I will buy them back for resale at the next auction, and I will not buy back a pair of vegetables, is that clearly understood? For one third of the initial purchase price, I will repurchase them after the buyer has finished with them. Provided that they are both still fairly capable of normal thought and speech. By this means, we can keep their usefulness going for what? Six months? A year? Five years? Who can tell? Suffice it that for the month of his prerogatives, each and every buyer will be able to squeeze every last drop of intelligence out of them."

Ian Quayle's mouth was dry as he heard Mayberry say: "This man knows about the upcoming sale by France of nuclear fuel to Pakistan; he knows of an Israeli plan to hijack the aircraft delivering it. He knows about Cuba's aspirations in Polynesia and of France's efforts to frustrate them, which are quite fascinating. I myself could question them, with persuasion..."

His voice was very hard. "It is quite apparent that Mr. Quayle suspects that I have a *personal* responsibility for the deaths of General Mancini and his daughter Carlotta. I repeat—he suspects it, but he can't be sure."

There was another little joke then: "Of course, should his suspicions ever become a conviction, then I suppose I ought to be cowering in a dark corner somewhere, to escape his just vengeance. But I am not. Because it might well have been an ex-cop named Bartolomeo Sassi, whose girl the General seduced."

There was some polite laughter, and he went on. "Like the fool he is, he has chosen to attack me on my home ground. And I choose to defer my response to his arrogance and to offer him, and his mistress Wendy Hayworth, for sale to my good friends here, to do with them what they wish to extract from them a whole slew of very valuable intelligence. And I start the bidding at a very foolish one million dollars. Do I hear one million?"

"One million," Madame Ging-Sen of China said, and Mayberry looked at her, a slight smile on his aristocratic face.

"I should perhaps tell you, Madame Ging-Sen," he said gently, "that Mr. Quayle's knowledge is almost entirely confined to Europe. The Far East is quite outside his sphere of interest."

She was very cold, an iceberg dressed up as a woman: "I do know my business, Mr. Norton."

"Very well, then. I have a million dollars, a trifle."

"I close the bidding," Colonel Rastopovitch said, "with three million dollars."

"Three and a quarter," Sheikh Mustafa of Bahrein said, and then, "three and a half," from Bulgaria.

"Three and a half," said Mayberry, and then "three seventy-five," from France's Colonel Moulins.

"Four," said Iran's Ayatollah Khassani, followed by a four and a half from Iraq and five from Syria, and Colonel Rastopovitch said once again: "Closing now. Seven million dollars, and the end of my bidding."

"I will wait for the second time around," Carlos the Jackal said mildly. "When they've already been softened up a trifle."

Madame Ging-Sen said, "Seven and a half."

"Going at seven and a half million dollars," Mayberry said equitably. "Do I hear more? No? Going, going...*gone!*"

He slammed down his gavel, and he said, "Mr. Quayle and Miss Hayworth have been sold to Madame Ging-Sen of China, for seven and a half million dollars. And the next item is the Libyan matter, what am I offered...?"

The Swedish giant slipped a handcuff over Ian Quayle's

wrist before he could even think of making a move; and how could it have helped him? He snapped the other bracelet over Wendy's wrist, and led the pair of them off, down the endless marble corridors and up the staircase to Quayle's room.

He thrust them down onto the bed, and he said roughly, "You sleep now, better you sleep."

He dragged up a chair and sat down, and took the pistol from his shoulder-holster, a 9mm Luger, and held it in his lap.

He said, "You stay there now, you don't give me no trouble. Tomorrow morning, I think, Madame Ging-Sen come for you, take you some other place. Best you sleeping now."

They sat disconsolately together on the bed, handcuffed together; and in a little while they lay down side by side and tried to make themselves more or less comfortable.

And later still, Ian Quayle said awkwardly, "Christ, I had far too much to drink this evening, I have to go to the bathroom..."

He raised his voice. "Sven? Would you unlock these cuffs for just a moment, please?"

Sven said coldly, "No, I will not."

"Nature calls, Sven! I have to relieve myself. The bathroom."

"Okay."

He lumbered to his feet, an ungainly monster of a man, and virtually dragged them both to the toilet. "There," he said, "do what you must doing."

"The cuffs," Quayle said tightly. "A moment of privacy, please? Just for a moment?"

"No. You pissing, then going back to bed."

"Oh Christ."

He said, wailing, "I'm sorry, Wendy. What can I do? Sometimes, you just can't hang on any longer."

"I know, don't worry about it, it's the least of our problems."

He hesitated. "And you? Are you okay? I hope to God you are, I couldn't stand it."

Wendy nodded. "Yes, I am. The female of the species has a larger bladder than the male, didn't you know that?"

"No, I didn't..."

"And besides, I didn't drink so much tonight."

"Oh, you're so smart! Hang in there..."

As he urinated in front of her, he thought that it was the kind of indignity that turns ordinary anger into fury.

And soon, they were back on the bed together, the lights on, with that damned Scandinavian giant watching them like one of the Hawks.

Ian Quayle twisted his body awkwardly, and laid a friendly hand on Wendy's breast, and he murmured, "Sleep, my love. It's the only thing we can do now."

"Yes, I know it. Are there any bright ideas in that fertile mind of yours?"

"Just one."

"Which is...?"

"That misfortunes always have their *limits*. Somehow, Wendy, we have to find them."

"And that's the most useless piece of philosophy I ever heard in my sweet life," Wendy said wrathfully, "shortly to be ended now. 'A limited use of mind-altering drugs,' Mayberry said. And you know what that means? It means that in a week or two from now, you and I are going to become semi-intelligent turnips! So what the hell are you going to do about it?"

"Shut up," Ian Quayle said. "We're on tape, remember? Just go to sleep, and let me *think*..."

CHAPTER 16

The night passed in worry, thirst, and frustration, and in the middle of it Quayle awoke from a half-sleep and saw that Wendy was wide awake beside him.

He said sourly, "There's nothing worse than nothing happening. I never could sleep with the lights on, how about you?"

"I hate it..."

Ian Quayle looked at the great stolid giant and called out, "Hey, Sven! Could we have the lights out, do you think?"

"No," Sven said.

He was ever watchful, so they turned themselves over and tried to find some sort of comfort in their handcuffs, and some kind of sleep.

The morning came, inevitably, and a maid was there with a breakfast tray which she set down on the bedside table. She drew back the drapes and said brightly, just as she'd always said in her long years of service here, "Another beautiful day, signori. And will you take your breakfast on the veranda? The jasmine there is so lovely..."

Quayle said sourly, "Oh shut up, for Christ's sake."

They sat together on the bed, uncomfortably, and drank cappuccino coffee from china bowls, and munched on hot rolls with butter and honey, and Quayle said, scowling, "Jesus, my underarm deodorant has given up the ghost. But we're not going to give this massive moron the satisfaction of watching us shower, manacled together, are we?"

"Definitely not."

Sven was still awake, but after a sleepless night his eyes were heavy, and they were wondering, both of them, if somehow this could be turned to their advantage; and Quayle muttered, "And where the hell is our new owner, do you suppose? We belong to Madame Ging-Sen now, so where is she?"

"Are you so anxious to meet with her again?" Wendy asked tartly, and he nodded. "Yes, I am! I told you already— nothing can happen that's worse than nothing happening..."

And then, a very strange and quite alarming kind of man appeared.

There was a stylized knock at the door, and Sven moved to open it, to admit a short, squat, dark-mustached man dressed in an ill-fitting gray suit, a fifty-four-inch chest at the very least, and a neck that could not possibly have taken a shirt with anything less than a twenty-inch collar. His hips were hardly broader than his waist in spite of that enormous mass of chest, and the overall impression was one of great physical power. He moved like a ballet-dancer, and must have been about forty years old.

He was accompanied by a tall and very wiry-looking Italian in his very early twenties, a skinny kid with masses of black hair falling all over his pock-marked face; he carried an Uzi machine-pistol, and stood respectfully a little behind his master, a bodyguard.

The newcomer stared at Ian and Wendy with very piercing small dark eyes, and he was suddenly smiling broadly.

"Well," he said affably, "good morning to you both! I'm Gordon Fest. I'd kind of like to ask after your wellbeing, but you must have spent a lousy night, right?"

His hand was outstretched, but he pulled up short and

turned to Sven. "Get those cuffs off," he said shortly, "We don't need them."

The Swedish giant fidgeted, and said deferentially, "I'm sorry, Mr. Fest, but my orders...I take orders only from Mr. Norton."

"You're relieved, Sven," Fest said mildly. "My own man is taking over now. Marcos. You know Marcos, I believe?"

"I know him," Sven said stolidly. "I do not like him too much."

"And I'm supposed to care about that? The handcuffs, Sven."

"I'm sorry, sir, but no."

Fest shot out a hand and gripped him by the collar, and the other hand went just as fast to his balls; and as the Swedish giant screamed out his pain, he found himself held high in the air, all two hundred and ten pounds of him, and then hurled bodily into a corner like a rag doll.

The gun fell from his grasp and clattered to the floor, and his eyes were on it; he even started reaching...

Gordon Fest did not move.

He said, with the ice in his voice, "All right, boy, grab it! Use it if you can! And I'll break all four of your legs, you animal."

Sven glared up at him, but suddenly all of his imminent violence was gone in badly-hidden fears. And as Fest said, "One more time...remove those handcuffs," he clambered sullenly to his feet.

"Yes, sir."

He found the key in his pocket and freed them, and Fest said, "Get the hell out of my sight now. Marcos takes over," and Sven was gone.

Gordon Fest grinned.

He took Ian Quayle's hand in a very gung-ho sort of grip, and he said, "We have a strange situation on our hands. That

Chinese broad bought you both, remember, for seven and a half million bucks. Hell, her whole allocation was only nine million! Stupid bloody woman, she was supposed to spend it on what the Chinese underground in Vietnam is doing. And frankly, Norton doesn't know too much about that, she got carried away."

The friendly smile was getting wider. "And so...Just to show her what a nice guy I am, I bought you from her, rounding the figure off to eight million, gives her a half-million profit to spend on other foolishness."

He was the very essence of charm. "I just couldn't bear the idea of this slant-eyed creature sliding bamboo needles under your fingernails and setting fire to them to find out stuff you don't really know about. They're very unimaginative, the Chinese."

"And I can't tell you," Ian said earnestly, "how very grateful we are. It was a nightmare! And you are what? CIA I imagine?"

Fest laughed, the nicest guy in the world. "CIA?" He echoed. "Hell, I wouldn't be found dead in bed with that bunch of goddam faggots. No, Mr. Quayle, I work for an outfit called Playtime Pursuits Incorporated. We manufacture, and market blow-up, life-sized plastic female dolls. They're very good if you're into that sort of thing."

"Er, yes," Quayle said awkwardly. "And may I present Mr. Gordon Fest, Miss Wendy Hayworth."

"We've met," Fest said, and turned to Wendy. "When was it, five years ago? In Washington? And how's your father, Miss Hayworth? For a bleeding heart liberal, he's doing okay with the new Administration. And how are you, honey? Still as gorgeous and sexy as ever, I see."

Wendy said coldly, "Mr. Fest...I've said it before, and I'll say it again. You're a monster."

Suddenly, with a movement so fast that Quayle could hardly follow it, Fest shot out a hand and gripped Wendy's face with murderous intensity, his iron fingers digging cruelly into her cheeks, holding her there easily as she screamed in pain, her eyes wide with shock.

"I am not a monster," he said. "I am an honest American citizen doing a job that has to be done, to prevent the maniacs from taking over the most advanced civilization in the world!"

Quayle, in shock himself, grabbed at Fest and screamed, "What the hell are you doing? Let her go...!" and Fest did just that.

He let go her face, and slapped her repeatedly, shouting, "Just to teach you, woman, to watch your tongue!"

She fell to the ground under his blows, and somehow to his surprise Quayle found himself on Fest's back, wrenching the chin up.

But Fest straightened his legs and did a back-flip with consummate ease, then picked Quayle up and drove his fist repeatedly into his stomach, one-two one-two one-two, like steel pistons.

Ian Quayle lay on the floor trying not to vomit, and he stared up at Fest and whispered: "For God's sake...aren't you American?"

"That's right," Fest said. "How bright of you to notice..."

"And we're...we're *allies*!"

"Allies!"

Fest stood over him, laughing, and he said, "Yes, that's true enough. But your outfit feeds my outfit a few teaspoons of chicken-shit once in a while, which is exactly what my outfit feeds your outfit. And you don't seem to understand, Quayle. Madame Ging-Sen bought you, can't you understand that? And I bought you from her! You're my property, Quayle, to do with as I please!"

He was pacing back and forth now as they both stared at him, and he said, "My people want to know what your people know, and you're going to tell me, one way or another. I can use drugs, which don't always work too good, or I can use physical persuasion, which is more reliable. Or I can use both."

But suddenly a very strange change came over him...

He looked down at Quayle, lying there on the floor still, and said with genuine concern in his voice: "You made a point there, Quayle, which I forget sometimes. Yes, we're *allies*! England and America, *friends*! And I was very harsh with you, wasn't I? Can you ever forgive me?"

He shot out a hand. Hesitantly, Quayle took it, and Fest applied pressure. His hand was a claw of carbon steel, crushing, cracking bones with its monstrous force, and Quayle screamed as he was forced to his knees.

Fest said gently, "London has already been informed that you're both dead, an unfortunate automobile accident. Your Robin Harris is weeping for your cadavers now, and you're mine! *Mine*! Non-people!"

He thrust Quayle aside, strode to the door, and opened it.

The new guard, Marco, was there; a tall, skinny cretin, red-lipped and possessed of the most fluttering eyelids in history. The Uzi was cradled in his lap, and Fest glanced at it, turned back to Ian Quayle, and murmured, "You do know what an Uzi can do, don't you? In seven tenths of a second, it can carve you in two, left to right or right to left across your stomach. And what we have here is two pieces of what was once a man dropping to the ground. And all that poor Marcos really knows is...how to point his gun and pull the trigger. So, beware of him! Idiots are always much more dangerous than those of us who are blessed with brains."

At the door, Gordon Fest turned back again.

"In a little while," he said, "we move to another place. To another safehouse, my own. Far safer than your place on Appia Antica."

He was grinning like a maniac.

"You think that house is *safe*? We knew about it the

moment your people signed that foolish lease. And when we arrive at your new destination...that is when the questioning will begin. And it will finish there too, because a combination of the right drugs plus a tightening cord around your forehead can achieve quite startling results. From both of you."

The look in his eyes was frightening, and he went on. "I just heard the tape. And I have to tell you that I rather like Miss Hayworth's phrase: *Semi-intelligent turnips*, she said, and I have news for you, Quayle! She was right. So think on it, my friend. At the end of a week, I'll know just about *everything* that's tucked away in your miniscule minds."

He was gone.

Ian Quayle said desperately, nursing a badly-bruised right hand, "So you know him. Who the hell is he, Wendy? He's an American, for Christ's sake! He can't be CIA, I won't believe it!"

Wendy went to the window and stared down on the rose garden; it was quite beautiful out there.

She was conscious that the guard Marcos was watching her every move, and she said quietly, "Gordon Fairweather Fest. We have a file on him in London yey thick. Like he said, he's President of Playtime, operating out of Montgomery, Alabama."

"He doesn't look like a business magnate to me. Blow-up female dolls or anything else."

"And Playtime is a cover for an agency so secret that even I don't know its mandate. What I do know is that they provide the CIA and the NSA, and all the other agencies with personnel, and with Intelligence too, to justify the high prices they charge for their services. They work absolutely outside of Government, Ian, with no control at all."

She was bitter, angry as hell. "They're not much liked in the Pentagon. But they do produce results. And that's all that counts in a world you're not accustomed to. But Fest himself...we know all there is to know about him. He's forty-two years old, and a health nut. He lives on almonds, raisins, and yogurt, good luck to him. But he does two hundred sit-ups every morning, can you believe that? Two hundred! I tried it myself once, and couldn't get past fifteen. He's studied Karate, and Savate, and Judo...Did you notice the burns on his hands?"

"No."

"When he fries an egg for his breakfast, he likes to stick his hand in the flame, and just hold it there till he's really convinced that he's tough. One of his minor weaknesses is to break bricks in two with the flat of his hand. I have this awful feeling that his backyard is littered with half-bricks. He also once swam across San Francisco Bay, all seven miles of it, with his hands and feet tied together. And it wasn't a publicity stunt at all, because he told *nobody* he was going to do it. It was just to impress himself, nobody else. And he *jogs*. But not just your everyday jogging; he straps twenty-pound lead weights to his Adidas running shoes."

"The man's a maniac," Quayle said.

"Yes," Wendy nodded. "And don't ever forget it."

Ian Quayle looked at the new guard Marcos and sized him up, and he said loudly, "That stupid bastard has been leering at you since the moment he arrived, have you noticed that?"

Wendy nodded. "I'm not blind..."

Marcos was sitting there with his Uzi nursed in his lap, staring at them blankly, and Quayle said, "Nothing to do till Fest returns, and I don't know about you...but now that we're out of our handcuffs, I'm going to take a shower. I honestly don't like sleeping in my clothes all night."

He looked at Marcos and said, "So if you don't mind, young man, we're going to get cleaned up now. Is that okay with you, you dumb-looking moron?"

There was only a blank look there, and a blinking of those girlish eyes, and Quayle said, "Great, he doesn't understand English."

"Or if his intelligence matches his pretty looks," Wendy said caustically, "he wants us to *think* he doesn't understand English."

"Maybe..."

He looked at her. "Suppose you take your shower first?"

His eyes would not leave hers, and she was sure she knew what it meant. She moved to the bathroom, and the guard said sharply, "*Aspetta*, wait!"

He went ahead of her and locked the communicating door to her own room and pocketed the key. He gestured broadly at her, and said, holding open the other door, "*La porta, sempre aperta*, all time opening door here, okay?"

"Okay. But if I catch you peeking, I'll bash your brains out..."

He did not understand what she was saying, it seemed, and he went and sat on his chair again, his machine-pistol resting across his knees.

Quayle paced back and forth, conscious of the young man's eyes on him. He threw him a glance and said, "Now is the time for all good men to come to the aid of the party. You understand?"

"*Si*..." Marcos said sullenly. "Am understand English good."

"Well, I'm very glad to hear that. Did you know that on occasion the quick brown fox jumps over the lazy dog?"

"*Capisco, capisco*, I understanding! Am learn English in school."

"In school? You mean you got yourself an education, you savage? But you're actually an asshole, aren't you?"

"Yes. Am understand."

Quayle was listening for the sound of the shower to come to an end, and when it stopped, he stood in front of Marcos, only a few calculated feet from him, and said earnestly, gesticulating with a raised finger, "To be, or not to be, that is the question!

171

Whether 'tis nobler in the mind to suffer the slings and arrows of outrageous fortune, or to take arms against a sea of troubles and by opposing, end them..."

Marcos was staring at him, wondering what this madman was talking about, and then...

Then, the diversion came.

Wendy came out of the bathroom carelessly wrapping a towel around her waist; and the young Italian's eyes went to her at once. He thought that in all of his young life he had never seen such a glorious figure, and his mouth dropped open.

It was the moment Quayle had been waiting for.

He grabbed the Uzi with both hands and wrested it away, and swung the butt round in a dreadful blow to the temple; and Marcos toppled from his chair and lay still.

Quayle looked at Wendy and muttered, "Put something on, for Christ's sake, you distract me too..."

"It worked, didn't it?" Wendy said as she slipped quickly into her clothes, and he nodded. He ran to the window and stared down onto the gardens, and said, worrying about it, "I don't see a single guard except the one at the gate."

"Only one?"

"There must be more in the gate-house. But how many, God alone knows."

"And the one...?"

"Watching the road, and he's way beyond the shrubbery. Is he going to see us?"

"Ian, we can't wait for dark. Fest might be back any time now."

"True, true..."

He went to the bed and pulled off the sheets, knotting them together by their corners, and he muttered, "The bed in the other room too, it's not going to be long enough...The key's in his pocket."

While she found it and brought the other sheets to

complete the rope, Ian undid the laces of Marcos' military boots, and used them to tie his thumbs and little fingers tightly together behind his back, tied them to his pulled-up ankles. He stuffed a rag torn from the man's shirt into his mouth and tied it there, and he said angrily, "Why don't I just cut the bastard's throat, can you tell me that? He's Red Brigades, for sure."

Wendy was fastening the improvised rope at the window, and she said impatiently, "We're wasting time, let's go...! You know where the Mini is?"

"How the hell should I? I parked it in the coach-house, if it's not still there I'll find another car and hotwire it, come on..."

They slid down the sheets to the ground, very quickly, and headed for the mass of oleanders that would give them shelter. They crouched there for a moment, listening, but there were no shouts of alarm, no signs of pursuit.

They ran swiftly to the coach-house, and there was the little red toy of a car. They climbed aboard, and roared at speed down the long driveway.

Predictably, the iron gates were closed and a guard was there. Peering at them and scowling as they skidded to a halt. Two others, sub-human all of them, were moving out of the gate-house, their hands on the butts of their holstered Smith and Wesson .38s.

Ian Quayle stuck his head out of the foolish little window and said amiably, "Mr. Norton ran out of champagne, we're going to find some more for him."

He was aware that it wasn't very bright; Lord Mayberry was scarcely the kind of man to send his guests for more drinks, even if his enormous cellars were ever to run as dry as Moses' Red Sea. But it was in situations like this that Ian Quayle was at his positive worst.

He heard Wendy muttering under her breath beside him, but then...

Then, as the guard turned to move to the gate-house

phone, he suddenly pulled up short, and he was staring towards the house, where the tell-tale white sheets were hanging from a third-story window. He reached for his revolver, and Quayle shouted, "Duck! Get down...!"

The car was a weapon now...

Ian Quayle shoved the gear-shift savagely into first, and saw the needle of the tach sweep swiftly to the red and over maximum as he drove at breakneck speed toward the gateman, catching him squarely in the midriff and throwing him high into the air.

He braked furiously, backed up for the briefest moment, and drove like a maniac at the second of them, his right foot on the floor.

He screamed, "I said duck, for Christ's sake, won't you ever listen to me...?" as a bullet crashed through their windshield.

He hit the man solidly, bumped over him, and swung round for the third assault.

Guard number three was poised with both arms held stiffly out as he fired, and fired again and again.

They saw him, briefly, up-ended six feet in the air before he fell to the ground and lay still, and Quayle said urgently, feeling the blood coursing down over his ear, "Are you all right?"

Wendy had lost all of her breath, and she stammered: "Yes, but you've been hit..."

"Forget it. Get the keys."

She leaped out of the soap-box and took the keys from the clip at the gateman's belt, and after a great deal of trembling and fumbling, she threw the gates open.

Quayle drove through, and when she was beside him again, he floored the pedal and *drove*.

There was rifle fire from the house behind them now, but they were a small and fast-moving target, and sheltered by hedges and trees.

But a missile of some sort *whooooshed* past them and hit the trunk of an oak ahead of them, exploding in a fury of flame and searing the Mini's paint as they sped past it.

A second exploded way behind them, and they were out of range now. Quayle was driving with his head incongruously stuck out the window, peering around the striated glass, and he swore softly, "And where the hell am I going to find a new windshield in Italy...?"

He looked at Wendy and grinned. "All right, luv?"

Wendy nodded. "All right, yes, I'm okay. But for Christ's sake watch where you're going, you're going to get us both killed."

He grunted. But a little later he pulled up under a hedgerow, punched out the remains of the shattered windscreen, four bullet holes in it, and threw it into the ditch at the side of the road.

And driving more sedately now, conscious of a throbbing pain in his head where a bullet had creased his skull, he seldom hit more than ninety miles an hour as he headed for Rome and the comfort of Leo's competent presence.

CHAPTER 17

The first thing Ian Quayle said to Leo was, "Our safehouse is blown. They know about it, they've known about it all along, ever since the lease was signed."

Leo almost exploded. "*Porco Dio*!" he said. "I told Mrs. *Maledetta* French that we should never sign a lease with a department of the British Government. But she overruled me. What can I say?"

"What you can say is...where the hell do we go now, Leo?"

There was a moment of hesitation, then: "We have another safehouse, an apartment on Via Salaria, just off Piazza Vescovio, facing the beautiful pines of the Villa Savoia."

"Fuck your beautiful pines," Ian said, "I don't want an apartment, it's too hard to escape from in an emergency. I want another villa."

Leo was a very worried man as he thought about it, and he said at last, "We could be safe in an expensive hotel on the Via Veneto, very close to the American Embassy. The manager there is a friend of mine, I could arrange it."

"Leo...!"

There was more deep thought, and at last: "Very well. Just over one kilometer down the road, still on Via Appia Antica, there is my own family villa, we have owned it for five generations now. I rent it out sometimes to tourists, but...it has been vacant now for more than a year, which means that financially I am suffering. Perhaps I could rent it to Mrs. French. Provided, of course, that she did not know it to be my own personal property. If she were to know this, then the rent would suddenly become miniscule, and I am a very poor man."

"I'll keep your secret," Ian Quayle said. "Provided it's truly safe."

"Oh, it will be. No lease, no signatures. Just a gentleman's agreement between you and me. And we are both gentlemen, are we not?"

Quayle said gravely, "That might well be, Leo."

And within four hours of frenetic night-time activity, the safehouse had changed its location.

No vehicles, Quayle was very insistent about this. They took with them only the all-important files (the gardeners staggering under their heavy loads,) as they went in the secrecy of the darkness from one house to the other.

Secrecy was all-important now...

Renata was there, and Claudine, and a newcomer...the infamous Bartolomeo from Trastevere, Renata's lover. There was a bandage around his head, but he was no more bellicose than usual; on the contrary, he sat lamb-like on the sofa with his arm around Renata, protecting her like a lion.

Leo said, beaming, "You wanted me to spring him, Mr. Quayle. And so, I sprang him. He is really the best possible bodyguard we can have for poor Renata, he is desperately in love with her. And in my expert hands...this man is clay."

"We say 'putty.' So, where's the punchline?"

"The punchline, Mr. Quayle, is that Bartolomeo is the head of a gang of street hoodles in Trastevere..."

"*Hoodlums.*"

"Yes, exactly. They are all pretty thieves..."

"Petty thieves..."

"Yes. Pretty thieves, and pimps, and burglars of expensive apartments. More than twenty of them who will follow him to hell and back. And this kind of underwear force always has access to information which is denied to the police, and even to MI6. But I am above it all, as always."

Ian Quayle thought about it, and then: "Ah yes. On top of it all. Good for you, Leo."

"Precisely," Leo said smugly. "Sitting above everything."

"And so...?"

"So...we put him to work now. Just tell me your most first priority."

"What I want to know before everything else," Ian said carefully, "is...if he can find out for us, the name of the man who actually planted that bomb in General Mancini's car."

Leo hesitated. He said awkwardly, "That might not be very easy, Mr. Quayle."

"And if he doesn't succeed," Ian Quayle said relentlessly, "then tell him that I will have London provide the Italian police with irrefutable evidence that he did it himself. The motive? Because General Mancini took his girl from him. That's the kind of motive any Italian court will readily understand. And believe you me...I'll make it stick."

Leo blinked his sad Spaniel eyes at him. "You are really a very devious man, Mr. Quayle, are you not?"

Ian Quayle said clearly, "*Someone* murdered the only woman I ever truly loved in my whole life..."

Wendy's calm eyes were on him, and so were Claudine's; and he went on: "So find this man for me, Leo! I'll take it from there. And there's something else might come in handy one day...Who is the Deputy at the Ministry of Justice who pulls all the strings?"

"You mean..."

"Just a Deputy, Mayberry told me in a moment of stupidity." He said sourly, "Brought on, no doubt, by his quite unwarranted contempt for my mental capacities. It seems that this man is a King-maker, that the Minister himself doesn't make a move without his approval."

"Ah..." Leo was beaming now. "You are speaking of Deputy Alfredo Aspremonte di Gioberti. The most corrupt man in a very corrupt Government. And, yes, Aspremonte is indeed the man behind the throne in the Ministry of Justice."

"You have a dossier on him, I assume?"

"Of course."

"I want it."

Leo could only nod, slowly, in the hope that the gesture would mean acquiescence to someone he greatly admired, but was frankly a little afraid of.

Through long experience, he knew that personal intrusions into matters of simple Intelligence sometimes signified the most dreadful calamity.

And that was what he was expecting now; with Ian Quayle its victim.

Wendy had long been aware that Claudine's reunion with her son was highly emotional, and that it wasn't merely a matter of that endemic Hungarian instinct, it was something more.

The two women—so widely separated by their individual philosophies—were in Claudine's room. And Wendy picked up a photograph from the bedside table and studied it. It was a snapshot of two people she did not immediately recognize.

But on closer study, she realized that the boy there was the young Ian Quayle, at age what, fifteen? There was a desperately sad look about him that brought tears to her eyes, a look almost of ill-concealed terror.

And the woman...?

Could it really have been Claudine Andrassy?

She was dressed in near-rags, her hair straggly and matted; but yes, it was Claudine indeed. And the child beside her was clutching her hand as though she were about to be dragged into Hell and only his intervention could save her.

The great Claudine Andrassy? Looking like the Witch of Endor? It made no sense at all.

Claudine, fixing her luxurious hair, was close beside Wendy, and she said quietly, "A press photograph, it's not very good, is it?"

"It tells the story," Wendy said, "and that's what matters. The time he rescued you from the Russians?"

"Yes."

"Budapest, October 1956. I wasn't even born then."

There was a generation-gap thing going on here, like the kids who knew nothing about World War Two except what they'd heard with the Remote Control switch-off, time to change channels and watch a game show...

But Wendy was older than her years. She said quietly, "I've read so much about it. It must have been awful."

"Dead bodies were scattered all over the streets," Claudine said. "And in the interests of hygiene they'd been sprinkled with lime. It turned them all into kind of marble statuary. Our M.I.T. news Agency was tele-typing for help, and none came. Then...it was shut down, by Soviet tanks. And Ian turned up, hardly more than a child...His father had been with him, but their plane crashed in Austria, and Harry was killed."

There was a terribly sad look in her eyes as she stared at herself in the mirror.

"Harry wasn't much of a father, or a husband either, come to that, but I loved him...I'd brought Ian up almost alone, so he spoke marvelously fluent Hungarian, and you know, I suppose, how determined he can be. It took him less than twelve hours to find the people he needed in the underground, to find me too. And almost before I knew it, I was being whisked out of the country. All it cost me was my jewelry, and the awful fear that Ian would be caught."

She was smiling suddenly, all her trials forgotten.

"But then...Ian was never the kind of monster to get caught quite so easily, was he? All through that terrible journey, I was wondering how I'd managed to raise such an expert in deception and connivance. But yes, he saved my life. Because, within a week, I would have cut my wrists, the coward's way out of intolerable humiliation and pain."

Emotionally, Wendy embraced her, and she murmured, "You're a wonderful woman, Claudine."

Claudine laughed. "Well, at least I raised a son I can be proud of! Even though he can be—and isn't that true?—a dreadful pain in the neck once in a while."

She kissed Wendy quickly on both cheeks, and said quietly, "Look after him for me, Wendy. He's all I have left now."

It was very early morning, and Ian Quayle was in the old stable of the new safehouse, serving as a sort of garage with almost no equipment at all. What use was an ancient horse harness when it came to a matter of fixing fenders?

Leo came to him, and said smugly, "Bartolomeo was out all night, Mr. Quayle, leaving his beloved Renata in my care."

"Oh? And what's that supposed to mean?"

"He found the man who planted the famous bomb. That was what you wanted, was it not? And what you want—I provide. It is a matter of my personal dignity."

"Good, good..."

"This idiot bomber's name is Volpone, a member of the Red Brigades. And the Red Brigades' High Command had him executed, so that he could never talk."

"Oh Christ."

"And you have a meeting with him thirty minutes from now, in the Colosseum."

Ian Quayle said patiently, "I have a meeting with a corpse? Leo, why don't you talk Italian? I'd understand you better."

Leo beamed. "They killed the wrong man. Shall we go? Better if we arrive a little early. To make sure, you understand, no sharping-shooters up on the walls, with highly-powered rifles or other nuisances."

"You are a good kid, Leo," Ian said earnestly. "Your car or mine?"

"Mine, Mr. Quayle. I have no wish that any of my friends see me in the wreck of your Mini."

"Your personal dignity again?"

"Precisely."

Fifteen minutes later they were at the Colosseum, and Volpone was already there with the same idea, his shrewd eyes constantly on the high walls and the dark shadows of the arches.

He was in his early thirties, ('Too old to be of much use to the Brigades,' Quayle thought,) a tough-looking sonofabitch with dark beetling eyebrows and broken yellow teeth.

He said, grinning furiously, "For twelve years now, every night I have a bottle of *Soave Bolla* wine in the Trattoria del Zio in Trastevere, always at seven o'clock. The same table in a corner of the patio. But this night, they got new waiter, he give my corner table to some other guy. So, I am angry. I go across road to Trattoria Da Meu Pataca, and I am drinking there. Soon, I am hearing rifle shot, and man taking my table fall, little round hole in his head. And when I am learning all of Trastevere weep and say '*Volpone is dead*,' I know this shot mean for me. I hide, *subito*, because I am a man of much sensitivity. But Leo find me."

"Where did you get the bomb, Volpone?"

182

Those beetle eyebrows were positively Satanic. "One thousand American dollars—I tell you."

Ian Quayle said patiently, "Let's knock off Leo's twenty percent," and Leo said at once: "I protest, Mr. Quayle."

"Okay, let's forget it. Leo's commission brings it down to eight hundred bucks. I'm prepared to pay three."

"Seven?"

"Five?"

"Maybe we saying six-fifty?"

"Okay, you have a deal, I'll go to six, take it or leave it. I can still leak the news, Volpone, that you're alive and well. And talking your ass off."

"Okay," Volpone said hurriedly, "Am agreeing. Six hundred and twenty-five dollars, you have one very good deal."

"Agreed. So who gave you the bomb?"

"My Red Brigades Commander. Same man try to kill me."

"And where did he get it from?"

It was the crucial question, and Volpone slowly shook his head. "Please believe me," he said, "I am knowing only his *nome di guerra*, is how you say? His codename."

"Which is?"

"*Bacca*," Volpone said. "*Bacca di Maggese*. I do not know his real name."

Ian said relentlessly, "And can you be sure of that?"

Volpone nodded. "My Commander tell me: '*Bacca* wants this man dead. Here is the bomb,' and he give it to me."

He was grinning suddenly, a maniac, and he said, "There was one woman in the car with Mancini, and I am not liking too much killing women, only if is necessary. But she is General's daughter, an enemy of the people, so is okay."

Quayle screamed, "Leo! Get him out of here before I kill him...I"

Leo hustled his informer away from there; and back at the

safehouse, he stared at Quayle and said somberly, "Your job is over now, Mr. Quayle. Better you go home now and make your report. I do not wish to be one of the mourning-people at your funeral."

Ian Quayle thought about his visit to the Morgue, etched into his mind for all eternity.

He said bitterly, "Have you ever seen a woman you once loved reduced to broken pieces of charcoal?"

"No sir."

"Then shut up," Quayle said, "because I *have*..."

The phone was ringing, a secret number, and Leo answered it and listened. He seemed to be in shock, and he was sweating and infuriated. He put the phone down and slammed a palm at his forehead in a wild Napolitan gesture, striding up and down, and for once in his life he seemed at a complete loss for words.

Wendy said patiently, "Okay, Leo, get it off your chest," and he threw up his arms with an oath: "*Puttana Madonna*! The call was from a stranger, and how did he know where to find me? Nobody knows we are here, *nobody*!"

"It seems," Ian Quayle said drily, "that you might well be wrong there..."

But then, there was something in Leo's look that told him of impending disaster, and he said, scowling: "Well? What did he have to say?"

Leo shook his head and gesticulated wildly, but he calmed down at last, even though his eyes were brimming.

He said slowly, "Something I did not want you to know about, because...because..."

He was stammering now, searching for the words. "Because of the pain it could cause you. I would have told you when...when this is all over, but, but..."

He took a deep breath and said, "There is a young girl on her way here. Her name is Pia, and she is Carlotta Mancini's daughter."

Ian Quayle stared at him. "Carlotta's daughter? Oh Christ! Then she really did marry after all..."

Leo shook his head slowly.

Claudine, alert as only a woman of her quality could be, was watching her son; and so was Wendy.

"No," Leo said, "she never married. She left London something like twenty years ago because she was pregnant. And she was afraid that the man who put her into that lamentable position might think that she was tricking him into the marriage she wanted so badly. And this was something she could never allow, you understand what I am telling you? And she wanted her child to be born in Italy, even though its father was an Englishman."

The blood was draining from Ian's face.

And Leo said, with that strange combination of sadness and satisfaction, "She'll be here soon. Pia Mancini. She's your daughter, Mr. Quayle."

Ian was trembling.

Wendy reached out and touched his hand. And Claudine took out her compact to examine her make-up in the little mirror. She said easily, "Well, it seems I'm a grandmother. Isn't that nice?"

It was a little after midnight when there was the sound of a car screeching up at the gate of the house they believed to be 'safe.'

And one of the 'gardeners' appeared, armed with a machine-pistol, and he said glumly, "*They* came, signor Quayle, and they brought a young lady with them..."

He was accompanying a very lovely young woman, and he said, not at all sure of himself, "*La Signorina Pia Mancini*, they said you were expecting her, and then they raced away at a very high speed. And there was no light on their number-plate..."

Ian Quayle stared at her, and he could not compose himself.

He approached the young girl, and took her hands in his, and he said quietly, "And do you know who I am?"

There was the slightest smile on her lovely face. "Yes, I know who you are. They told me, Papa."

Papa?

The tears were streaming down his face as he took her in his arms and hugged her tightly.

Claudine, Wendy, even Renata, were all watching the drama and it was very far removed from the prosaic business of the League of Hawks.

He whispered, "And how was it that they found you? Will you tell me that?"

Her smooth, unwrinkled forehead was furrowed now, and she said hesitantly, "I don't really understand it, Papa."

Papa again...!

She went on: "I was kidnapped, I think that's the only word for it. Four men with stocking masks on their faces burst into my room, and my roommate..."

She sighed. "My roommate, her name is Giselda, is a very strong and opinionated woman, she's ten years older than I am. Anyway, she went for them with a cast-iron skillet, and one of them hit her on the side of the head, very hard, and knocked her out. And then...they tied ropes around my arms and legs and carried me out to their car."

Quayle was in anguish. "And did they...did they...?"

"No, Papa," Pia said. "There was a little search for my breasts, nothing worse than that. They told me: 'We are taking you to your father, child.' And that is what they seem to have done."

"And do you know," Ian Quayle asked, "just why they should have done that?"

186

"No, I have no idea at all. But I'm glad for it."

"As I am too..."

But it worried the hell out of him. What sort of a gesture was this? What could it possibly mean?

He was soon to find out.

CHAPTER 18

It was in the early hours of the morning that the answer came.

There was a telephone call which Leo sleepily answered. He listened for a while in absolute puzzlement, and went at once to Ian Quayle's room.

He found Wendy with him, and he was terribly embarrassed, but he said, unsure of what was happening now, "A call from one of my friends in the police, Mr. Quayle. It seems that the Morgue was broken into tonight. Someone stole the remains of General Mancini and his daughter. And why? Can you answer me that? What could there possibly be of use to us there? I am quite mystified."

Ian Quayle scowled. "What do you mean, *stole* them?"

"Precisely that, Mr. Quayle. There was a large cardboard box containing the remains..."

"I saw it," Quayle said tightly. "Go on."

"And it seems that three armed men broke in and took them away. It does not make any sense at all. There is nothing in charcoal that can help us in the least. How can further examination of ashes help us now?"

Ian Quayle said coldly, "So help me God, Leo, if you say the word charcoal, or embers, or ashes, just one more time...as God is my witness, I'll beat the fucking shit out of you. So shut up!"

Leo was greatly abashed. "Yes, of course, forgive me."

"Get lost, Leo," Wendy murmured, less than half awake. "Do us a favor and get lost."

And then, she was suddenly wide awake...She sat up in the bed and said sharply: "What? They stole the Mancini remains?"

"*Si, signorina...*"

Wendy thought about it, and she said at last, "I don't like it one bit! It opens up all kinds of quite horrible possibilities."

Ian stared at her, brushing the sleep from his eyes.

"Such as..."

"*Think*, Ian," she said impatiently. "I know that's not something you're accustomed to, but think for once in your life! Two and two invariably make four, have you ever thought about that?"

She closed her eyes and murmured politely, "Goodnight, Leo. And goodnight Ian too. One fine day you two might just wise up..."

The wising-up came very soon.

At the earliest sign of the glorious sunrise, there was that screeching of tires outside on the lovely Via Appia Antica again.

A parcel was thrown over the gate, and the gardener was there once more, bringing it to them, lugubrious as ever. "Addressed to signor Quayle," he said.

It was gift-wrapped, and there was even a scarlet ribbon around it, a cute little bow there, and Wendy said urgently, "Be careful, Ian, it might be a bomb..."

He shook his head. "No, it weighs nothing at all."

He tore the gift-wrapping apart and stared at a cardboard box there he had seen before in a dreadful moment of trauma. He flipped open the lid, and saw a mass of charcoal and half-incinerated bones, with blackened skulls as well, and he felt the nausea coming over him again.

There was a note there, hand-written on parchment that was headed: *Thaddeus Norton, Antiquarian.*

It read:

'There are three more women in your life, Quayle. Claudine Andrassy, your mother; Wendy Hayworth, your mistress; and now Pia Mancini, your daughter, whom we have sent you for one of those nice, old-fashioned family reunions.

And this can happen to all of them, it's really very simple for us to arrange, quite cheaply. So...you will now return to London, and you will tell them nothing. Be grateful, Quayle, that I chose not to have you killed, this too would have been very easy.

And the reason for my forbearance? Also very simple. I may need you again one day, aren't you lucky?'

The note was even signed: '*Your dear friend and admirer, Bacca.*'

Pia was a sweet and utterly charming youngster. Tall and slender, she had her grandmother Claudine's good looks, and a great deal of her character too.

She said, smiling in answer to Claudine's question, "What do I do for a living? I am a ballerina with the *Balleto Romano*, following in your footsteps, Nonna, though not yet so very famously, I still have troubles with my *pointes*."

The '*Grandma*' struck Claudine to the heart, and she said quietly, "Then perhaps I should take you under my wing. I must return to Paris very soon now, and will you come with me?"

Pia threw her father a quick glance, and said, "I would like that very much. Papa...?"

Ian nodded. He was torn between two urgent desires—the need to be with his newly-found daughter now, and the more desperate need for her safety.

He turned to Leo. "In Paris, can we arrange for police protection?"

"Of course," Leo said. "We have a very good man there, he's been an MI6 agent for more than seven years. His name is Pleyer, Inspector Pleyer."

Ian Quayle grunted. "Yes, I met him. And he struck me as being a man of some competence. When's the next plane to Paris? There's a certain urgency now."

Leo looked at his watch. "It leaves in fifty minutes, Mr. Quayle, Flight 32. But it is not possible for you to catch it...However, there is another at seven-fifteen this evening."

"Call Inspector Pleyer," Ian said, "and tell him that I want protection to begin at the airport, on the arrival of Flight 32. And from then on...round the clock."

He looked to Pia and to his mother, and he said gently, "We leave *now*. So pack your bags as quickly as you can. I'll give you three minutes..."

His speed on the highway was frightening, and at the airport gate he ignored the pleas of the announcer on the speaker: "Flight 32 for Paris is leaving now..." and embraced them both.

"Paris," he said, "just give me...a couple of days, no more. And then—we'll all be together again."

Claudine, in distress, was shaking her head, worrying about him. "Ian," she whispered, "you're so *impetuous*..."

"But careful too. Don't worry about me, either of you. The day after tomorrow...in Paris. And never forget how much I love you both."

The girl there was hurrying them off. "Please, *signore*, we have to close the gate now."

He watched them run for the plane, and his heart was very heavy.

191

* * *

Back at the safehouse, he said to Leo, "You called Inspector Pleyer?"

Leo nodded. "Yes, of course. And please be assured, Mr. Quayle, they will be safe now. Our Paris office has a very high reputation. They will be safe."

"If they're not," Ian Quayle said, "then I will personally cut Inspector Pleyer's bloody throat from ear to ear. It might almost be worth another phone call to tell him that."

Leo said mildly, seeking information, "Have you honestly ever killed a man, Mr. Quayle?"

Quayle thought about it, and he said at last, sighing, "No, I never have, Leo. I guess I'm just trying to work myself into a state in which I'd accept it if it ever becomes necessary. Which it might..."

He was wrapped in thought for a while, and he said at last, very tightly, "I need a handgun, Leo. Something like a P38, I think."

Leo sighed. "I do have a few unauthorized handguns here, Mr. Quayle. And yes, there is a Walther P38 among them. I hope you know how to use it."

"You pull back the barrel once," Quayle said tartly, "and then pull the trigger again and again and again, pointing it where you want to do the most damage...And maybe I'll need a cyanide gun too, do you have them?"

Leo was very unhappy. He said miserably, "Yes, I have three cyanide guns, but they are very rigidly controlled. By the London Office. There is a form to be filled out with six copies, it goes to Mrs. French in London, and she always finds reasons why I should have said no."

Quayle was beside himself. "Fuck Mrs. French," he said, "and fuck her damned bureaucracy! I want a cyanide gun, and that's the end of the discussion! So get it for me!"

"Then please, excuse me..."

He was gone, to search out the weapons. And Bartolomeo, shoveling Leo's pasta into his mouth, said sourly, "You are not understanding, Mr. Quayle, the true bad of these people. They kill you now for sure."

"You're wrong," Ian said. "They know that I can be useful to them. They know me well, I'm afraid! They know that if I ever had to submit to torture...I'd talk my bloody head off...They know that I'm just not the rank-name-and-number type. And it's very sad, isn't it? But some of us, Bartolomeo, are not made of concrete. Some of us are made of clay. Clay can be molded very easily."

"And they know that, Mr. Quayle. You are in very greatest danger now."

"Maybe. Sometimes we have to confront it, head-on."

Wendy was staring at him, deeply perturbed, and she whispered, "Ian? Would you mind telling me just what you're up to? You're not thinking of returning to Florence, I hope? I mean...A P38? A cyanide gun...?"

"That is exactly what I am thinking of," Ian Quayle said. "And this time...I will go alone."

Leo was back with the weapons, and he was deeply troubled. He said, "The P38—*niente problema*. But the cyanide gun..."

He was waving forms into Ian Quayle's face, and he said, almost weeping, "Paragraph four, Mr. Quayle. I am supposed to state the reason."

"Under para four," Ian said, "write: '*The murder of Carlotta Mancini.*'"

He checked out the weapons, the P38 was easy. But it was the first time he had ever actually seen a cyanide gun, even though it had figured quite often in his research.

It was a Parker ball-point, just a very good writing instrument. But press the clip, and it emitted a stream of cyanide gas under high pressure, seven milligrams of it to one touch of the button; and the killing dose, he knew, was one-point-five milligrams.

Ian Quayle fell silent and into a kind of reverie. They knew that he was thinking of that terrible cardboard box; and they left him to his introspection.

Then, a cable arrived from Mrs. French in London, addressed to "*Leo for Quayle*".

Leo got out his code-books and went to work, and fifteen minutes later he handed Ian the deciphered message. "She likes what you have done," he said enigmatically. "She wants you home again in her bosom."

The message was short and to the point:

QUAYLE FROM DEPUTY DIRECTOR STOP WE ARE PLEASED WITH YOUR PROGRESS AND AWAIT YOUR FULLEST REPORT WHICH CAN ONLY BE WRITTEN, IN LONDON STOP EXPECT YOUR IMMEDIATE RETURN FOR CONSULTATION CQR MESSAGE ENDS.

"CQR" was MI6 nonce-terminology that was intended to mean: This message is of the utmost importance, and Ian Quayle grunted. "CQR indeed," he said caustically. "But there's one thing that bloody woman doesn't realize."

Wendy felt a contraction of her heart-muscles. She knew the answer, but she asked the question anyway, one of her very womanly weaknesses. "Which is...?"

"I found out," Ian said calmly, "exactly what I came here to find out. The identity of Carlotta's murderer. Now...I have to do something about it."

"No!" Her voice was very sharp. "No, we've been ordered home! From now on, bringing Mayberry to justice is a matter for the Italian police. They'll get a copy of your report, you know that!"

Ian Quayle thought about it for a moment or two, and then dismissed the idea.

He said at last: "Get a cable off to London, tell them I'll be home when I'm good and ready, not before. And send it FRO, For Recipient Only."

"Ian," Wendy said patiently, "you're Grade Five. Grade Five doesn't have access to FRO. Grade Five isn't even supposed to *know* about FRO."

Ian Quayle sighed. "Nothing I hate more," he said, "than the demon Bureaucracy. But you're what? Grade Four, I imagine..."

"Actually," Wendy said, "Grade Three. Okay, I'll send Mrs. French your message under my code. She's going to hate both of us for it. Even more than she does now."

"Are you crazy?" Ian Quayle said, exasperated. "No! It goes to Robin Harris! Didn't you listen to what Leo had to say? There's a double agent in the London office! Someone, there, is going to start wondering why I don't want to go home yet, someone is going to be very upset about it!"

He calmed down a little, and said quietly, "There's no one else I trust there now. Especially not Mrs. French."

"You're so wrong!" Wendy said. "With all her faults, Mrs. French is not only the best brain we ever had—she's one hundred percent loyal too, she's nobody's double-agent, I'd stake my life on it!"

"Very well," Ian Quayle said sourly, "so Mrs. French is acceptable. Now give me one of your famous thumbnail sketches of Robin Harris."

"Robin Harris," Wendy said obediently, "is quite probably the most *gentlemanly* English gentleman you ever met in your life. But he was up at Cambridge with Burgess and Mclean, and later on he became a close friend of Kim Philby's. Philby, McLean, and Burgess, they all defected to Moscow."

Quayle hated it. He said sullenly, "That was a long, long

time ago, and Robin Harris is not the enemy of the moment. Mayberry is."

"So leave him to the Italian cops! Let *them* take care of his bloody Lordship!"

"No," Ian Quayle said flatly. "Bacca told me in so many words of the protection he has, in high echelons of Government."

"The infamous Deputy Aspremonte?"

"Precisely."

"Then he's the man we have to get to first."

"No."

He said clearly, "I'm leaving for Florence again, *now*. And you will stay here, with Leo for protection, until I come back. That's when I'll return to London. And I'll be able to add to my report...the satisfying news of Bacca's death."

He hesitated only briefly, and then: "And I will never forgive you for what you did."

Wendy stared at him, and he said abruptly, "Mrs. French is pleased with my progress? How did she know about it, Wendy? You instigated that cable, didn't you? I can't imagine Mrs. bloody French being concerned about my safety."

"Yes," Wendy said at once. "I knew that you wouldn't listen to me. I hoped that perhaps you might obey an order from your boss."

"Ha!" Ian said.

Without another word, he stalked out of the room.

And a few moments later, they heard the battered Mini taking off, its tires screeching out their anguish as he floored the pedal.

Wendy said furiously, "Well, don't just stand there, Leo! Do something!"

Leo raised his arms in that Neapolitan gesture of complete helplessness. "What *can* I do? When that man gets an idea into his mind...You said it yourself."

"For starters," Wendy said, "you can give me that file on

Deputy Aspremonte. Where does he live? Here in Rome?"

Leo shook his head. "No, he has a villa in Fiesole. That's just a few kilometers from Florence."

She speed-read the forty pages of the file in a little under three minutes, and she said abruptly, "Okay, let's go. We'll take your BMW, but I'll drive, I'm probably one hell of a lot faster than you are."

And five minutes later, they were on their way, the souped-up mill roaring through a custom straight-through exhaust. They managed to side-swipe two parked cars and a lamp-post before they even left Rome's outskirts, and Leo was wailing.

But Wendy Hayworth knew *exactly* what had to be done now.

She was always very good at this sort of thing; she thought of it as 'feminine intuition,' but actually it was more a matter of long and careful training in one of the best undercover agents' school in the world.

It was a place called 'The Academy of Advanced Technology,' innocuous as hell, in Purley, Surrey, England.

But in actual fact, it was a training-ground for the agents of MI6 who were graduating to the coveted rank of Grade Three. And Wendy had passed their courses with flying colors, third from the top of one hundred and sixty-two alumni.

CHAPTER 19

On the long drive to Florence, Ian Quayle's blind rage had turned to a cold, overpowering hatred.

There was murder in his heart, and he wondered for a moment if he could actually kill a man. But then he thought of his beloved Carlotta, and he knew that—sensible or not—revenge was all that mattered now.

But when he had left the outskirts of the town and was approaching the heavily-wooded area around the villa, there was a very considerable surprise waiting for him.

The whole area was crawling with police cars.

It was dark now, and there were very few street lights here, and as he slowed down he began to realize that his little Mini, battered, pock-marked with bullet holes, with no windshield and its once immaculate paint-work singed and blistered, was more distinctive than ever.

There was a disturbing sort of feeling that something was terribly wrong, but after a moment's careful thought he dismissed it as a symptom of paranoia and thrust it from his mind.

There was a cop stepping into his path and sternly holding up a white-gloved hand, so he pulled to a halt and stuck his head out of the window. "*Que ce*? what is it?"

The cop came round to the side and looked the car over.

"*Licenza*," he said severely, as though a major crime had been committed, and Quayle reached for his driver's license and handed it over. "It's English," he said. "Good in Italy for three months."

The cop studied it earnestly, and then raised his voice and shouted, "Capitano...! *E lui*, it's him...!" and he was suddenly fumbling for the Beretta pistol at his belt, taking an unconscionable time to get it out of the cracked leather holster.

Ian Quayle put his hand to his head. "Oh for Christ's sake..."

And then Captain Arrigo was suddenly there out of the darkness, peering at him, and he said, "Well, signor Quayle! I will confess to a surprise. When they told me you might be returning here, I did not really believe it. I had a somewhat higher estimation of your intelligence."

"When *they* told me...?"

Wendy and Leo? To '*save*' him? It made very little sense, just enough to be possible if, convinced as they both were that he was headed for suicide, they had decided that police interference was the only answer to a problem that was exclusively theirs and not his.

But he said sourly, checking on it, "They? Who the hell is *they*, Captain Arrigo?"

There was quite a long silence. And then Arrigo said. not very comfortably, "I am sure I am not supposed to tell you this, Mr. Quayle, but out of my personal affection for you, out of my great admiration for what it is that I know you are trying to do, even though it is a hopeless endeavor...My orders came from one Deputy Aspremonte in person, the most powerful man in our Government today. And sometimes, a humble police officer has to do what he knows is wrong. I'm sorry. I have a warrant for your arrest."

Unobtrusively, Ian Quayle depressed the clutch and slipped the gear-shift silently into reverse. He said tightly, "I have the right to know what the charge is, I believe."

"Attempted murder," Arrigo said, and as Quayle stared at him he went on. "The attempted murder of Durante Fresco."

"Great. I never even heard of him."

"He was a guard at signor Norton's gatehouse. The warrant states that you deliberately drove your car at him, and broke his back." He said apologetically: "And there are two other charges of the same kind, in respect of the other two guards."

There was that silence again, and Arrigo said heavily at last, "I'm not supposed to tell you this either, but all three of them are from the Red Brigades and on our list of most-wanted terrorists, all of them wanted for murder, kidnapping, bombing, and various other offenses. But according to Deputy Aspremonte it is still attempted murder."

"Well," Ian Quayle said harshly, "my department has friends in high places too. I'm returning to Rome now, we'll find a sensible answer to this damn nonsense at the British Embassy."

"No, Mr. Quayle," Captain Arrigo said. "You are under arrest. Step out of the car, please." He turned to the constable beside him and said: "*I ferri*, the handcuffs."

Ian Quayle screamed, "Handcuffs...? You're out of your mind, Arrigo!"

He took his foot off the clutch and floored the accelerator, and the Mini leaped back like an angry panther. He did some fancy gear-shifting and spun the car around and headed away from there fast, back in the direction he'd come from. And before he skidded round the curve in the lane he heard three belated pistol-shots behind him, heard too Arrigo's furious shout: "*Non si spara*...No shooting!"

He drove on for half a mile or so, and flicked his headlights on briefly as he bulldozed the powerful little bomb off the road and deep into the shrubbery, spinning the wheels and rocking it back and forth until he was sure that it was well-concealed.

A police car hurtled past him as he sat there in his hiding-place, its two-tone siren wailing, its Christmas lights flashing to tell the whole world that the cops were coming. Another followed it, and then another...

He just sat there for a few minutes, wondering what the hell he should do now. He thought of Carlotta for a while, torturing himself, and of Claudine and Pia, now safely on their way back to Paris.

The thoughts of his daughter steadied him, and he found himself almost in a good mood again. She was so sweet, so very lovely! She had trouble with her *pointes*, but she was now in the skillful hands of the world's most competent teacher, his own mother, who had once been the greatest *Prima Assoluta* ever to set foot on a stage...

He thought of her final performance when, crippled and in the most terrible agony, she had somehow finished the show and had taken her bows to a standing ovation which went on forever.

There were grown men and women in the audience whose tears were streaming down their faces, knowing the truth, as they applauded her in a frenzy.

And Wendy, poor Wendy, who wanted so much to control his life.

Did he truly love her? Did she truly love him? Ought he perhaps to marry her one day? Would she accept him as a husband? He thought perhaps not.

These were the women in his life whom Bacca had threatened. Pia and Claudine would be safe in Paris, surely? But Wendy?

Poor frustrated Wendy would be relying on Leo for her protection, and was he up to it? So what would she be doing now? Sitting impatiently in her corner chair with her interminable stitching...looking after that strange creature Renata, certainly, as she wondered how her sometime lover was faring on what she regarded as a suicide mission...

The thought pulled him up short.

No! Wendy would not just be sitting there, she wasn't the type! So, what would she be up to now?

He could not possibly have known it, but Wendy was already in position for her counter-attack; she was only a few miles away, in a place called Fiesole.

In the moonlit gardens of Deputy Aspremonte's Fiesole villa, Wendy and Leo were crouched in the darkness among the cypress trees.

They were watching the front door, and Wendy whispered in the silence, "I don't believe it. There *has* to be a sentry there somewhere. At least one cop, so where is he?"

"We will find him," Leo murmured. "Follow me..."

Together they crept through the huge peonies and the clumps of fern towards the rear of the house where the kitchen was.

Wendy stepped on a soft mass of animal flesh and fell to the ground, and as she picked herself up she stared down at the biggest goddam Dobermann she had ever seen, not an ounce less than a hundred pounds in weight.

The dog squealed once, very lightly, at this intrusion on his sleep, stuck his nose in her behind and almost threw her off her feet again, and then went happily back to sleep.

They found the kitchen window, half-open, and there, seated at the huge scrubbed-pine kitchen table was the sentry they had been searching for, a nice-looking young man with masses of dark curly hair and a dimple in the middle of his chin.

There was a bowl of pasta in front of him, and a bottle of white wine, and he was shoveling down the *tagliatelli* as though he hadn't eaten for a month.

Beside him, a woman was sitting on the edge of the table,

in her forties, perhaps, not bad-looking; and with his free hand the cop was idly stroking her thigh under her full skirt as though it wasn't of very great importance.

They heard him say: "You are a very good cook, your pasta is...delectable, as always."

She simpered, a forty-year-old schoolgirl. "I am very good at everything I do, *mi' amore*, my love. As you must know."

The young oaf nodded, forking food into his mouth. "Yes, I know it. There's no one like you."

Wendy sighed. 'Christ,' she whispered, "I can't stand it! Any minute now, he's going to screw her on the table. The moment he finishes his damned pasta. Don't we have work to do?"

"Follow me," Leo whispered.

He led her along the wall of the villa and found a suitable projection, the coalhouse.

Together, hand over hand, they climbed up to the second story, a ledge there, no wider than the breadth of a man's hand. They steadied themselves as they moved cautiously along it, and in a little while Leo found a window he could open...

And thirty seconds later, they were in the house, on the second story where the bedrooms would be. They found a sliver of light coming from only one of the doors in the long corridor, and Leo touched Wendy's wrist in the darkness and whispered, "This is it, I am sure. Do we know what we have to do now?"

"I know," Wendy said, and threw open the door.

Deputy Alfredo Aspremonte di Gioberti, the most powerful man in the Italian Government, didn't exactly seem to live up to his reputation.

'Clothes make the man' was the tailors' cliché; and stark naked, Aspremonte was a shadow of his publicity.

His flesh was aspirin-white, and he was very skinny, not a muscle showing anywhere, even though he wasn't much more than sixty years old.

And this was the formidable Deputy of whom all Italy stood in awe?

There were two young girls in bed with him, a huge four-poster bed from the seventeenth century. They were both Italianate gorgeous, with half-grapefruit breasts and skin as smooth as ivory, and they were staring at the intruders.

The Deputy reached out a skeletal arm for the bell-pull, but there was a pistol in Wendy's hand, pointed straight at his parchment forehead.

"Don't dare touch it," she said.

His hand dropped away, and he was ready to listen, scared half out of his wits.

"Keep a gun on him, Leo," Wendy said. "I don't trust him."

"Okay."

Leo's nine millimeter was aimed straight between Deputy Aspremonte's eyes; the two girls were shrinking, covering themselves under the sheet as though this were somehow the time to prove how chaste they were.

Wendy held up a sheaf of papers, and waved them under Aspremonte's nose.

She said clearly, "You want to know how much I know, Deputy? This house was a gift to you from Lord Mayberry...you have a profitable rice field on the river Po, also a gift from Mayberry. There are also three apartments in town which are used as brothels, another gift from the same source. We know your profit on them, down to the last lira, and wouldn't your political enemies like to raise a few questions about this at the next Cabinet meeting? We also know about your four separate bank accounts, including the one in Switzerland. So shall I continue? Or will you agree to my demands?"

The Deputy was white as a sheet. Who were these people? How could they possibly know so much? The man seemed to be keeping carefully silent, but he *looked* like an Italian—and worse, like a damned southerner.

But the woman...Her Italian was easy and correct, but he fancied there was the slightest trace of an accent there. English? Or American?

Did it matter?

He was not entirely a fool; he had not reached his high degree of power through stupidity, and he said carefully, "Will you tell me who you are?"

Wendy shook her head. "No, I will not."

"You seem to be well-informed, though of course I deny everything you have suggested. So what are those demands?"

"You'll find out when the time comes."

"A blank check? You must be mad..."

"No, we just hold *all* the cards."

"And what do I receive in exchange for my cooperation?"

"Your secrets will remain secrets," she said sarcastically. "In other words, I'll see that your reputation remains immaculate. And you really have no choice at all. So, put some clothes on, for Christ's sake! You are coming with us to Florence, you'll be needed...at a certain villa outside the town."

"And you must surely know," Aspremonte said mildly, "that you will never leave this house alive."

Wendy waved the file again. "If we do not," she said, "then by tomorrow morning a copy of this file will be on the Prime Minister's desk. Another with the Premier, and a third in the hands of your mortal enemy the Minister of Defense. So let's go, we're wasting a very precious commodity...*time*."

Slowly, the Deputy climbed into his clothes as his agile mind searched for a way out of this dilemma, and found none.

The policeman in the kitchen heard their march down the stairs, and he was there at once, his tunic buttoned up now and his machine-pistol at the ready. But the Deputy said curtly, "It's all right, there is no trouble, go back to your post."

"*Si signor Deputato, subito...*"

Outside, the somnolent Dobermann opened an eye to look at them; and a few moments later Wendy was pushing the BMW to its maximum, and the tires were screeching.

Leo said plaintively, "Why can't I drive my own beautiful car, Miss Hayworth?" And Wendy answered: "Women drivers, Leo, they're a menace, didn't you know that? And that's what we have to be now. A menace. So bear with me..."

The tarmac rolled by under their headlights; and there was still a great deal of danger on the curves of the winding road, taken impossibly fast.

CHAPTER 20

It took Ian Quayle less than twenty minutes to fight his way, as silently as he could, back through the woods to the high brick wall that surrounded the Villa delle Rose.

He came to it at last, and he wondered how the hell he could ever climb over it, it was something like ten feet high.

But he was thinking of Carlotta again, and so he crept like a thief in the night along its base until he came to a tree that offered promise. It was an oak, and very impressive. Its spreading branches reached over the wall, and he knew that this was his way in. Only, he wasn't very good at climbing trees, and it took him nearly half an hour of frustrated effort to get up there onto one of the limbs that overhung the garden, and then there was a drop of what he thought in the darkness might be twenty feet or more.

Would his ankles stand up to it? He knew they wouldn't.

But by a piece of commendable and Tarzan-like effort, he managed to drop onto the top of the wall itself to lessen the final descent to the ground inside the estate. And there was a problem; in the European fashion, the top of the wall was thick with shards of broken bottles cemented in there to inhibit just this kind of intrusion.

The blood was coursing freely down his legs as he dropped to the ground and found himself where he wanted to be—in the grounds, finally, of the Villa delle Rose.

He looked at the luminous dial of his Omega; nearly three o'clock in the morning, and would the house be asleep? He thought not. Mayberry, perhaps, yes; he was too fond of his nocturnal pleasures. But Bianca? He could picture her prowling, gun in hand, looking for one of her enemies.

And that monster Gordon Fest! Would he have left once the auction was over? Quayle hoped to God that Fest wouldn't be there too...

The lights in the house were subdued, dimmed to the very minimum but on everywhere. And there was nothing in the world, he reflected, that inhibited breaking and entering so much as a light here and there.

There were brighter lamps in the grounds, shining nicely on the fabulous roses that had given the villa its name. But they were easy to avoid as he snaked his way through the dense shrubbery to the walls of the house itself.

And why were there no dogs here?

Was Mayberry perhaps not a dog fancier? There were plenty of people around who hated dogs, hated the way they destroyed the manicured lawns with their pounding feet, hated the way they would tear up a hedge if a rat took shelter there.

He looked up at the second floor, only part of it semi-lit, and tried to figure out which was Mayberry's bedroom, and he still did not know what he had to do next.

To find a way to it, he thought, burst in and use his Parker ball-point cyanide gun, a swift stream of gas at a range not less than ten feet, and it would all be over.

It all sounded so simple. But common sense took over, and he knew it wouldn't be. There would be guards, no doubt, everywhere.

He stared at the balconies up there, and worked it all out. The room at the end of the corridor. But was he on the right side of the villa? Yes, he was sure of it. The last wrought-iron railings then, the access to Mayberry's bedroom.

He found an iron pipe close enough beside it and wondered if he could successfully climb it. But he *had* to.

He was acrophobic too, terrified of heights and edges that had *terra firma* more than a few feet below him. Hell, he couldn't even climb a twelve-foot ladder without worrying about it.

Once, he had braved the phobias to climb onto the roof of his Surrey cottage to find a leak in the dense thatch, and had stayed up there in abject panic, not more than fourteen feet from the ground before plucking up his courage sufficiently to set foot on that damned ladder again and climb painfully down.

These were not the easiest of the phobias, and someone— who was it? Paula What's-Her-Name? had told him earnestly: "See a hypnotist, Ian, you can be cured, I know it."

But he wasn't the type, take it or leave it, to seek out that kind of help.

Biting his tongue to drive away the fear, he began the slow climb, wishing he were twenty years younger.

And he had hardly taken hold of the pipe when out of the darkness behind him came the most terrifying sound, a multiple *warp-warp-warp* at very high volume. There was a flurry of white feathered fury below him, and a powerful beak struck at his ankle, almost fracturing it.

Geese!

Geese, the ancient watchdogs of the Chinese, far more reliable—and dangerous—than the best of dogs. They would react to the very slightest intrusion, and their strong beaks, at the end of immensely powerful necks, could wreak havoc.

Unlike a dog, geese continued to fight long after you shot them dead. Like the headless chicken, their bodies still had enormous potency long after death had overtaken them; and perhaps worst of all, their furious croaking could be heard for a very long way around.

And as if in answer to Ian Quayle's thoughts as he scurried inexpertly higher, the full lights in the room above him went on.

He found safety from the howling geese on the balcony, grateful for the security of the railing, and he heard the door inside there open and slam shut. The drapes were drawn, but he found an opening in them and peered through it, and he saw the lovely Madame Ging-Sen in the four-poster bed there, sitting up and staring at the now-closed door.

Was it the right room? There was only one way to find out...

He waited for just a few moments, and then quietly opened the French doors and stepped into the room, and his P38 was levelled at the bridge of her nose.

She stared at him, only momentarily in shock, and then sort of snuggled comfortably down under the blankets, covering herself only casually, entirely composed and sure of herself.

She murmured: "Oh, so it's you...He thought it might be that maniac Gordon Fest wandering around the grounds at night, which is not allowed here."

So Fest was still here then...It was something Ian Quayle wanted to know.

"By '*he*,'" he said, "you mean Mayberry?"

She was puzzled. "Mayberry? Who is Mayberry?"

"I should have said Thaddeus Norton. Is he your lover tonight?"

She was completely unfazed. "Yes. And he's very, very good. I wonder if you might be better..."

She was smiling, fluttering her eyelids again. "And why don't you put that gun away? I can't do you any harm."

"And I have to make damn sure you don't," Ian Quayle said. "Forgive me."

He tucked the gun into his belt, and tore one of her sheets into strips. He bound her wrists first, and then her ankles, pulling them up behind her back to a slip-knot around her swan-like neck.

"Don't struggle too much against that," he said amiably, "you might just strangle yourself..."

He was very much aware of her nakedness, and of the perfection of her long, lithe body, the color of old ivory, and so was she. She took it all in stride, and when he had finished, she said quietly, "And now that you have me bound so abjectly...what are you going to do with me? Do I know already?"

"I'm going to take a rain-check," Ian Quayle said coldly. "So shut up."

He stared down at her, and even though she was an enemy, he could not hate her. He said slowly, "You asked me once, remember, *how* I would remember you? Perhaps it will be like this. In my fantasies."

"*Fantasies*?"

A lovely woman, calm and even contented in spite of her present humiliation, she whispered, "No, you will not live to enjoy them, the odds against you are far, far too great." There was a certain sadness on her, and she said quietly: "This is farewell forever, Mr. Quayle, they'll kill you now. A great pity. Truly, a great pity."

"And I do not like all this, believe me..."

He stuffed a gag into her mouth and bound it tightly in place, and set her just so in the bed. On an impulse, he touched her splendid breast and then kissed it before bringing the blankets up to cover her body.

He said, sighing, "Yes, a pity, and I hate it."

And then, he was gone.

The corridor was empty and only dimly lit, and he searched everywhere for cameras and found none as he made his careful way to the Grand Staircase and down it.

And at the bottom, he almost ran into trouble...

Mayberry was there, with Captain Arrigo, and he dropped quickly to his belly and lay on the stairs, in sudden panic, hidden by the balustrade.

The two of them were pacing back and forth, and he heard Mayberry say clearly, "It's that damned maniac Fest, I'm sure. You can't hold that man down for five minutes. But then, on the other hand, it just might be that idiot Quayle."

"No sir," Arrigo said, "it is definitely not Mr. Quayle."

They had stopped only a few feet from the bottom of the staircase; another pace or two and Quayle would certainly have been discovered.

But the police Captain went on. "Mr. Quayle is trying to escape us by driving to Rome, to the British Embassy. Well, his car is very fast, and he's a good driver. But even so..."

Ian Quayle could almost hear Arrigo's broad shrug. "Three of my cars are right behind him, and we've set up roadblocks everywhere. I promise you...within the hour we will have taken him."

"I want him alive," Mayberry said harshly. "He's no good to me dead."

Was there a touch of reluctance in Arrigo's voice?

He sighed and said, "Yes, of course, I understand that, sir. Deputy Aspremonte's instructions were very clear. And I am his servant."

"And *he* is *mine*," Mayberry said. "Never forget that, Arrigo! You've waited a long time for promotion, haven't you? You just might find it coming your way soon. With Quayle's capture."

"Ah...after all these years!"

"So get back to your duties, Captain. Search the grounds thoroughly. Fest or Quayle, the geese will tell you where he is. And if its Fest...be very, very careful how you handle him. He's impetuous, violent, and competent. He's perfectly happy to kill anyone he thinks might be in his way. So be warned."

"Yes, sir."

They turned away and moved from the foot of the staircase. Ian Quayle waited till he heard a door close behind them, waited some more, and then found his way cautiously to the entrance to the *Gran' Salotto*. He eased the door open gently, and went inside.

The lights were very dim here too, but he was sure that they were enough for the constant cameras. And in the half-light he saw three or four of the tiny pin-pricks of light that he thought were glass and that Wendy had said were perhaps diamonds. He saw the painting of Tancred just above the light-switch and knew what he had to do now.

He wormed his way on his belly to the nearest table, reached up to unscrew the bulb in the lamp there, and dropped his stainless steel pocket-knife into the socket; he fancied he heard a *plop* as all the lights fused, and he was on his feet in a flash.

In the sudden darkness he found the painting of Tancred, close by, that had worried Wendy so much, and by God, she was right, it was on a hinge, and with a certain amount of jiggling...

('You have to jiggle' the morgue attendant had said.)

With a certain amount of jiggling, the portrait-door swung open, and there was indeed a box beneath it, just as Wendy had suggested.

There was little time left now. With the fusing of the lights there was an electronic *beep-beep-beep* going on everywhere.

But this was very important to him now.

He used his pen-light, and wondered how long it might be before all the lights came on again, full force, and exposed him to the cameras.

Had he already been discovered? Was the lovely Madame Ging-Sen right when she'd said, '*This is farewell forever...*'?

He just didn't care, because his thoughts were only of

Carlotta.

And there, under his flashlight, there was indeed a switch of the simple pull-down, pull-up type, above which was an inscription, punched out on tape: '*Non si tocca mai*, not to be touched, ever.' And beneath it, in the same red tape: '*Pericolo della morte*, danger of death...'

But it was the cast-bronze inscription that interested him more. In old-fashioned curlicue, it read: '*Barras-Massena, Toulouse, France.*'

Barras-Massena!

Now, Ian Quayle knew...

Those *beep-beep-beeps* worried the hell out of him. He found a closet to hide in, aware that the whole house was on alert now, that they'd be coming for him soon. The closet was filled with filing cabinets, and he crouched down between them, and waited, and *thought*...

Barras-Massena, of Toulouse, France.

His researcher's mind was at work, and everything was falling into place.

Barras-Massena! He's almost forgotten them, a highly secret firm that manufactured armaments for the French Government. And what was it, seven years ago? No, only five and a half, they'd come up with the ultimate weapon.

The only problem was—*it didn't work.*

It was a kind of laser beam, yet not a laser, that shot a little over a million volts for a distance of seven hundred and twenty feet, or almost two hundred and twenty meters, incinerating everything in its path.

It was meant to destroy approaching enemy tanks, and on paper it was marvelous. But its heat was such that it had to leave the source, and home in on the pinpoint of a diamond.

And who the hell was going to stick industrial diamonds on the sides of rampaging tanks?

Moreover, after eight point two seconds, the whole damn

thing—because of the twelve thousand degree heat—self-destructed and had to be rebuilt at enormous cost.

And so, after a long period of experimentation, the whole project had been dropped, a multi-million disaster.

Ian Quayle remembered it now.

Barras-Massena had sought shelter in bankruptcy, and nobody—not the French DGE, not the American CIA or NSA, not the West Germans' Directorate of Weaponry, not even England's MI6 had been able to find out who finally bought all of their high-tech experimental equipment.

And here it all was, in Lord Mayberry's 'architectural computer,' and ready for...for what?

Research, and the memory that went with it, was the whole of Ian Quayle's being.

And how could it help him now?

He just squatted there, uncomfortably, and worried about it.

And wondered, too, what the hell he was doing here.

CHAPTER 21

It was absolutely no good at all just sitting there.

But the dark in the closet was comforting; darkness to Ian Quayle always brought with it a sense of security, and even the pervasive scent of the oiled-oak filing cabinets there seemed to add a homely touch, reminding him of his cottage in England.

Could he perhaps spend an hour or so safely in hiding? Hiding even from his own fears at the thought of the terrible danger he was in?

Could he hope against hope that Mayberry would give up the search and return to his own room, where he could be found and become a victim at some other, better time?

No! In God's name, no!

Madame Ging-Sen, his mistress for the moment, was bound hand and foot in his bed, so that it seemed *that* brief interlude was obviously a very serious mistake.

And yet, what else could he have done with her? Cut her throat and toss her out into the rose garden? No, again! His fight was only with Mayberry and his thugs.

So, the time to act, the time to stifle his awful fear was now, not at that mythical better time, which could not possibly ever come.

Was it his imagination? Or was he actually trembling?

He rose slowly to his feet, and took the pistol from his

belt. He remembered an embrasure in the corridor outside Mayberry's bedroom, a trio of tall potted ferns there, thick enough to hide him, perhaps, if he were careful.

Then...a couple of quick shots, one to the head and one to the heart, and then two more in case he'd missed the first time around...

He wasn't too bad with a hand-gun, actually.

He'd worked out once in a while at the Alfa Gun Club on Ham-Bone Lane in London, not with any serious intent but just for the hell of it because a girl he'd dated once was a National Champion with rifle, revolver, and pistol, and he'd sort of been trying to keep up with her.

It was from her that he'd learned the art of instinctive aiming, none of this peer-down-the-sights bullshit; use the gun-barrel like an index finger, because when you point at something instinctively you're always dead on target if your coordination's as good as it ought to be.

Two shots then, from the fern-forest of the embrasure, followed by a rapid run to the staircase, down it, out through the front doors or—if they were locked, no time messing around with bolts and dead-locks, but a foot through either of the windows at its side...A race across the grounds, *to where?*

There was that damn ten-foot wall with the broken glass cemented in along its top...

There was the gate, of course, but the sub-human race was guarding it, and could he perhaps hold them up with his gun and force them to open it?

Not very likely...

One guard would come to see who it was, and whether he had a gun in his hand or not, the others would be in the gatehouse, and surely not sleeping. With rifles or revolvers or blood bazookas at the ready!

The problem of the wall was not an easy one.

Not easy?

It was *insurmountable*, he thought, with a little flash of humor at his own weak wit. And with typical Ian Quayle philosophy, he thrust it all to the back of his mind with the consolation: "Well, we'll cross that bridge when we come to it, and play it off the cuff."

He knew that it was a very perilous way to think; but he had a murder to commit now, and that was all that mattered.

He silently turned the brass knob of the door, and God dammit, it was the kind of lock that could only be opened from the outside; the knob turned, but the bolt stayed home. His probing finger found the tiny hole in its center where you could insert a spike of some sort to free it, a very small screwdriver, or one of Wendy's bobby pins.

He tried his pen-knife, but the blade was too broad. He tried the Parker cyanide gun, but that was too thick to penetrate deeply enough, and under his breath he cursed the makers of modern door hardware.

For God's sake, this was supposed to be a four-hundred-year-old villa! So what the hell were they doing with twentieth-century hardware?

And while he was wondering just how he could escape from his involuntary prison without making enough noise to wake the bloody Dead, he froze...

There was the sound of a door being opened out there in the Salotto, and then being softly closed again.

And then . . . *Silence.*

It was hard not to clear his throat. He could still feel the blood from those damn pieces of broken bottles seeping into his pants, and in his imagination there was a great pool of blood on the floor, spreading out into the room and betraying his presence there.

He knew that his imagination was running away with him, and he controlled himself with an effort, holding his breath and not daring even to swallow.

And he heard Gordon Fest's hateful voice, from far across the room. It was quiet, and yet loud and clear: "Okay, Quayle, I know you're in here someplace. So why don't you show yourself? And we'll have a nice, friendly little chat..."

Silently, Ian Quayle transferred the Walther P38 to his left hand. And with his right, he found the cyanide gun and held it loosely at his side. And he *waited.*

He hardly heard the padding of rubber-soled shoes, but at last the door to his closet hiding place was flung open, and Fest was there, grinning like a maniac.

Quayle shot out his left hand, the gun held at eye-level, pointed straight at the bridge of the nose. And Fest was laughing...

He said, happily, "Okay, you fucking wimp! Let's find out now if you have the guts to kill a man in cold blood! I doubt it! Let's see if you're man enough to pull that trigger! Right between the eyes, it'll blow the top of my head right off if you're using the right ammo, which I doubt too!"

He was the happiest man on earth, laughing his contempt for a lesser being, and he said, "Shoot me, Quayle! I don't even have a gun in my hand, you see how easy it's going to be?"

Nearly two hundred years ago, that master spy Joseph Fouche, father of all modern espionage, had said drily: *"If you wish to kill a man, first engage him in conversation. It's so much easier when you have his full attention..."*

And that was precisely what Fest was doing now.

"You seem to have forgotten, Quayle," he said blandly, "that you're my property now, I *bought* you, remember? From that Chinese whore who just wanted you as a slave in her bed. Spending her impoverished Government's hard-earned foreign currency on her own pleasures, it's not right, is it?"

Even as he spoke, he swept that menacing gun-arm away with a lighting movement, and he shouted, "And I'm going to take your balls out with a pair of shears and ram them down your throat..."

Ian Quayle let the automatic clatter to the ground with the blow.

He took a deep breath as he fell under Fest's violent assault, with carbon-steel fingers digging into his neck to crush his Adam's Apple.

He brought up the Parker ball-point in his right hand, and pressed the clip. The stream of cyanide gas hit Gordon Fest squarely in the face, and he gasped in shock, quite the wrong thing to do now.

And Ian Quayle struggled to his feet and stared down at his no-longer adversary, writhing in death now for only a matter of seconds until he lay still.

He had killed his first man ever, and he was in a terrible state.

He thought of the report he would have to make to Mrs. Bloody French:

'Gordon Fest, American, President of an undercover Agency called Playtime something-or-other that serves the CIA and the NSA and perhaps other secret organizations as well. In a moment of anger, undoubtedly compounded by fear, I killed him with one of your damned cyanide guns...'

It was more than he could stomach, and he said aloud, "Wendy, where are you when I need you...?"

And there was Gordon Fest lying dead at his feet. The dark eyes were still open with a kind of hateful malignancy in them, and Ian Quayle could not bring himself to close them.

But there were more serious problems now. All the lights suddenly came on at full power, the fuses fixed, and the other door to the Salotto was slowly opening.

Ian Quayle stared as Mayberry entered the room, smiling broadly. But the smile faded as he saw Fest's dead body lying there, and he said incredulously, "What? Have I underestimated you, Quayle? By God above, I was about to hire Mr. Fest as my deputy, it would have been a mistake, wouldn't it? I mean...people who can so easily be killed by idiots honestly have no place on my staff."

The savage Bianca was close behind him, armed with her favorite Beretta 9mm, and Quayle wondered if it was perhaps the same one he had tossed out into the rose garden.

And did it matter? He thought not.

Behind them, three, four, six more of the thugs were moving in, seeming to fill even that huge room with their ominous presence. They spread out in a broad semicircle facing Ian Quayle, nursing their Uzis as though they were ready for business, ready for mayhem, ready to satisfy their own personal craving for violence; most of them flaunted the red neck-cloth the Red Brigades wore when there was no need to hide their affiliation.

Mayberry said mildly: "Bianca...that pen in his hand is a cyanide gun," and there was a lapse of no more than a split second.

Ian Quayle heard the sound of the Baretta, and he held up his right hand and stared at it, the Parker shot out of it and blood flowing everywhere. There was no pain, *yet*. There was just numbness, a feeling that his right hand did not exist anymore.

"We keep him alive, Bianca," Mayberry said, "that will be enough for the moment."

"Better if he lose a knee-cap," she said angrily, and Quayle threw himself at her, using his body as a battering-ram. He heard the shot again, and felt the burning pain as a bullet creased his thigh and went on to shatter the base of a marble pedestal.

As he fell, he saw Mayberry strike her viciously on the side of her face, sending her stumbling, heard the furious shout: "No! You will obey my orders, always...!"

Sven moved forward and kicked him savagely in the groin, then lugged him up to his feet, picking him up with one hand as though he was a goose-down pillow.

The giant's voice was low and controlled. "Maybe you let me take care of him, Mr. Norton," he said. "I know better than that woman."

"Just show him how much we dislike him, Sven," Mayberry said, recovering his habitual equanimity. "Let him learn the disadvantages of his arrogance."

The giant slung his Uzi over his shoulder, and drove his huge and powerful fist into Quayle's solar plexus, sending him reeling across the room and staggering into the door. He collapsed on the floor in agony, and dragged himself to his feet again.

The pain was coming into his right hand now, and the blood was coursing like a mountain stream. His thigh hurt like hell, but the worst pain of all was in his chest, and he wondered if a couple of his ribs were broken, perhaps puncturing a lung. The whole room was swaying crazily around him as he tried desperately to hold on to his consciousness, and he brushed at the light switch and flicked it off.

The main lights went out, and he heard someone yelling; was it Mayberry? The words were lost in the stars that flashed in front of his eyes, and he was dimly aware that Sven, bellowing his laughter now, was advancing on him once again.

With his good left hand he tore the Tancred portrait-frame open, and clutched at the handle there; and this time, he heard Mayberry's scream in all of its importance:

"No...! In God's name no...!"

His desperate grip on the handle was made of steel as he fell to the ground; and then it seemed that all his pains were suddenly brought to nothing as he tugged it down with his fall and felt the double blades of the switch strike home.

Was there a safety-zone, for God's sake?

Yes, there *had* to be, close by the switch, because whoever was throwing it had no intention at all of committing suicide, but rather, in one fell swoop, of eliminating in one way or another certain enemies who might be apparent among the very violent and dangerous people gathered there.

How did it work? Ian Quayle just didn't care anymore.

And with the *click* of the contact, all Hell broke loose...

Bright red beams were shooting across the room in all directions, leaving and homing in on those miniscule diamond points in short sharp bursts. There was a strange hum, quite subdued, sounding like the beginnings of a Gregorian chant from a hundred holy Druid voices and growing quickly in intensity as the system heated up till it became the high-pitched, ear-splitting sound of massed and manic violins.

But, lying there on the ground, trying to struggle to his feet or at least to his knees, Ian Quayle watched those stabbing rays in horror; some of them were no more than two feet away from him; but this was, as he had surmised, the 'safe zone...'

And nowhere else in the room was safe.

He saw Lord Mayberry, who was now calling himself Thaddeus Norton, literally exploding, almost in slow motion, as a dozen or more of those stabbing rays caught him in the stomach, the back, and the chest. That marvelously athletic body, very nearly naked now as the clothing atomized into nothing, was bursting apart, blistering into explosive bubbles as it swelled enormously, boiled from the inside out.

He saw the eyeballs blown across the room, saw the skull explode and scatter shattered bone and gray matter all over.

He turned his horrified eyes to the side, and saw Bianca's pot-roast body in pieces on the floor, mixed in with what was left of Sven and Marcos; and then, with a final appalling crescendo, the violins and the fireworks stopped, and the infamous Barras-Massena 'ultimate weapon' had at last proved its limited worth, and had self-destructed within its expected allocation of eight point two seconds.

It was no good on enemy tanks; but its million-plus volts and twelve thousand-degree heat sure as hell worked on flesh and bones.

In the awful sudden silence, the *Gran' Salotto* was like a battlefield, with bits and pieces of what had once been people lying there annihilated, bloated, blistered, and boiled. There was not a single one of them left alive.

And for a while, Ian Quayle blacked out, completely.

CHAPTER 22

But when he recovered his senses, he knew that it could not have been for very long. There was the gray light of the dawn streaming in through the windows, tinged with the early morning gold so beloved by the Florentine painters of a past era.

And now, three more guards were moving cautiously into the Salotto, and they were all staring open-mouthed at the shattered bodies, with no blood anywhere in evidence; the blood had all been vaporized.

They were all armed, drawn there no doubt by the penetrating sound; but they were no menace at all now, even though, Ian Quayle was sure, they were all from the Red Brigades or from something even worse.

He pulled himself to his knees, wondering if he could walk now or even stand up decently, and he stared at them for a moment, and he said, pointing, "*That* was your boss, Thaddeus Norton; that's Bianca, and Sven, and Marco, all that's left of them. And don't anybody touch anything, because..."

He looked at their faces, and said, "Because it may be contagious."

And for good measure, he added, emoting, "*Tutto all'intorno da noi non c' e que la morte*, there's only death all around us."

It was a quotation from one of Dante's essays on Hell.

But he was quite sure they wouldn't know that, and he didn't care at all.

He staggered to his feet, and found that his left leg wasn't working very well. He pulled a sixteenth-century saber from the wall to use as a cane, and stumbled his way out of there, leaving them all staring after him in acute bewilderment.

The fresh air was a blessing as he took great deep breaths of it to fill his lungs. He held his shattered right hand chest high in an effort to lessen the awful pain and the bleeding, and wondered how long his wounded leg would hold out. He was barely conscious as he stood there, swaying from side to side.

And what to do now?

How was he to get past the guards at the gatehouse, who would have been quite ignorant of the happenings in the house.

They would be new, no doubt, replacing the three he had crippled with his Mini-born assault, and would they be more amenable to the only power he had left now, the power of *reason*?

He doubted it, severely. And where the hell was the Mini, anyway?

He began his painful way down the rose-bordered path, and he fell, almost blacking out again.

An ancient saber was not the best walking cane in the world, but when he pulled himself up on it, unsteadily, a pew peril faced him...

Police Captain Arrigo was emerging from the shrubbery, surrounded by half a dozen cops, and there was a gun in his hand, the standard Police issue, the Beretta 9mm pistol.

He took one look at Quayle, and holstered his gun, and he said slowly, not without a certain sympathy, "I see that you've been hurt, Mr. Quayle, quite badly. *I ferri*, the handcuffs will not be required now. But I still have a warrant for your arrest, on a charge of attempted murder."

Ian Quayle could hardly steady himself. He said, "Ah,

yes, a Red Brigades bastard named, what was it? Something-or-other Fresco?"

He was seething, not himself at all now, and he said, holding himself in check by an effort of will, "And you can now add successful murder charges, Captain Arrigo. I just killed Lord Mayberry. You know who he was?"

"No, I think not."

"You know him as Thaddeus Norton. He's dead, and I killed him..."

Common sense took over, and he said clearly, "Correction. Thaddeus Norton, together with hords of his bodyguards, was killed by the accidental triggering of a device he had installed to wipe out all of his guests, should there ever be the need for it. And I have to tell you, Arrigo...he really wiped them all out, himself included. Go take a look, you might just pick up some meat for your supper."

Police Captain Arrigo didn't have the faintest idea of what he was talking about, so he fell back on the book that he had studied so well as a Sergeant, pushing for promotion some twenty years ago.

He said, as though reading a set piece, "Under the powers invested in me under Article 135 of the Italian Penal Code, I place you under arrest. You will now accompany me to the Magistrate's Court in Florence, where formal charges will be made. You have the right to the services of a lawyer, at your own expense, to be present when said charges are read, and thereafter."

His voice was far more gentle as he mentally put the book away, and he said, "One sees, Mr. Quayle, that you are in urgent need of very considerable medical attention. But the hospital ward of the prison in Florence is staffed by some of the best doctors in Italy." He sighed. "I sometimes wish I had access to them myself. My arthritis, you know, it's really most punishing. But this is a privilege reserved, in our Police Department, only for officers of more senior rank..."

There was the unhappy sigh again, and then: "So...you will come with me now, please."

"You're a persistent sort of bastard, Arrigo, aren't you?" Ian Quayle muttered. "And you're still going to have to take me by brute force."

He raised the saber in a threatening gesture, quite prepared to fight all of them to the death; but without its support he fell to the ground again, helplessly. And he blacked out once more.

Captain Arrigo shouted, *"Para-medici, presto!"* and within moments the paramedics from the police squad were there, wiping away blood and binding up his wounds and popping pills into his mouth.

And when he came round again, it was because Captain Arrigo was holding up his head and pouring copious quantities of heavily-fortified wine down his throat from his Sergeant's water bottle.

Ian Quayle heard the friendly, comforting voice: "Marsala, Mr. Quayle, it cures everything, even the *malaise* of defeat. And are you ready now to accompany me to the prison?"

Quayle gulped down the wine, feeling much the better for it, and he said sourly, "I told you once before, Arrigo, and I tell you again; you're going to have to cart me off there forcibly. And, by Jesus Christ, when the British Ambassador's finished with your Minister of Justice...I swear to God, Arrigo, you're going to be a fucking Corporal again."

Captain Arrigo raised his voice and shouted, "Three men, *subito*! Three men to carry Mr. Quayle to my car! And he is badly hurt, he will be handled gently!"

They were already lifting him up when the headlights of a car approaching at speed illuminated them starkly. It was being driven by some kind of a maniac, and it turned on its own length as it skidded to a halt, a BMW, one of the best cars ever made in modern times.

Leo stumbled out first, his face ashen, and he said loudly, for all the world to hear, "God save us all from women drivers...!"

Wendy was next out, and she threw open the rear door and said harshly, "Out, you sonofabitch! And do what has to be done now...!"

His Excellency Deputy Aspremonte climbed out of the car with all the dignity he could muster; he didn't much like being called a sonofabitch, but he wrote it off as a matter of protocol.

And then Wendy saw her Ian Quayle, and she ran to him in a state of absolute panic.

He was seated on the ground, unable to rise, and she threw her arms around him and wailed, "Oh my poor darling, what have they done to you...?"

And then he blacked out again.

She saw the huge mass of blood-stained bandages on his hand and his thigh, with the pants split all the way down for easier access to a wound that was far more serious than he had thought.

Captain Arrigo said to her apologetically, "We've done all we can, Miss Hayworth. And I assure you, in prison, he'll have very expert attention."

Wendy Hayworth ignored him completely and turned to her hostage.

"Okay, *Deputy*," she said sourly, "this is where you ensure the continuance of your goddam reputation! Such as it is!"

At the sight of the greatly-feared Aspremonte, Captain Arrigo had snapped to servile attention.

He said awkwardly, "This man, Excellency, is the notorious Ian Quayle, whose arrest you wanted. And I have executed it as you wished."

But there was more grist for his longed-for promotion now, and he went on:

"My men are in the villa, and it seems that Mr. Norton is dead, together with several members of his staff. We don't yet know how they died, but our investigations might prove that Mr. Quayle was responsible. Your orders, Excellency, are always my most ardent wishes."

It was quite a speech, and Aspremonte was staring at him incredulously. He whispered, "Norton...*dead*?"

"Si, Eccelenza...Though how he died is quite beyond our comprehension."

That ancient, syphilitic voice was hoarse. "You are sure? There can be no mistake?"

Arrigo could not resist it. "He looks like the beginnings of the meat for a *salsa Bolognese*, Excellency. Several hundred kilos of it all over the floor."

"Oh my God..."

Wendy still had her arms around her lover, almost nursing him like a baby. She looked up and said tightly, "Go to it, Deputy. You think we brought you here just to rubber-neck?"

Aspremonte took a long, deep breath, and cleared his throat. He said, quite a speech too, in careful and very serious tones:

"There are matters of diplomacy involved here, *Commandante*, matters of which a Major of Police can have no knowledge at all, and of which the whole Police Department— indeed, the public at large—must remain ignorant. Do I have your full attention?"

"Sir!" Arrigo said, clicking his heels, and Aspremonte went on:

"These events *did not happen, Commandante*! You yourself will see to it that there are no, repeat, no leaks to the Press! Anyone of your men who talks out of turn will find himself on the morrow begging for bread on the streets of

Trastevere, is that clearly understood?"

"Ha!" Leo said loudly. "Corrupt bureaucracy is at work again, I love it..." and the Deputy ignored him completely.

Captain Arrigo was still at rigid attention, and the wheels in his head were spinning wildly.

"Clearly understood, Excellency," he said. "But, with respect, I am not *Commandante della Polizia*, not a Major. I am merely a humble Captain."

"The Official Gazette," Aspremonte said, "is published monthly by our illustrious Government. Its next issue, I believe, is due in two weeks' time. If you peruse it well...you will find notification of your promotion."

Arrigo was beaming. He clicked his heels again, and saluted, and wondered if he should perhaps also make a bow of some sort.

The Deputy said, pressing home the point, "This night's events are wiped off the slate of history. And since Mr. Quayle is not even present...he will go free."

"Mr. Quayle?" Arrigo asked blandly, "I do not think I know the name, Excellency. Who is Mr. Quayle?"

"Good," Aspremonte said. "Allow me only to add that your promotion is well-deserved. I see a fine future ahead of you, Arrigo. The next step after *Commandante* is *Colonello*. And a Colonel of Police has enormous power. And is it not power that we all want?"

Leo said, feeling that his position entitled him at the very least to a bystander's opinion of what was going on, "There is a lesson here for all of us, is there not? It is...that in Government, intelligence does not count for much. What is of importance is...*duplicity*. Am I right?"

The Deputy turned those cold old eyes on him, and the Northern-Southern enmity was very apparent now as he said, not too unkindly, "For a damned *Napolitano*, my dear friend, you do seem to have occasional flashes of wisdom. You are absolutely right. Artfulness is all that matters in Government."

Leo fell silent, and the Honorable Aspremonte looked at Wendy and asked gently, "Well, have I kept my end of our little bargain?"

Wendy looked up at him and nodded. "Yes, you have," she said. "For an unprincipled old fart, you're okay, Excellency."

"Then...you will keep yours?"

"Of course, and you know it."

"So...will someone drive me home now?"

"Ah yes," Wendy said. "There are two young ladies waiting for you, I remember! And won't you have exciting stories to tell them?"

"My lips are sealed," Deputy Minister Aspremonte said. "So be it. We will have other matters to talk about. They're not very bright, you know."

"And they don't have to be, do they?" Wendy said with a certain amount of sympathy, and he took her hand in his and said earnestly, "So Thaddeus Norton is dead! I'll have to find someone else, won't I?"

For some moments, Ian Quayle had been unconscious and lost to the world, suffering the most agonizing pains. But he recovered now enough to hear that last comment, and he shouted, "The man who killed Carlotta is dead! And so is the League of Hawks...! They're all dead! Finished!"

"Ssshhh," Wendy said, embracing him tightly. "The Mini must be here some place, do you remember where you left it?"

"Of course..."

The stars were exploding again, but he pulled himself together and said, "Five hundred yards to the west of the main gates, hidden in the shrubbery there."

"Then we have to drive you there."

She turned to Leo. "Can you take the Deputy back to his villa? And drop us off at the Mini, I'll drive him back to Rome now, and the American Hospital there."

232

She looked at Ian and said, almost crying now with relief, "Don't worry, my love. In ten years' time you'll be as right as rain, and all this will have been forgotten."

"The world's greatest comforter," Ian Quayle murmured; and he lapsed back into coma.

It took them nearly half an hour to find the Mini and to extricate it from its hiding place; Ian Quayle was a great help, unconscious all of the time on the back seat of Leo's BMW.

But at last they found the little car and maneuvered it onto the road, a disaster of a once-beautiful machine.

Ian Quayle recovered enough to assert his lost authority, and he said unsteadily, "And I will drive. There is nothing...nothing worse in...in the whole world for a civilized...civilized man, than the...the inability to drive his own car. Unless it be...unless it be because of...of too much indulgence in Mother's Ruin. Which...which is to say...the jolly old bottle."

"Shut up, Ian," Wendy said, and he tried to struggle out of the BMW by himself.

Not entirely unexpectedly, he fell flat on his face in the dirt, and they helped him to his feet and stuffed him into the Mini's passenger seat.

He was still suffering from the effects of the paramedics' pills, given perhaps too liberally, and he muttered, "Christ, I have to be driven home..."

The awful pain had given way to a kind of numbness, and when he touched the wound in his thigh to see how it was coming along, and then pounded at it furiously, he felt absolutely nothing at all.

The pills!

He closed his eyes, and let himself lapse into something between sleep and coma.

He heard, or thought he heard, Wendy saying quietly, "Take the Deputy Minister home, Leo, I'll drive Ian back to Rome. And I'll see you there as soon as you can make it."

She sighed. "Ian's efforts haven't exactly been, well, orthodox. So let's get together and decide what lies we have to tell London. He's not licensed to kill, you know, and you and I aren't licensed either, to kidnap senior Italian Ministers out of their rotting-beds and...and *blackmail* them into doing what we want them to do. So let's all get our story right. And we have to tell her *now*, before any more damage can be done, about that double-agent working out of the London Office."

She was staring down in anguish at Ian Quayle, dead to the world, she thought . . .

But he opened one eye, and it stared at her. He said weakly, "The question...question of the double-agent. That is something you will say nothing about, either of you. That is a matter I will discuss in person, and in secrecy, with Robin Harris, when I finally make it back home. Till then—there will only be silence."

Wendy said tartly, "Don't give me orders, Ian Quayle! You're not my boss, I'm yours, remember?"

He grunted, and closed that accusing eye again, and said, out of the void, "And that too, is a matter we will discuss when the time comes. And now, if you don't mind, I'm going to sleep..."

Sleep? Ian Quayle was out cold.

Slowly, finding their way where they were headed in that fantastic Florentine light of the early dawn, a light that had driven artists out of their sensibilities for more than three hundred years, the two cars went on their way.

Rome, splendid Rome, was ahead of them, with its ancient *Via Appia Antica*, the civilized world's most historic thoroughfare.

For Ian Quayle, and for Wendy Hayworth, it meant some

kind of safety.

At least...for a while.

THE END

ABOUT THE AUTHOR

Alan Lyle-Smythe was born in Surrey, England. Prior to World War II, he served with the Palestine Police from 1936 to 1939 and learned the Arabic language. He was awarded an MBE in June 1938. He married Aliza Sverdova in 1939, then studied acting from 1939 to 1941.

In January 1940, Lyle-Smythe was commissioned in the Royal Army Service Corps. Due to his linguistic skills, he transferred to the Intelligence Corps and served in the Western Desert, in which he used the surname "Caillou" (the French word for 'pebble') as an alias.

He was captured in North Africa, imprisoned and threatened with execution in Italy, then escaped to join the British forces at Salerno. He was then posted to serve with the partisans in Yugoslavia. He wrote about his experiences in the book *The World is Six Feet Square* (1954). He was promoted to captain and awarded the Military Cross in 1944.

Following the war, he returned to the Palestine Police from 1946 to 1947, then served as a Police Commissioner in British-occupied Italian Somaliland from 1947 to 1952, where he was recommissioned a captain.

After work as a District Officer in Somalia and professional hunter, Lyle-Smythe travelled to Canada, where he worked as a hunter and then became an actor on Canadian television.

He wrote his first novel, *Rogue's Gambit*, in 1955, first using the name Caillou, one of his aliases from the war. Moving from Vancouver to Hollywood, he made an appearance as a contestant on the January 23 1958 edition of *You Bet Your Life*.

He appeared as an actor and/or worked as a screenwriter in such shows as *Daktari*, *The Man From U.N.C.L.E.* (including the screenwriting for "*The Bow-Wow Affair*" from 1965), *Thriller*, *Daniel Boone*, *Quark*, *Centennial*, and *How the West Was Won*. In 1966-67, he had a recurring role (as Jason Flood) in NBC's "*Tarzan*" TV series starring Ron Ely. Caillou appeared in such television movies as *Sole Survivor* (1970), *The Hound of the Baskervilles* (1972, as Inspector Lestrade), and *Goliath Awaits* (1981). His cinema film credits included roles in *Five Weeks in a Balloon* (1962), *Clarence, the Cross-Eyed Lion* (1965), *The Rare Breed* (1966), *The Devil's Brigade* (1968), *Hellfighters* (1968), *Everything You Always Wanted to Know About Sex* (*But Were Afraid to Ask)* (1972), *Herbie Goes to Monte Carlo* (1977), *Beyond Evil* (1980), *The Sword and the Sorcerer* (1982) and *The Ice Pirates* (1984).

Caillou wrote 52 paperback thrillers under his own name and the nom de plume of Alex Webb, with such heroes as Cabot Cain, Colonel Matthew Tobin, Mike Benasque, Ian Quayle and Josh Dekker, as well as writing many magazine stories.

Several of Caillou's novels were made into films, such as *Rampage* with Robert Mitchum in 1963, based on his big game hunting knowledge; *Assault on Agathon*, for which Caillou did the screenplay as well; and *The Cheetahs*, filmed in 1989.

He was married to Aliza Sverdova from 1939 until his death. Their daughter Nadia Caillou was the screenwriter for the film *Skeleton Coast*.

Alan Caillou died in Sedona, Arizona in 2006.

DON'T MISS ANY OF MICHAEL KASNER'S HARD HITTING MILITARY NOVEL SERIES

BLACK OPS

Formed by an elite cadre of government officials, the Black OPS team goes where the law can't - to seek retribution for acts of terror directed against Americans anywhere in the world.

3 BOOK SERIES

Armed with all the tactical advantages of modern technology, battle hard and ready when the free world is threatened - the Peacekeepers are the baddest grunts on the planet.

4 BOOK SERIES

CHOPPER COPS

America is being torn apart as criminal cartels terrorize our cities, dealing drugs and death wholesale. Local police are outgunned, so the President unleashes the U.S. TACTICAL POLICE FORCE. An elite army of super cops with ammo to burn, they swoop down on the hot spots in sleek high-tech attack choppers to win the dirty war and take back America!

4 BOOK SERIES

FROM CALIBER BOOKS
www.calibercomics.com

CALIBER
BOOKS

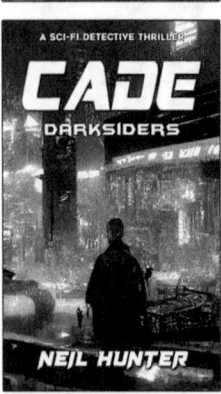

CALIBER COMICS GOES TO WAR!
HISTORICAL AND MILITARY THEMED GRAPHIC NOVELS

**WORLD WAR ONE:
MO MAN'S LAND**

ISBN: 9781635298123

*A look at World War 1 from
the French trenches as they
faced the Imperial German
Army.*

**CORTEZ AND THE FALL
OF THE AZTECS**

ISBN: 9781635299779

*Cortez battles the Aztecs
while in search of Inca
gold.*

**TROY:
AN EMPIRE UNDER SIEGE**

ISBN: 9781635298635

*Homer's famous The Iliad and
the Trojan War is given a
unique human perspective
rather than from the God's.*

WITNESS TO WAR

ISBN: 9781635299700

*WW2's Battle of the Bulge
is seen up close by an
embedded female war
reporter.*

THE LINCOLN BRIGADE

ISBN: 9781635298222

*American volunteers head
to Spain in the 1930s to
fight in their civil war
against the fascist regime.*

**EL CID:
THE CONQUEROR**

ISBN: 9780982654996

*Europe's greatest warrior
attempts to unify Spain
against invading foreign
and domestic armies.*

WINTER WAR

ISBN: 9780985749392

*At the outbreak of WW2
Finland fights against an
invading Soviet army.*

**ZULUNATION:
END OF EMPIRE**

ISBN: 9780941613415

*The global British Empire
and far-reaching influence
is threatened by a Zulu
uprising in southern Africa.*

AIR WARRIORS: WORLD WAR ONE #V1 - V4 *Take to the skys of WW1 as various fighter aces tell their harrowing stories.*
ISBN: 9781635297973 (V1), 9781635297980 (V2), 9781635297997 (V3), 9781635298000 (V4)

CALIBER COMICS GOES TO THE EDGE!
Science Fiction and Horror themed graphic novels

ALSO AVAILABLE FROM CALIBER COMICS

QUALITY GRAPHIC NOVELS TO ENTERTAIN

THE SEARCHERS: VOLUME 1
The Shape of Things to Come

Before *League of Extraordinary Gentlemen* there was *The Searchers*. At the dawn of the 20th Century the greatest literary adventurers from the minds of Wells, Doyle, Burroughs, and Haggard were created. All thought to be the work of pure fiction. However, a century later, the real-life descendents of those famous characters are recuited by the legendary Professor Challenger in order to save mankind's future. Series collected for the first time.

"Searchers is the comic book I have on the wall with a sign reading: · 'Love books? Never read a comic? Try this one! ....money back guarantee..." - Dark Star Books.

WAR OF THE WORLDS: INFESTATION

Based on the H.G. Wells classic! The "Martian Invasion" has begun again and now mankind must fight for its very humanity. It happened slowly at first but by the third year, it seemed that the war was almost over... the war was almost lost.

"Writer Randy Zimmerman has a fine grasp of drama, and spins the various strands of the story into a coherent whole... imaginative and very gritty."
- war-of-the-worlds.co.uk

HELSING: LEGACY BORN

From writer Gary Reed (Deadworld) and artists John Lowe (Captain America), Bruce McCorkindale (Godzilla). She was born into a legacy she wanted no part of and pushed into a battle recessed deep in the shadows of the night. Samantha Helsing is torn between two worlds...two allegiances...two families. The legacy of the Van Helsing family and their crusade against the "night creatures" comes to modern day with the most unlikely of all warriors.

"Congratulations on this masterpiece..."
- Paul Dale Roberts, Compuserve Reviews

DEADWORLD

Before there was The Walking Dead there was Deadworld. Here is an introduction of the long running classic horror series, Deadworld, to a new audience! Considered by many to be the godfather of the original zombie comic with over 100 issues and graphic novels in print and over 1,000,000 copies sold, Deadworld ripped into the undead with intelligent zombies on a mission and a group of poor teens riding in a school bus desperately try to stay one step ahead of the sadistic, Harley-riding King Zombie. Death, mayhem, and a touch of supernatural evil made Deadworld a classic and now here's your chance to get into the story!

DAYS OF WRATH

Award winning comic writer & artist Wayne Vansant brings his gripping World War II saga of war in the Pacific to Guadalcanal and the Battle of Bloody Ridge. This is the powerful story of the long, vicious battle for Guadalcanal that occurred in 1942-43. When the U.S. Navy orders its outnumbered and out-gunned ships to run from the Japanese fleet, they abandon American troops on a bloody, battered island in the South Pacific.

"Heavy on authenticity, compellingly written and beautifully drawn."
- Comics Buyers Guide

SHERLOCK HOLMES:
THE CASE OF THE MISSING MARTIAN

Sherlock is called out of retirement to London in 1908 to solve a most baffling mystery: The British Museum is missing a specimen of a Martian from the failed invasion of 1899. Did it walk away on its own or did someone steal it?

Holmes ponders the facts and remembers his part in the war effort alongside Professor Challenger during the War of the Worlds invasion that was chronicled in H.G. Wells' classic novel.

Meanwhile, Doctor Watson has problems of his own when his wife steals a scalpel from his surgical tool kit and returns to her old stomping grounds of Whitechapel, the London

CALIBER PRESENTS

The original Caliber Presents anthology title was one of Caliber's inaugural releases and featured predominantly new creators, many of which went onto successful careers in the comics' industry. In this new version, Caliber Presents has expanded to graphic novel size and while still featuring new creators it also includes many established professional creators with new visions. Creators featured in this first issue include nominees and winners of some of the industry's major awards including the Eisner, Harvey, Xeric, Ghastly, Shel Dorf, Comic Monsters, and more.

LEGENDLORE

From Caliber Comics now comes the entire Realm and Legendlore saga as a set of volumes that collects the long running critically acclaimed series. In the vein of The Lord of The Rings and The Hobbit with elements of Game of Thrones and Dungeon and Dragons.

Four normal modern day teenagers are plunged into a world they thought only existed in novels and film. They are whisked away to a magical land where dragons roam the skies, orcs and hobgoblins terrorize travelers, where unicorns prance through the forest, and kingdoms wage war for dominance. It is a world where man is just one race, joining other races such as elves, trolls, dwarves, changelings, and the dreaded night creatures who steal the night.

TIME GRUNTS

What if Hitler's last great Super Weapon was – Time itself! A WWII/time travel adventure that can best be described as *Band of Brothers* meets *Time Bandits*.

October, 1944. Nazi fortunes appear bleaker by the day. But in the bowels of the Wenceslas Mines, a terrible threat has emerged . . . The Nazis have discovered the ability to conquer time itself with the help of a new ominous device!

Now a rag tag group of American GIs must stop this threat to the past, present, and future . . . While dealing with their own past, prejudices, and fears in the process.

www.calibercomics.com